THE FIANCÉ HOAX

FAUX LOVE BILLIONAIRES

CRYSTAL MONROE

Copyright © 2023 by Crystal Monroe

All rights reserved.

No part of this book may be reproduced in any form or by any electronic or mechanical means, including information storage and retrieval systems, without written permission from the author, except for the use of brief quotations in a book review.

Cover Photo by Wander Aguiar Photography.

DESCRIPTION

Daddy's best friend is my new fake fiancé.
No one knows it's a scam.
And then the bastard gets me pregnant.

Cooper Pierce, single dad and chiseled by God.
Blue eyes that could melt panties like superman.

My cutesy boutique is on the edge of bankruptcy.
And Cooper just flew in with his red cape and meticulously carved six pack to save the day.

With one teeny tiny little catch.
He needs me to play wifey for three months.

So I'll wear his fat 4.3 carat diamond ring.
And fall in love with his two adorable little daughters.
But his fierce protective streak makes it hard to stay out of his bed.

Daddy wants to kill Cooper.
Cooper doesn't know I'm having his baby.
I can't wait for the next family reunion!

1

FELICITY

"Felicity, you look absolutely ridiculous."

I pushed the thick-framed glasses up my nose and adjusted my wig. "But do I look like someone who's not *me*?"

Lauren studied me from the passenger seat. "Yes, actually. Your little disguise is silly, but it's working."

"Good." I looked in the rearview mirror and arranged the frizzy blonde curls I was sporting. "You'll help me keep an eye out for my dad, right? He can't find out I'm here."

Lauren and I climbed out of my old clunker and stood on the grassy parking area facing my childhood home.

"Of course I will," she said. "But I still don't understand why you need to hide from your father."

I adjusted the neckline of my dress. It was my own design—a long, midnight blue gown with a flared skirt. For a moment, I worried that wearing one of my own creations would blow my disguise.

But that was silly. Dad had no idea what the clothes I made looked like.

"He doesn't want me asking one of his fancy investor

friends for help." I glanced at my best friend. "You know that, Lauren."

"I know. And I'm sorry, sweetie." She stood beside me and gave my arm a squeeze.

We watched as the guests arrived in their Bentleys and Maseratis, making my old sedan stick out like a sore thumb. At least my dress was up to speed.

These were my dad's friends and clients. The well-dressed couples headed toward the party on the gorgeous estate where I grew up.

"I just don't get what he has against helping his daughter out," Lauren said. "You're so talented, Felicity. You just need a little cash to keep your store open until your fashions take off."

I nodded tightly as I thought of the business I'd poured my heart and soul into for three years.

The one I was about to lose.

Lauren gestured at my dad's huge house. He lived here alone, ever since I moved out at age eighteen.

"Your dad obviously has more than enough to spare. Plus, he knows the top businesspeople in LA. I'm sure any of them would love to invest in your shop." She clicked her tongue. "But ol' Marsh Hayes won't even let you ask one of his buddies for help."

I did my best impression of my father's deep, booming voice. "No handouts. Not even for you, Felicity. *Especially* when you're all mixed up in that fashion design business."

"He makes it sound like you're a drug dealer." Lauren giggled. "What a hardass."

"Exactly." I grabbed my clutch and squared my shoulders. "Which is why I'm gonna sneak into this party, find some rich investor to save my business, and escape before Dad catches me."

Lauren smiled as we crossed the parking area. "It's on." She wore a little black dress that showed off her long legs.

The other guests at the party entered through the front door of the house, where the butler received them and led them to the backyard. But I didn't have that luxury.

"Let's sneak in through the side," I muttered to Lauren.

We kept to the shadows as I found the path on the far side of the house.

"I still can't believe you grew up in this *mansion*," Lauren whispered. "It's crazy! You came from a rich family, and now you're totally broke!"

I squinted as we walked in the dim light, trying not to trip on a rock.

"I mean, you drive a 1998 Plymouth Breeze," Lauren continued. "You live in a moldy apartment. And you're about to lose your boutique!" She shook her head sadly.

I looked at her. "You know, you're not helping."

"Sorry. I just think your dad's kind of a jerk. No offense."

"None taken." I resisted the urge to scratch my head. "I'm just salty I couldn't afford a better wig."

Soon, we reached the low stone wall that enclosed the backyard. I pulled Lauren to the side, where we hid behind a large tree.

"We'll climb that stone wall when no one's looking," I said. "Then we'll join the party and blend in with the guests."

"Got it," Lauren said confidently. She twisted her long red hair into a bun.

I snuck a peek at the gathering in the backyard.

The party was packed. The finest from Los Angeles' business world mingled, drank champagne, and ate hors d'oeuvres delivered by tuxedoed waiters. Soft lighting illuminated a full bar and clusters of tables with white linens. A string quartet played upbeat music.

Ruth, my dad's executive assistant, had outdone herself.

As I gazed at the elegant party, I felt like a hungry dog looking in a butcher shop window.

But this wasn't my world anymore. It never had been, really.

A rush of nervousness flooded me. This event was *extra* fancy. If Dad found out I was crashing his party, he'd be furious.

"You okay?" Lauren asked.

I nodded, slipping the handbag strap over my wrist. "Let's do this."

I lifted myself up onto the stone wall. It was about chest high—nothing crazy. Still, I was glad I'd worn flats. Lauren gave me a thumbs-up sign.

I paused at the top, straddling the wall with my dress hiked up.

What the hell am I doing?

Going after my dreams, dammit.

Carefully, I lifted my other leg over the wall. I planned to hop down and land on the other side, conveniently hidden by some large rosemary bushes.

But my dress caught on one of the stones. As I tried to free it, my leg tangled in the fabric. I panicked, flailing wildly until I landed on the ground with a loud thud...

Catching the attention of some guy standing by the pool.

Shit, shit, shit.

I lay there for a moment with my eyes closed, praying he wouldn't be interested in coming over to investigate.

No such luck.

"Are you okay?"

I opened my eyes and almost gasped.

The Fiancé Hoax

A gorgeous, incredibly sexy guy—no, *man*—towered above me.

Are you for real? I thought to myself.

I almost said it out loud, but apparently I still had some sense left.

His muscular frame was almost unbelievable, with massive shoulders and arms that were practically bursting from the tailored suit he wore. He was older, but it only made him sexier.

Distinguished.

Powerful.

And his eyes? Oh, good Lord, those intense blue eyes bore deep, *deep* within my soul. It was a miracle I remembered how to speak.

"Yep. I'm just fine," I squeaked.

He bent down and offered me a huge, strong hand. I put my hand in his, and he helped me to my feet.

Once I was standing, he retrieved my fake glasses from the ground where they'd fallen and handed them to me. I put them back on, my face feeling hot to the touch.

"Thank you," I said, my gaze sweeping over him.

His brown hair had lighter streaks in it, as if he'd been to the beach recently. Tattoos on his forearm peeked from under his jacket sleeve.

He was gorgeous.

"No problem." His deep voice made me shiver. "Are you sure you're okay?"

Our eyes met, sending butterflies through my stomach.

"I'm sure."

I made myself look away, twisting around to check my dress for damage. It was torn at the hem, but nothing I couldn't repair later.

"Does, uh, your friend need a hand climbing over that

stone wall?" he asked. "I wouldn't want both of you injuring yourselves tonight."

I looked back at Lauren, who watched us from atop the stone wall with wide eyes. Snapping back to reality, she swung her legs over the wall—much easier to do in a shorter skirt, I'm sure—and hopped down without a hitch.

"Thanks. I'm good," she chirped.

I looked up at Mr. Hottie and forced myself to maintain eye contact. "Well, thank you for your help. We'll just be getting back to the party now."

An amused smile appeared on his full, luscious lips. "Getting *back* to the party? You mean you were here before?"

I scoffed. "Of course we were."

"So you originally came in through the front door like the rest of us," he said, clearly skeptical.

Lauren fidgeted beside me, but I felt strangely confident. He might be the most handsome man I'd ever seen, but he wasn't going to shame me for sneaking into my dad's party.

I was ready to die on this hill, dammit. Bad wig or not.

I lifted my chin. "Certainly we did."

"So the climbing over the wall thing?"

I crossed my arms over my chest. "The ladies' room was full. And if you must know, I have a small bladder. My friend was kind enough to keep me company."

He chuckled. "I see."

I nodded, preparing to make my escape from his interrogation. "Glad we got that out of the way. Now, if you don't mind—"

"Um, Felicity?" Lauren muttered under her breath. "Isn't that Ruth?"

I looked past the guy's giant shoulders to see Ruth, my dad's assistant, standing twenty feet away in her pantsuit. She narrowed her eyes suspiciously in our direction.

Shit.

I stepped back, trying to hide behind Mr. Hot Detective.

"So, how do you know Marsh?" I asked him, hoping to stall for time. I desperately needed him to stay put until Ruth moved on.

His eyebrow arched. "Marsh is my attorney. He's the attorney for most of the guests here tonight." He looked me up and down, and heat flooded my core. "Is he yours, too, since you're on a first-name basis with him?"

I swallowed. "Yes, of course he is. He's the best, after all."

"The best attorney for investors, absolutely."

I fidgeted with the platinum-blonde hair of the wig. My mouth was dry. "So, you're an investor?"

He nodded, that amused smile back on his face. "Yes."

I smiled warmly and extended my hand. "I'm Felicity, and this is Lauren."

He shook both our hands. "Cooper Pierce."

I gulped. "Of... Pierce Investing?"

"That's the one."

Lauren and I exchanged a quick glance. I could not *believe* my luck.

Cooper Pierce was the number-one investor I wanted to chat with tonight.

I'd heard my dad talk about him before. Cooper owned a very successful investment company. Best of all, he was known for taking chances by investing in small businesses.

Dad never mentioned what an absolute hottie he was.

"Are you both investors, too?" Cooper asked with a smirk.

Lauren laughed. "No, I work in a flower shop. And Felicity's a badass girl boss."

I raised an eyebrow at my friend. Lauren was not sticking to the script tonight. At all.

"I own a clothing boutique," I blurted. "I sell my own fashions that I design and sew myself." I opened my clutch and retrieved a business card, handing it to Cooper.

He looked at it, his face neutral. "Moonstone Boutique," he read.

"She's wearing one of her designs," Lauren offered.

His eyes fell on my dress and moved down slowly, taking it in.

God, why did that feel so naughty?

And *so* good?

"I don't know much about fashion," he said. "But it's a nice dress. Not the best for climbing stone walls in, though."

"Thank you." I ignored his last comment. "My specialty is vintage-inspired bohemian for the free spirit, with a modern twist."

"How many employees?"

I blinked. "None. Just me." I didn't mention that I couldn't afford to pay anyone.

"Where's the store?"

I dug my phone from my purse and brought up my photo app. I'd created a folder with pictures of the store. I passed him the phone, and he flipped through the images.

"It's right downtown," I said. "A darling little building. Tons of natural light and a good location."

"Felicity makes beautiful clothing," Lauren offered as he returned my phone. "All our friends love her designs. And she has a group of dedicated customers. Small, but dedicated."

I elbowed Lauren and cleared my throat. "I have a devoted clientele who appreciate creative designs. Women who want to wear one-of-kind pieces love my store. Plus, everything is made from natural, sustainable fibers."

He rubbed his jaw, nodding absently.

"And I studied fashion design in college," I added.

God, I probably should have worked on my elevator pitch before this party.

"But *not* business," he said.

"No, not business." I took a breath. "But I'm learning! And I do everything on my own. Designs, sewing, sales, accounting."

"Answering the phone, ordering supplies, cleaning the bathroom." Lauren counted on her fingers. "The girl's a workhorse."

"It's a labor of love." I lifted a shoulder. I wanted to come across as casual. Not desperate. "And I've managed to keep my doors open for three years."

"But her landlord's increasing the rent on her store," Lauren chipped in. She scoffed and shook her head. "Damn rent hikes. No one recognizes genius anymore."

"So, you'd like me to invest in your business," Cooper said.

"Yes." I nodded quickly.

It was shameless, but I couldn't help myself.

He studied my dress for a moment, his eyes lingering on my curves. Heat pooled between my legs.

Something told me he was studying more than just the dress.

And God help me, I wanted him to.

"It would be a smart investment," I added. "All I need is a little more time to get some traction. If I could afford advertising, it would change everything."

Lauren nodded. "Once word gets out about Moonstone, *forget* about it. You won't be able to keep the customers away."

I waited with bated breath, but Cooper was silent. Finally, he removed his phone from his pocket and typed something on the screen. Lauren and I looked at each other as he read and scrolled.

What the hell? Is he really on Facebook right now?

As the silence dragged on, my stomach twisted. My anxiety turned to annoyance. The least he could do was say no. Instead, he was ignoring me altogether, scrolling through his social media.

I sucked in air, about to tell him off. The nerve—

"Boutique fashion design sales will increase by eighty percent in the next five years," he said, still reading on his phone.

Oh. He was researching my industry.

"Yes, that's correct," I said. "And my clothes are designed for an upscale market. Women who appreciate unique pieces no one else will be wearing."

"And who have lots of money," Lauren added.

He read a bit more on his phone, then pocketed it. I held my breath, waiting for him to turn me down.

He leveled his gaze on me. "Want to go somewhere to discuss this? There's a diner down the road open now."

"Really?" I chirped. Then I composed myself. "I mean, yes, of course. I'd love to discuss this further."

I peered around his shoulder. Ruth was no longer standing nearby, but I spotted my father on the other side of the pool, laughing and talking with several of his clients and their spouses. He hadn't spotted me, but if I walked in his direction, he might see me.

And now that I thought about it, a platinum-blonde wig wasn't the best way to blend in.

Cooper went to the stone wall and turned toward me and Lauren.

"Ready?" he asked.

I frowned. "You're going to climb over the wall?"

"We all are. You don't want to walk through that party, do you?" He smirked. "Your dad might see you."

I blinked. "How did you know—"

He extended his hand toward me. "Here, I'll help you over so you don't twist an ankle this time."

2

COOPER

Felicity Hayes was like nothing I'd imagined.

Her father, Marsh, hardly spoke of her. But when he did, I got the impression she was a spoiled, clueless brat.

The young woman I just met was nothing like that. She was smart, competent, and passionate.

A little scattered and clumsy, yes.

But sexy as hell.

And totally off-limits.

Which was why it was wrong of me to imagine pulling that dress up around her waist and burying myself between her legs.

Yep, very wrong.

But as I waited for her to arrive at the diner, I could think of nothing else.

This was just a business meeting like any other. We'd discuss a potential investment—nothing more.

Get her tight little body out of your damn head.

I gulped down the rest of my ice water, trying to banish the image of her straddling that wall from my head.

I'd seen pictures of Felicity in Marsh's office. But she was a kid in those framed photos—an awkward teenager.

When had she grown up into a stunning young woman?

Okay, she was a woman who wore goofy wigs and snuck into her dad's parties.

I'd fucked with her just a little by pretending I didn't know who she was at first. I couldn't resist. It was too much fun.

Outside, an ancient Plymouth sedan pulled into a parking spot. The driver parked and turned off the headlights. Felicity stepped out of the car and rummaged in the backseat for a stack of sketchbooks.

She moved across the parking lot in her blonde wig and long blue gown, fumbling with the purse and books she carried. She was alone this time. I'd have her all to myself.

As she hurried toward the entrance, Felicity stumbled and dropped one of the sketchbooks. A stack of papers flew out, carried by a gust of wind.

I heard her yelp as she chased them down, giving me a prime view of her heart-shaped ass.

Ripe, delicious, and full. The type of ass that could drive a man crazy.

Not me, though. Not her. Not my closest friend's daughter.

Finally, she collected her things and bustled inside the diner.

"Sorry it took me a few minutes," she said as she arrived at my table. "I had to drop Lauren off at the bus stop. Then my papers flew across the parking lot outside."

"I noticed."

She dropped a fistful of loose papers and her stack of notebooks on the table. Breathless, she collapsed in the booth across from me and pushed the blonde curls out of her face.

"So, can I show you some of my designs?" She shuffled her papers, which seemed to be mock-ups of the clothes she made.

I hid my smile behind my hand. "Your, uh, *hair* is falling off your head."

Her hands flew to her head, where her wig was off-kilter. "Oh, God, how embarrassing." Her big hazel eyes went round, her face bright red.

Fuck, she was adorable. It only made me want her more.

I leaned across the table and spoke in a low voice. "Why don't you take off that ridiculous wig?"

She froze. Then with a sigh, she removed the mess of blonde frizz and tossed it on the booth beside her.

"Good call," she said. "That's much better." She shook out her real hair and flashed me a smile.

I swallowed, lost in the movement of her rich, silky brown mane. What I'd give to run my hands through that hair, then pull her close...

The waitress appeared, bringing me back to my senses. *Get a grip, Cooper.*

We each ordered coffee, then she turned her doe eyes back to me.

"How'd you know I'm Marsh's daughter?" she asked.

"He's mentioned you. Said you were into fashion or something." I glanced at her designs. "And the fact that you were sneaking into his party wearing a disguise kind of gave it away."

She blushed again, looking down at the table. "Yeah, I guess so."

I pulled at my collar. When did it get so hot in this place?

The waitress brought us the coffee, and Felicity added several packets of cream and sugar to hers.

"So, tell me about your business model."

She tucked a strand of chestnut hair behind her ear.

"I mostly focus on the creative side of things. By night, I design and sew. I have my sewing machine set up right in the store. By day, I sell the clothes I make."

"But what about your business plan?"

"Sell as much as I can?" She winced.

I sighed. "What about your profit analysis?"

She blinked. "Um..."

"How do you know how much material to order? How much product to make every month?"

"Oh, that." She lifted a shoulder. "I wing it. I'm pretty intuitive."

I nearly choked on my coffee.

"*Intuition* is your business model?"

She cringed. "Is that bad?"

I sighed. "Very bad. You need data, Felicity. Numbers. What's your profit margin?"

"Okay, I know that one. It's around five percent."

"That's terrible. What about your markup—how much do you price the products over wholesale?"

"Twenty percent. I think." She scrunched her face up.

I set my coffee cup down. "Felicity, you're *giving* your clothes away."

"No, that was just once or twice to *one* lady. And she swore she'd pay me back after she paid off her credit card."

I raised an eyebrow. "So you're *literally* giving your clothes away? Let me guess. You're giving your favorite customers discounts, too."

Her eyes darted to the side. "I have to make sure my fans come back, don't I?"

I leaned back in the booth. "That's not how it works. When you price the clothes, you need to factor in your time making them. The rent, utilities, all of it. It's not just the cost of the fabric."

"You must think I'm an idiot." She buried her face in her hands. "Lauren's always telling me I'm too generous to the customers."

"I don't think you're an idiot. I think you've got some... *interesting* ideas when it comes to running your business."

She looked up. "I thought if I was nice to them, they'd become loyal customers."

"Pay your bills first, then you can be generous."

She nodded sheepishly.

I sipped my coffee. "You need to learn how to manage a business. And at least get a portfolio to keep your designs in so they don't blow away at the first breeze."

"Okay, good points. But look at these designs." She shuffled through the papers and showed me several drawings. "This is where I'm strongest. Creating unique clothing. You can't find this just anywhere. This is gold, Cooper."

She met my eyes when she said my name. For a second, there was something there. Something between us.

I liked my name on her lips. Blushing, she quickly looked away.

"You could have the best clothes in the world," I said, "but without business sense, you'll fail."

She looked down, her face falling.

"You're running your business all wrong, Felicity."

She bit her pouty lip.

"I mean, a rent increase shouldn't make or break you if you're prepared," I said. "You need to have emergency funds. Some kind of Plan B."

"I know. I'm terrible at business, honestly." She sighed. "I guess I thought if I had the talent and the skills, I could make the store a success."

I shook my head. "Talent's not enough. You need a business plan, a marketing strategy."

"Okay, you're right. I'm just saying there's potential here. If I did all that and had some money to advertise, I know I could turn Moonstone into something... magical."

Her eyes met mine, the light catching the ring of gold in her irises. I didn't blink, and this time, she didn't look away.

"I can feel it, you know?" she asked in a breathy voice.

Her lips parted.

Were we still talking about clothes?

I leaned in a little, focused on her plump, pink mouth. Fuck, I wanted to kiss her.

"Yeah, I can feel it," I murmured. "Do you want to get out of here?"

She blinked at me, confused.

Damn it. I'd pushed too far.

The buzz of my phone in my pocket startled me. I grabbed it and swiped the screen to answer.

"Yeah?" I snapped, sounding more annoyed than I meant to. "Oh. Hi, Inga."

I studied Felicity's face as I listened to the woman on the other end. Felicity looked flustered, and she busied herself with collecting her papers and stacking them neatly.

"Okay, you're right down the road," I said to Inga. "Why don't you come over to Greene's Diner? The more, the merrier."

I ended the call and pocketed the phone. Felicity's lips were tight, and she avoided my eyes.

I ran a hand through my hair. "So, where were we?"

She narrowed her eyes. "I was just leaving."

"So soon?"

"Yes. You have some nerve, Cooper Pierce. Did you just invite me to go home with you? And you invited *Inga*, too—who sounds like a Swedish supermodel." She narrowed her eyes. "Did you think I'd agree to a... a *threesome*?"

Her face was flushed with anger as she gathered her things.

"Felicity—"

"I should've known better than to think you'd help my business without wanting anything in return."

She slid out of the booth and grabbed her stack of sketchbooks and papers. With a huff, she spun on her heels and headed toward the door.

She paused, then returned to the table. "I forgot my wig," she bit out and snatched up the frizzy mane of blonde hair.

"Wait, Felicity," I said.

But before she could retort, the front door of the diner flew open. The commotion caught her attention.

Felicity watched as Inga, my middle-aged nanny, entered. Running around her and tearing across the room were two rambunctious little blonde girls.

I rose to my feet, and my two daughters ran into my open arms. Inga hustled to keep up behind them.

"I'm sorry, Cooper," Inga said as she approached my table. "John said it was urgent. You know I'd normally never do this, but—"

"Don't worry about it," I said as I lifted my younger daughter in my arms. "Go take care of your husband. I'm just glad the movie theater you took the girls to was nearby."

Felicity watched with her mouth hanging open.

"Oh, Inga, this is Felicity, a local business owner."

Inga smiled and shook Felicity's hand. "How do you do, dear?"

"Felicity, this is Inga. My *nanny*."

Felicity flushed red and shook Inga's hand. She gave Inga a warm smile. "It's nice to meet you, Inga."

"You too, Felicity. I'd love to stay and chat but my husband needs me at home." She looked at me before hurrying toward the door. "Thanks, Cooper."

"See you soon," I said as Inga left.

I turned to Felicity with a grin. She gave me an apologetic look and fidgeted with her books.

"Felicity, let me introduce you to my daughters."

Eva was already standing before Felicity with a big smile on her face. "My name's Eva Pierce. I'm eight years old."

Felicity grinned as she shook her hand. "Hi, Eva, eight. I'm Felicity."

She turned to Lily, who buried her head against my neck.

"And this one is Lily," I said. "Say hi, Lily."

Lily turned to face Felicity, and a timid smile appeared on my daughter's face. "Hi."

"Hello, Lily. How old are you?"

Lily hid her face again.

"She's six," Eva answered. "She's shy."

Felicity nodded. "Oh, I understand. Eva and Lily. Eight and six. It's so nice to meet you both."

She looked at me, a trace of guilt on her face. *Sorry*, she mouthed.

I grinned at her. She'd been sexy as hell when she was angry.

Eva looked up at me. "Daddy, Inga said that Mommy canceled our spring break visit. We're not spending a week with her?"

"No, sweetheart, you're not." I brushed her hair out of her face. "I'm sorry."

"She always cancels." Eva crossed her arms over her chest with a pout, and Lily pressed her head against my neck.

"Let's talk about this at home," I said.

Felicity looked at the girls sympathetically, then at me.

"Their mother and I are divorced," I explained.

"I see," Felicity said.

"What's that?" Eva pointed at the wig Felicity clutched in her hand.

"Oh, this. It's a wig." Felicity looked down at the frizzy mass.

"Were you wearing it?" Eva asked.

"Yes."

"Why?"

Felicity looked uncomfortable. "I was, um, hiding from someone earlier."

Lily lifted her head and squirmed out of my arms. I set her on her feet. She investigated the wig cautiously. "Like hide and seek?"

"Exactly like hide and seek," Felicity said.

Lily's face brightened. "That's my favorite game."

Felicity kneeled down to Lily's level so the girls could see the wig better. Eva touched the hair with curiosity, and Lily followed suit.

"I like freeze tag," Eva announced. "Or dodgeball." She began to play with Felicity's real hair. "Your hair is much prettier than that one."

"Oh, thank you." Felicity smiled up at me as Eva started to braid her long hair.

"What's that stuff?" Lily asked, pointing at the stack of papers and sketchbooks in Felicity's arms. Eva let go of Felicity's hair as she peered at the drawing on top.

"These are my sketches. Drawings."

Lily's eyes lit up. "You like to draw?"

Felicity nodded. "Uh-huh. I draw pictures of clothes, and then I make them."

"You make *clothes*?" Eva asked.

"Yep. With a sewing machine." She moved to the table and laid out some papers for the girls to see.

The three of them climbed into the booth, one girl on either side of Felicity. Eva and Lily peered at the drawings, fascinated.

"Ooh, that's a cool dress!" Eva chirped. "And that one, too!"

"Felicity's a fashion designer," I said. "She has her own store."

But the girls had lost all interest in what I had to say. I slid into the booth opposite them and watched.

"What's that one?" Lily pointed.

"That's a winter coat."

"It's much nicer than the coats Daddy makes us wear," Eva said. "He makes us wear *boring* clothes."

"Hey, I keep you warm, don't I?" I asked. "A winter coat just has to keep you from freezing. Six- and eight-year-olds don't have to be fashion models."

My daughters weren't listening. "Daddy has such boring taste in clothes," Eva said.

"Yeah," Lily agreed.

Felicity laughed.

"This is so cool," Eva gushed. "I didn't know anyone made their own clothes!"

"Me neither," Lily said.

"Daddy never takes us to see cool stuff like this," Eva complained.

I rolled my eyes. "Yes, you two live *such* a deprived life."

Eva looked at the blue dress Felicity wore. "Did you make that?"

"Uh-huh."

Eva touched the fabric on Felicity's shoulder and beamed. "Wow!"

I watched as the girls pummeled Felicity with several more questions. She was good with them. Really good.

The girls were totally at ease with her. And Lily? I'd *never* seen her open up to someone new so quickly.

It was amazing.

But I didn't want to scare Felicity off. My daughters were energetic, and they could be overwhelming to people. After several minutes of questioning, I decided to wrap things up.

"Girls, it's time to say goodbye to Felicity."

"Just five more minutes! Please, Daddy?" Eva begged.

Lily looked up at me with puppy dog eyes.

"Sorry. It's already past your bedtime. But maybe you can see her later. Felicity, would you like to come by our place tomorrow to discuss your business over lunch?"

Eva beamed. "And play with us?"

"I'd love to," Felicity laughed.

"Yay!" Eva cheered. Lily was quiet, but a smile crept across her face.

Felicity gathered her belongings again. I got her phone number and texted her our address.

"See you at noon," I said. "And for the love of God, put those designs in a folder so they don't blow away."

"I will," she said, biting her lip.

Holy shit, I wanted to taste those full, plump lips. I wanted to taste every inch of her perfect body.

But I never slept with business associates.

And Felicity had no idea what kind of business deal she was about to get into.

3

FELICITY

"How about this one?"

Lauren scrunched her nose up. "No way. Too stuffy. You don't want to look like a librarian, do you?"

I stood before the mirror in a suit jacket and slacks. "I don't want to look like an exotic dancer, either. This is a business lunch. With children involved."

"But you *do* want him to jump your bones, right?" Lauren grinned.

"Absolutely not! I just want him to invest in my business."

Lauren lifted an eyebrow. "Uh-huh. I know that look on your face."

I took refuge in the closet, hiding in the racks of clothes. "There's no look on my face!"

Lauren followed me, close on my heels. "Yes, there is! You want to bang this guy!"

"I do not!"

She raised both eyebrows expectantly.

I bit my lip. "Okay, maybe I've thought about it once or twice."

"Once or twice? Uh-huh."

Dammit. I couldn't hide a thing from Lauren.

"Okay, fine." I closed my eyes. "I want Cooper bad, Lauren. *So* bad."

"I knew it!"

Ever since last night, he was all I could think about. I knew it was wrong, but I couldn't help it. The way he leaned in and got close...

It was enough to leave me breathless.

"You should've seen him with his daughters at that diner!" I gushed. "I never knew single dads could be so hot."

"I know, right? It's something about how protective they are." She smiled dreamily. "And what about that tattoo peeking out under his sleeve? The bad boy vibe mixed with his big shot business look is *hot*."

"He's incredible." I sighed. "And... I think he wanted to hook up last night."

Lauren blinked. "Shut. Up. You're just *now* telling me this?" She pressed her hands to her chest. "Moi? Your best friend and housemate?"

I paused. "It was so weird. I think he regretted it as soon as he asked me. What does that mean? He's attracted to me... but he doesn't want to be?"

"He probably thinks you're too young or something," Lauren said with a dismissive wave of her hand. "How old is he?"

"Forty-two. And yes, I learned that by stalking him online."

At twenty-six, I'd never dated anyone over thirty. But compared to Cooper, every twenty-something guy I knew looked like an immature boy.

Lauren laughed. "So, you're younger. Big deal. He'll get over that."

"Or he realizes it's dumb to sleep with a business contact." I shook myself out of my daze. "Which means I have to get the whole thing out of my head right now. There's no way I'm sleeping with Cooper Pierce."

"Why? Who says you can't mix business and pleasure?"

"I do. My boutique comes first. If I start sleeping with my investor, it could mean all kinds of trouble."

I plucked a salmon-colored dress from the rack and started changing into it.

"And all kinds of fun."

"Absolutely not. Besides, I don't even know if he's going to invest in Moonstone yet. That's what this meeting is about."

I stood in front of the mirror. It was a structured dress that fell to my knees. Appropriate for a business casual lunch, but feminine enough to feel pretty.

"That's one of my favorite designs of yours." Lauren smiled. "Wear that one."

"Salmon dress it is." I put in small hoop earrings and grabbed a purse.

"You got this, babe. This guy's going to save your boutique. And he's *totally* going to give you mind-blowing orgasms. Hopefully not in that order."

"Dream on." I stepped into my heels and rolled my eyes. "You're not working today?"

Lauren shook her head. "Got the whole weekend off." She looked over my shoulder as I stood before the mirror. "You look beautiful, Fel. Knock 'em dead."

∽

My nerves were through the roof as I parked my car at Cooper Pierce's house.

No, *mansion*—a sprawling estate in the ritzy Brentwood area of Los Angeles.

It put my dad's house to shame.

"Thank you for not breaking down," I mumbled to my car as I stepped out of it. The Plymouth looked ridiculous parked in front of this house.

Cooper's front door flew open. Eva shot out like a bullet.

"You're finally here!" she called, running up to me.

"Hi, Eva." I laughed.

She came to a stop and looked at my car, confused. "What kind of car is that?"

"It's, um, a Plymouth Breeze."

She frowned. "I've *never* seen a car like that before."

"They haven't made those in, what, twenty years?" A deep voice from the door made us both look up. "Now *that* was a good business decision."

Cooper stood in the doorway with a smirk.

"Are you insulting my car?" I asked. Eva grabbed my hand, and we walked toward him.

"Wouldn't dream of it," he said, holding the door open as we stepped inside. "Come in. Monica just got lunch ready."

"I take it Monica's another employee of yours?"

He nodded. "The housekeeper." Then he leaned in and lowered his voice so only I would hear. "Don't worry. I don't have any Swedish supermodels waiting to ambush you."

His breath was warm on my skin, and his voice made goosebumps appear on my neck.

Clearing my throat, I stepped inside with Eva on my heels.

"Look, Felicity, I'm wearing a dress like yours!" She twirled in her hot pink dress, flaring the skirt out.

"That's beautiful!" I exclaimed. Eva tugged on my hand and led me through the elegant foyer and into a massive, gorgeous living room.

Lily was sitting on a large sofa with a picture book. "Hi, Lily!" I said.

"She's wearing a blue dress. Like the one you wore yesterday," Eva said.

Lily slid off the couch and gave a spin to show off her dress. I smiled and clapped my hands.

These girls were a delight. Eva was fearless and outgoing. Lily was shy, but sweet and gentle. They were both adorable.

"Wow, what beautiful dresses!" I said. "And you said your dad bought boring clothes for you."

"This is the good stuff," Eva said. "You should see the play clothes he picked out for us." She rolled her eyes.

Cooper laughed. "Okay, girls, Inga's going to take you to the park now while Felicity and I chat."

"Can I show Felicity our room, Dad?" Eva asked.

"Maybe later."

Inga entered the living room from the kitchen with her purse over her shoulder. "Okay, girls, get your jackets in case it gets cold." She gave me a big smile. "Hi, Felicity."

"Hey, Inga. Is your husband okay?"

"Oh, thanks for asking, dear. He's fine. We have to monitor him for heart trouble these days, but thankfully it was a false alarm."

"Glad to hear it."

Inga smiled at me, then corralled the girls to the foyer. They got their jackets, shouted their goodbyes to Cooper and me, and left through the front door. With them gone, it was suddenly quiet.

Cooper turned to me. Our eyes met.

He looked amazing in his button-down shirt, the sleeves rolled up to reveal meaty forearms. The edgy tattoos on one arm, paired with his overall wealthy businessman look, made me weak in the knees.

Look away, look away.

"Hungry?"

"Uh-huh," I squeaked.

And then I realized he was referring to food.

4

COOPER

"So, where did we leave off last night?" I asked between bites of my Indian korma.

Eva and Lily ate mac and cheese with Inga earlier. I wanted to speak to Felicity alone.

Felicity dabbed her napkin at her mouth. "You were saying I had no business sense." She shifted uncomfortably in her seat.

"Look, I'm blunt, Felicity. That's how I got to where I am now. But I know what I'm doing. You need customers to get inside your store, and you need to make enough money to keep your business running."

She sighed. "If only it were that easy."

"It can be."

We ate in silence for a few moments. Finally, I looked at her.

"Why are you driving that ancient car?"

"It took me months to save up for that thing. I got a good deal on Craigslist." She stabbed a chunk of chicken with her fork and shrugged. "Times are tough. I put every extra dime I have into Moonstone."

I watched her for a moment. Felicity was unique, and it wasn't just her looks. She wasn't at all like how her father talked about her. He described her as lost and aimless.

This girl was totally different. Brave. Resilient. Special.

It took guts to ask her dad's clients for a loan to save her boutique. She was passionate about her business. I could relate to that.

Then there was the magnetic pull I felt toward her...

I shook the thought out of my head.

"You know, I would never let one of my daughters drive a heap of junk like that. Why hasn't Marsh bought you a new vehicle?"

Felicity looked down at her lap. "My father doesn't believe in parents helping their adult children. Especially when they go into a business he doesn't approve of."

"Wow."

She shrugged. "I'm used to it. He *did* pay for my college tuition. So I'm thankful for that. But since graduation, I haven't expected any help from him."

I nodded. "It makes sense on a certain level. He didn't come from wealth—he worked for everything he has. I guess that shaped his ideas about helping his daughter out."

She pushed her food around on the plate. "I guess so."

"Still, though. It wouldn't kill him to help you a little. He could turn things around for you with a loan. Hell, just paying for some business courses would help. Anything."

She nodded. "I know."

"In all the years I've known him, I never would have guessed he would be such a stickler with his only child."

She looked up. "So you've known him for a while?"

"Yeah, we go back. When I started my investing business, I hired him as my lawyer right away. Over the years, we became friends. He was there for me when my wife and I split up."

She dropped her fork. "Marshall Hayes? *My* father was there for you?"

"It was surprising to me, too. I didn't know the guy had it in him. But he felt he could relate. You know, with losing your mother."

Felicity's face fell slightly. She looked away.

I cringed. What a dick thing to say.

"Shit. I'm sorry to bring up a delicate subject. And it's not the same thing as my divorce. Obviously."

"No, it's okay. It's been several years since Mom passed." She took a long gulp of her tea. "I'm just surprised my dad could provide emotional support to anyone."

"Yeah, he's not all bad."

"So you two are really... *friends*?"

"Yes. I guess you could say I'm his closest friend."

Felicity shook her head, bewildered. "I had no idea you and my dad were so tight. He keeps his life private from me." She chuckled. "I didn't even know he had any real friends. Besides his business associates and partners."

"So I take it you two aren't the best at communication?"

"*My dad* is not the best at communication," she said. "At least not when it comes to his own daughter."

"Yeah, I can see that."

We finished our meals in silence. I cleared our plates from the table and sat back down.

It was *go* time.

"Look, Felicity. You need some cash to keep your boutique afloat. You also need to learn how to manage a business."

She leaned forward, holding her breath.

"I can help you with all that," I said.

Her face opened up into a big grin and she clasped her hands together.

"Really? That's wonderful, Cooper. You won't regret this! Your investment will be well spent." She pulled a notebook from her bag and began to flip through pages. "What are the terms of an arrangement like this? I did some research, and I was seeing anything from thirty to fifty percent. But it all depends on what your process is. What were you thinking?"

She looked up at me. She was beaming, and it was adorable. I wanted nothing more than to scoop her up and carry her to my bed.

"I'd like to have a non-traditional agreement."

"Oh." She leaned back a little. "What kind of agreement?" She narrowed her eyes suspiciously.

"Don't worry. I'm not going to ask you to sleep with me in return for investing in your business."

"Okay..."

"My ex-wife, Gen, is suing me for custody of my daughters."

The words were heavy in my throat. I stood up and began to pace through the room.

"They've lived with me for the past two years," I said. "Gen's never been the most dedicated mother, to put it lightly. But now she says she wants the girls to live with her. She wants child support, of course. She spent her divorce settlement, and now she's out of money. So she's trying to get the girls."

"That's awful," Felicity breathed. Her hands were clasped over her heart.

"Yeah." I sighed. "My ex-wife has... problems."

Felicity nodded silently, watching me pace.

"The girls don't want to live with her. Gen has never

been interested in being a mother to them. It hurts them terribly."

"I'm so sorry, Cooper. I can tell the girls really love you. This must be difficult."

I nodded. "Very."

She exhaled. "So where do I come in?"

"I have an attorney specializing in family law. He says the judge handling my case is tough. Judge Graves wants children to be in a two-parent household. But when that's not available, he almost always grants custody to the mother. Even when that particular mother has never been very maternal."

"Uh-huh," Felicity said slowly.

I sat at the table and leaned in toward her.

"I need you to pretend to be my fiancée."

5

FELICITY

I nearly fell off my chair.

"You want me to do *what*?"

"Pretend to be my fiancée."

I rose to my feet so quickly the chair toppled over underneath me. Now it was my turn to pace back and forth across the kitchen floor. "Yeah, I got that part. I just can't believe you're asking me to do... *that*."

"Think of it as a business arrangement." He folded his hands calmly on the table.

I recoiled. This was all so easy for him.

"I was expecting you to ask for a portion of my sales. Not some kind of escort service."

He laughed. "I'm not asking you to provide sexual services, Felicity."

I rolled my eyes. "Oh, that's a relief."

"Unless, of course, you *want* to provide them."

I spun on my heels and glared at him. A smile crept across his face. The bastard thought this was funny.

"I'm just asking you to play a role. Go to the custody

hearing with me, make some appearances with me in public. Pretend to be madly in love."

"And you think this will make the judge rule in your favor?" I scoffed.

"Yes, I do. I think this is the only way I have a shot in hell. My attorney agrees."

I shook my head. This was too crazy. "Is this a joke, Cooper? Did my dad put you up to this or something?"

"I'm totally serious. And I'd prefer we keep your dad out of it."

"But... why me? I'm sure you know a lot of single women you could ask instead."

For some strange reason, my throat closed up when I said the last part.

Why on earth would the idea of Cooper dating a lot of women upset me? I didn't even know the guy.

"Because you're perfect for the job. You're charming, articulate, and attractive. And my daughters like you."

My face grew warm at his compliments. I looked away.

"But I'm not successful," I added.

"Not yet. But you're creative and passionate about your business. I have no doubt your boutique will be a success in time."

My heart lifted a little at his words. "You sure know how to flatter a girl, Cooper Pierce."

He flashed me a charming smile, and I looked away before I got lost in his gaze.

"You *are* single, right?" he asked. "I haven't heard your dad complain about some guy you're seeing lately, so I assumed you were."

Oh, God. My dad spoke to him about my love life? My face felt even hotter.

"Yes, I'm single," I muttered.

"Perfect."

"So my dad doesn't know you want me to do this?" I asked.

"No," he said. "He'd kill me if I knew I was suggesting it to you."

"So you would... what? Keep it a secret from him?"

"Ideally, yes." He sighed. "But if he does find out, he knows what I've been through with Gen. He won't like this arrangement, but he won't sabotage it."

He stood up and crossed the space between us, standing in front of me. My heart raced to be so close to him. His spicy cologne invaded my senses.

"Help me keep custody of my daughters, Felicity. If you agree, I'll invest in your business. Moonstone Boutique will be a success. I guarantee it. And you'll keep all your profit. No loan repayment. No need to share your income with me."

I blinked, staring at him. I was woozy all of a sudden.

"And you'll be helping my daughters out, too. Gen is not fit to be a mother. She wouldn't provide a stable environment for the girls."

"How long?" I breathed.

"Three months."

He was even closer now, looking down at me. So close I felt his breath on my skin. Wetness pooled between my legs. My lips parted, my breath caught in my lungs.

At that moment, I would have agreed to almost anything he said.

"Okay."

"You'll do it?" His face lit up.

"I'll do it."

Cooper took my hands and squeezed them. His gaze lingered on my lips. He leaned in a tiny bit.

For a second, I was sure he was going to kiss me.

But he pulled back, letting go of me and taking a step away as he pulled his phone from his pocket.

"This is great, Felicity. We're going to make a good team." He grinned as he started swiping through apps on his phone.

I took a deep breath. I was still a little unsteady on my feet.

"You'll have to move in, of course," he said. "I'll set up the moving company now to help you."

"Wait, what?" I gripped the edge of the counter. "I have to move in *here*?"

He looked at me. "We need to keep up appearances. Most engaged couples live together, after all."

"That's... I didn't know I'd have to move in."

He looked at me over his phone. "We need this engagement to look believable. If there's a shadow of doubt, it will hurt my chances in court."

I chewed my lip. What was I getting myself into?

"You'll have your own room. I don't think anyone will be checking to make sure we sleep in the same bed."

The thought of sharing a bed with Cooper made my mouth water.

"You'll be totally comfortable here," Cooper said. "Think of it as a vacation. I assume your apartment is on the same... level as the Plymouth Breeze?"

"Pretty much."

"Then you might enjoy your time here. Monica is an excellent cook. She'll make anything you want. She comes to work six days a week, so you won't have to worry about meals or housekeeping, which will free up your time to focus on your business. Plus, the girls already love you."

"They do?"

He nodded. "Absolutely. Lily is never that talkative with new people. She warmed up to you very fast. Eva, too. They'll love having you around for a few months."

I smiled, tracing the edge of the granite counter. "That part sounds fun."

He returned to tapping on his cell phone. "So, when should I schedule the movers? How about tomorrow? I'd like to start immediately."

I swallowed.

The whole arrangement was insane. I was doing something crazy already. Why not embrace it and go totally off the deep end?

"Sure." I threw my arms in the air. "I can move in tomorrow."

I took a sip of water, sneaking a peek at his muscled body.

How could I possibly share a roof with this man for three months?

6

COOPER

I stood in the doorway and watched as Felicity drove away in her car.

I'd managed to do it.

I didn't know how, but I'd miraculously convinced this gorgeous young woman to pose as my fake fiancée.

Suddenly, all of the problems that had been plaguing me were solved.

With Felicity wearing my ring, I'd have a good shot at keeping custody of the girls. Plus, I'd get to work on a new business project. That was a relief—I'd felt stagnant in my work for so long.

And the girls would finally have a maternal figure in their life, even if it was temporary.

Inga was the closest thing to a female role model they had. I was thankful for her—Inga was great. But she had kids of her own. Her family came first, of course.

Eva and Lily would love getting to know Felicity.

But while I had solved my existing problems, I'd also created several new ones.

Namely, I'd have to figure out how to explain this to my daughters. And somehow keep it from my best friend.

But the biggest challenge? Keeping my hands off my fake fiancée.

I had some time before Inga returned home with the girls. Without a further thought, I ran upstairs and slammed the door to my bedroom behind me.

Shedding my clothes on the way to the bathroom, I turned the shower on full blast to cold.

I stepped inside the freezing spray of water. I gritted my teeth.

Get your friend's daughter out of your filthy mind.

I leaned forward and pressed my palms against the shower wall. I'd have to freeze the image of Felicity out of my head.

But those round hips, that long brown hair I wanted to wrap around my fist... Those pouty pink lips that would look so good wrapped around my cock.

Damn it.

Not even a cold shower could help. My hard-on was more persistent than ever.

With a sigh, I shifted the shower valve to hot water. I wrapped my hand around my shaft and began to stroke the length.

Earlier, in the kitchen, I'd wanted to unbutton that pretty pink dress she was wearing. I would pick her up and put her on the counter to dive between her legs. I'd taste her sweet honey and make her writhe around and beg for more.

My mouth watered at the thought of sucking her perfect flesh and making her orgasm under my tongue.

Then I would set her on her feet, turn her around and bend her over the counter.

I stroked myself in the shower and increased my speed.

The Fiancé Hoax

I'd grab her by the hips to lift that perfect ass into the air. Spreading her cheeks, I would enter her slowly, teasingly. I'd reach around and play with her perfect, bouncy tits.

Then I'd push myself inside her walls all the way, making her moan and gasp. I would pump in and out of her tight body until I filled her sweet, hot little pussy with my cum.

"Oh, fuck," I muttered in the shower. I clenched my cock tighter as it throbbed and pulsed.

My release shot across the shower. I moaned, clenching my teeth. I pumped my length, squeezing the last few drops out.

Holy *shit*. Fantasy sex with Felicity was better than most real sex I'd had in my life.

I cleaned up the shower and myself. But there was no way to get rid of the disgust I felt for myself.

Felicity was my friend's daughter—and now my business partner. I had to get her out of my head.

I towel dried my body and my hair, styling it the way it had been before. I dressed in the outfit I had been wearing earlier so no one would suspect anything.

Then I went downstairs and put the lunch things away. Just as I finished, the front door flew open and the sound of excited voices and commotion entered the house.

"Daddy! Daddy!" Eva shouted. "Where are you?"

I headed toward the foyer, where the girls were removing their shoes at Inga's prodding.

I smiled at the chaos they created in their wake. "I'm right here, silly goose."

"Hi, Daddy," Lily said as I bent down to her level. She and her sister reached up to hug my neck. I picked them both up, one in each arm, and spun them around.

"Whee!" Eva squealed.

I moved to return them to their feet, but Lily clung to me. "Again!"

I spun them around again, then set them down.

"Where's Felicity?" Lily asked.

"She had to go home," I said.

"Aww, man," Eva said. "I wanted to show her my room!"

Lily looked disappointed, too.

"I'm sure you'll see her again soon." I looked at Inga. The smile on her face was obvious, even though she was halfway hidden as she rummaged in the hall closet.

"Yay!" Lily clapped her hands.

"Now let's play airplane!" Eva shouted. "I go first because I'm older."

Inga laughed as she put away their jackets. "You girls are going to wear your father out."

"Okay, one round of airplane each," I said. Both girls cheered and clapped their hands.

I picked Eva up and lifted her over my head, moving around with her as she spread her arms and legs wide like an airplane.

"Make the noises, Daddy," Lily advised.

I made the airplane noises and the girls giggled.

Inga smiled as I set Eva back down. "You're almost too big for that, Eva."

Eva shook her head. "No, I won't be too big until I'm at least eleven, right, Daddy?"

I laughed. "We'll have to see about that. Okay, Lily, your turn."

I lifted her up and flew her around the room with the appropriate sound effects.

"One more time!" Lily asked.

I shook my head. "No, that's all for now. I need to talk to

you girls about something. Why don't you go wait for me in the living room?"

"Okay." Eva looked at her sister. "Race you!"

The two girls shot down the hall.

"Careful not to break anything!" Inga called after them. "They're like two tiny bulls in a china shop," she said to me with a laugh.

"Thanks for taking them to the park, Inga. We're good for the rest of the day. Why don't you cut out of here a little early?"

"I appreciate that, Cooper. I'll see you on Monday." She grabbed her jacket and opened the front door.

"Sounds good. Thanks, Inga." I shut the door behind her and took a deep breath.

In the living room, the girls were chasing each other around the sofa and laughing hysterically.

"Okay, you hooligans," I said. "Come sit down next to me."

I patted the couch cushions, and they plopped down on either side of me.

"Did you have fun at the park?" I asked.

"Uh-huh. I went down the slide fifteen times!" Eva exclaimed.

"I went down six times, Daddy." Lily said. "But I like the swings better."

"I jumped out of the swing when it was really high," Eva said.

"Be careful doing that, little duck," I said.

"I thought I was a goose!" She broke into belly laughter.

Lily looked at me, her blue eyes round. "When's Felicity going to come back?"

"That's what I wanted to talk to you two about." I swallowed. "I have some good news for you. Felicity is going to come stay with us for a while."

Lily's eyes grew large, and Eva sprang to her feet.

"Really?" Eva asked.

"Yes. She'll move in tomorrow."

Eva and Lily let out a chorus of cheers and shouts.

"OMG! Yay!" Eva exclaimed. She and Lily high-fived each other. "We love Felicity."

Lily nodded her head in agreement.

"She's so cool and funny and pretty," Eva said.

"And nice," Lily added. "Do you think she'll take us to the park?"

I shifted in my seat. I knew the girls liked Felicity, but I wasn't expecting this much enthusiasm.

"I'm not sure about that yet. We'll have to see when she gets here."

"Will she stay with us forever?" Lily asked.

"No, not forever," I said gently. "For a few months."

"Oh," Lily said, thinking it over. "Is she going to be our nanny?"

"No, Felicity won't be your nanny," I said. "Inga is still your nanny. Felicity will be… spending some time with us."

How could I explain this to them? I didn't want to lie to my daughters.

"I care for Felicity very much. I like her," I told the girls. Somehow, that part came naturally. "Even though I haven't known her very long."

Lily seemed to decide that was acceptable, and she nodded. "What room will she be in?"

"The spare bedroom next to mine," I answered.

Eva was strangely quiet, and she studied me.

Lily crawled into my lap. I cuddled her and answered her questions about Felicity. I told her that Inga would still pick them up from school, and that hopefully Felicity would eat dinner with us, but I didn't know her schedule yet. Finally she wiggled free.

"I'm going to go check on my bean sprout," she said.

"Good idea."

She'd brought home a tiny plant from her first-grade class and kept it in her bedroom. I watched as she ran upstairs.

Eva was still quiet.

"Are you okay with this, Eva?"

She thought about it, looking out the front window. "Yes. I like Felicity. It'll be fun to have her here."

I nodded. "Yeah."

She looked at me, her face tilted to the side. "Is Felicity going to help you win so we can stay with you?"

My heart just about leapt out of my chest.

I'd always known Eva was smart. But I never expected her to figure this out so easily.

I nodded slowly. "Yes, she is."

"Oh," she said. "I hope it works."

"Me, too."

"We don't want to live with Mom." Eva looked down as she traced the seam on the sofa cushion.

"I know, baby. I'm doing everything I can to keep you girls with me."

"Okay," she said with a nod. "Good."

She gave me a quick hug, then ran off to play.

I exhaled, leaning back in my seat. I hoped I was doing the right thing.

But there was no other option. If I didn't fake an engagement, my lawyer was sure I'd lose my daughters.

Gen would get custody of them. Their lives would be uprooted. They'd live in an unstable home with a mother who didn't know how to give them love. And who knew how many random men she'd bring into their lives.

I would never forgive myself if that happened.

No. That wasn't *going* to happen.

I had to do this to protect my daughters. They wouldn't be safe with Gen.

7

FELICITY

"Are you sure this is for the best?"

I raised an eyebrow at Lauren. "Weren't you telling me I should jump his bones just a few hours ago?"

"Yes," she said. "And I still think you should. But that doesn't mean you should move in with the guy and pretend to be engaged."

She folded the sweater I handed her and tucked it in the suitcase on my bed.

"It's just for three months." I grabbed an armload of clothes from my closet and laid them on the bed.

Lauren shook her head. "Faking an engagement to win a custody battle? That sounds serious, babe."

"It *is* serious. Those little girls belong with their dad, from what I can tell." I begin to fold a peasant blouse. "Besides, this is the only way I can get Cooper to help Moonstone."

"I just don't want you getting tangled up in some big emotional mess." She blew a strand of red hair out of her face. "I don't want you getting hurt, Felicity."

I smiled and squeezed her shoulder. "I appreciate your

concern, but you don't need to worry about me. I'm not going to fall in love with Cooper."

She looked at me. "What if you get attached to his daughters? It might be hard to spend all that time with them and then have to leave."

"I can handle it. I like those girls a lot, but I've never been great with children. Even in high school, when I was desperate to earn money to buy clothes and my allowance wasn't enough, I didn't babysit. I worked in fast food instead of taking care of other people's kids." I laughed. "I've got this."

My chest tightened. I was mostly confident about this plan, but I couldn't help feeling a little nervous.

Lauren looked at my desk in the corner. It was cluttered with sketches and fabric samples—work I'd brought home from the boutique.

"Do you want me to start packing this stuff?"

"Nah. I'll do it after the clothes."

She shook her head. "I don't know how you can stand to be so disorganized."

I chuckled. "Now you sound like Cooper."

Lauren turned to me, her face long. "I'm going to miss you, Felicity."

"Hey, come here." I wrapped her in a hug. "I'll only be gone for three months."

"I know. But this moldy dump isn't going to be the same without you around here."

"At least you won't have to deal with me leaving a mess in the common spaces," I offered.

"That *is* a major perk."

My phone rang, and I looked at the screen.

"That's my dad. I better take it."

Lauren headed toward the door. "Tell Marsh he throws a

mean party." She grinned at me over her shoulder as she left.

I chuckled. "Thanks for your help with the packing!"

I took a long breath, then swiped the phone to answer.

"Hi, Dad."

"Hello, Felicity." I could tell right away he was angry. "Did you sneak into my party last night?"

Oh, shit.

Should I deny or confess?

"I, uh, well..."

"Ruth says she saw you and Lauren there."

I sighed. Time to confess and apologize.

"Yes. I snuck into the party."

"Damn it, Felicity. These events are strictly for my business associates and clients."

"I know, Dad. And I'm really sorry I did that. It's just, I was desperate—"

"Your mother and I raised you better than this. What the hell were you thinking? Sneaking into an invitation-only event? These parties aren't for me to have a good time and drink champagne. The point is to network and secure my business ties."

"I know, Dad. I know how important your law firm is to you. That's why I wish you could understand why my boutique is important to me."

He snorted. "So *that's* why you snuck in? I should have known. Felicity, you can't go around my back soliciting my clients to bail out your failing business."

A lump pressed against my throat. "A lot of businesses struggle their first few years. It doesn't mean I should give up on my dreams."

He snorted. "If your dreams are based on nothing more

substantial than cotton candy and clouds, then maybe you *should* give up on them."

Tears threatened to spill from my eyes. But I wouldn't let myself cry on the phone with my father. He would just see it as another weakness of mine.

He was so fixated on making me fend for myself that he couldn't understand how much he was hurting me.

"Felicity, I've told you over and over. Fashion design is not a reasonable career path. It's nearly impossible to make a name for yourself in that industry. And you're combining design with retail. Which you know nothing about, by the way. That boutique of yours was doomed to fail from the beginning."

"I know your opinion about it, Dad." It took everything I had to keep my voice from breaking.

"*And* you know I warned you not to ask any of my investor friends for help. But that's exactly what you tried to do last night, isn't it?"

I clamped my eyes shut. I had to get off the phone before I broke down.

"I'm sorry, Dad. It won't happen again." I paused. "I need to run now. Can we talk later?"

"Fine. Talk to you later."

The call ended with a click before I could say goodbye. I tossed my phone on the bed and then collapsed onto the comforter beside it.

My chest ached. Why did he have to talk to me like that? Would it kill him to believe in me for once?

I let a few tears fall then I dried my eyes and forced myself to get out of bed. I knew my dad loved me. He just had a funny way of showing it.

And maybe if I could save Moonstone Boutique, I could show him that my dreams meant something.

I headed toward my desk and gathered all the paperwork and drawing supplies. My mind raced with a dozen worries.

Could Cooper really save my business? What if my father was right? What if this boutique was a pipe dream all along?

Despite my nerves, a smile crept over my face.

I could hardly believe I'd be moving in with Cooper Pierce. Living under the same roof as that Adonis was thrilling enough. But I was excited to spend time with his daughters, too.

It was surprising because I'd never been crazy about kids. Still, I found myself thinking about Eva and Lily a lot.

In fact...

I sat down at my desk and started sketching a jumpsuit for Eva and a dress for Lily. I smiled as my pencil moved across the paper. They would look so cute in these designs.

I reached for my brightest-colored markers, filling in the outfits with bold color. I could imagine Eva playing on the playground in the jumpsuit and Lily dancing around in the little dress.

I looked at the rough drafts. Not bad. Now, about those winter coats...

Grabbing a fresh sheet of paper, I furiously blocked out designs for children's outerwear.

I had never designed clothes for children before. Kids weren't my target market. But this was surprisingly fun and stress-relieving.

And since my big move into Cooper's house was just hours away, I could use the relief.

I knocked on Cooper's door the next afternoon.

He opened the door, and I realized I'd somehow forgotten how huge he was.

Well over six feet with shoulders that filled the doorframe, he stood before me looking hotter than ever. Rugged, even, with his button-down plaid shirt and the masculine stubble on his face.

God, I could just imagine him chopping wood in the forest somewhere. He'd come inside the cabin after a long day, all sweaty and hot. I'd be in the kitchen, baking pies in a frilly apron. He'd lift me up and carry me to bed, or to a bearskin rug...

"Where are the movers?"

His question startled me from my fantasy. I blinked.

"Oh. The movers. I told them I didn't need their help." I looked back at my Plymouth. "Everything I needed fit into my car. It seemed silly to use them."

"Okay, then I'll help you bring it in."

It took us three trips to bring my suitcases and work files from my car upstairs to my new, temporary room. It was a spare bedroom next to Cooper's room.

He set my suitcase down inside the closet, then walked across the hardwood floor. I snuck a peek at the endless expanse of his shoulders and back as he reached up to open the curtains.

Sunlight flooded the space. It was a beautiful room, with powder blue walls and tasteful, modern furnishings.

"See, I promised you your own room. I trust you'll be comfortable here?"

"Absolutely. This is perfect."

He walked to the desk and picked up a stack of paperwork. "I'd like you to read this soon."

"Of course."

I glanced at it, thinking it would be an agreement for the engagement. But instead, it was all about Cooper's investment in Moonstone Boutique.

I flipped through the pages. "There's no mention of the engagement?"

"No. Couldn't risk putting it on paper. But it's implicit in your acceptance of the contract."

"Okay. I'll read it later." I set it down on the bed. "What about ground rules between you and me?"

He folded his arms across his broad, strong chest. "Such as?"

I fidgeted with my hair. "Well, I think we should agree on what I'm required to *do,* exactly, as your fiancée."

"You'll need to make public appearances with me. Play the part of an adoring fiancée in love. And it needn't be high-profile black-tie events. After I report my engagement status to the court, my attorney says Gen's lawyer's office might start watching me for any indication it's fake. So we'll need to be seen together doing everyday things like any engaged couple."

"Okay. That sounds reasonable." I swallowed. "What about... physical contact?"

The corners of his mouth curved into a slight smile. A naughty smile, even.

"While we're in public, yes. Only tasteful contact, of course. Holding hands, lingering gazes, my hand on your back. That sort of thing."

My mouth salivated. "No kissing, then?"

He paused, then took a step closer. "I think there should be kissing to make it believable."

He looked down at my lips, his blue eyes deep and intense. I could get lost in those eyes forever and be happy.

"Don't you?" he murmured.

My nipples hardened and pressed against the thin fabric of my blouse. "Mmm-hmm." I cleared my throat. "A few pecks on the cheek, though, right? Nothing crazy."

"Of course not."

"And nothing more than kisses." I took a step away and reached for the contract. If I kept staring at him, I'd lose all control. "We have to agree not to sleep together."

He smiled. "I can agree to that. I'm a professional, after all."

"Good."

"And one more thing," he said. "Let's not get emotions mixed up in this."

"What do you mean?"

"How should I put this?" He rubbed his jaw. "We should avoid getting attached to each other. This arrangement has a time limit."

That stung a little.

"Fine with me."

He studied me. "Emotions make it complicated. With my daughters involved, I'd rather keep it simple and straightforward."

I nodded. "I'd prefer that, too."

"And your dad wouldn't be happy to hear I was sleeping with his daughter."

"No, he definitely would not." I shuddered.

"And obviously, we can't date anyone else during the three months you're here."

"Right," I said. "We have to keep up appearances."

"So it's settled. Three rules. No sex, no falling in love, and no dating anyone else."

I extended my hand to shake his, displaying confidence I didn't feel. "It's a deal."

Why did it feel so wrong to agree to those first two rules? *No sex, and no falling in love.*

It probably had something to do with how amazing it felt to touch his hand.

I wanted more from Cooper Pierce. A lot more.

But Cooper clearly didn't.

Too bad. Get over it, Felicity.

This was a business deal. I was lucky to have his help with Moonstone.

No use wanting some guy who was light years out of my league. Better to get it out of my head completely.

"Oh, one more thing." He reached into his pocket and retrieved a small velvet box.

Cooper opened it to reveal a gigantic, beautiful diamond ring.

"I'll need you to wear this."

I sucked in air as I gazed at the massive rock. "For God's sake, Cooper. It's huge."

Our eyes met, and we burst into laughter.

I knew we were thinking the same thing: *That's what she said.*

"But it *is* pretty," I said. I slid it onto my finger and held it out to admire the sparkle. It wasn't quite my style, but I could admit he had good taste.

"It looks good on you," he said with a smile.

His eyes lingered on my face for a long moment. Then the doorbell rang.

Cooper took a step back. "Come on. Time to make your first appearance as my fiancée."

He left the room quickly. I followed, my heart thundering.

His *fiancée*.

Even though it wasn't real, the word sent goosebumps down my flesh.

Downstairs, Cooper stood at the door and glanced at me before slowly swinging it open. From his tense body language, I could tell the person ringing the doorbell was not a welcome guest.

I paused on the landing of the stairs, unsure where to go.

A beautiful woman in her early forties stood before him. She was thin and statuesque, with long honey blonde hair that fell in curls down her shoulders. She wore workout clothes that highlighted her toned, svelte body.

Cooper's jaw tightened.

"Hello, Gen."

8

FELICITY

"Hello, Cooper," she said with disgust in her voice. "Where are the girls?"

"They're upstairs."

With a huff, she leaned around him and shouted, "Eva! Lily! Mommy's here!"

Her eyes fell on me, then narrowed. "Cooper, I told you not to have your women around my daughters."

Oh, shit.

Cooper's *women*?

Her words made my stomach sour. Not only did her condescending attitude rub me the wrong way, but thinking of Cooper with a lot of women made me feel ill.

And that was silly. Because it shouldn't. Obviously.

Cooper reached his hand out toward me. I crossed the foyer to stand beside him.

"Felicity, let me introduce you to my ex-wife, Geneviève Barra. Gen, this is Felicity Hayes."

"Nice to meet you, Gen." I smiled and extended my hand.

She fixed me with a blank stare and gave me a limp handshake. "Charmed."

Footsteps behind us drew our attention, and we all turned to see Eva and Lily racing down the stairs.

They were dressed for an outing with blue jeans, T-shirts, and sneakers on. Eva's golden hair was pulled back in a ponytail, and Lily wore her light blonde hair in pigtails.

Adorably, each girl had a small pink backpack over her shoulders. They were packed for a day with their mother.

"Mommy!" Lily exclaimed.

The little girl ran to her mother and reached her arms up, clearly wanting Gen to pick her up. But Gen only bent down to give each of them a quick hug. Then she straightened up.

"Hi, Mommy," Eva said.

"Hi, girls. How are Mommy's princesses today?"

"Great!" Lily gushed. "Where are we going today, Mommy? Will you take us to the arcade? Please?"

"I can win a teddy bear this time," Eva said hopefully. "Last time Dad took us, I got triple points at basketball."

Gen pursed her lips. "I'm sorry, girls, but we'll have to reschedule. I'm afraid Mommy has to cancel our visit today."

Lily's face fell. "We don't get to visit you today?"

"Not today, sweetheart. Something very important came up. But we can go to the arcade next time. Okay?"

Lily's bottom lip trembled. She was fighting back tears. "Okay, Mommy."

Eva stood there stoically. She barely seemed surprised. "Yeah, maybe next time," she muttered.

Those poor girls.

My heart was breaking for them. I wanted to scoop them

up and hold them both. But it wasn't my place to do that, so I stood with my feet glued to the marble floor.

I could almost feel the anger and frustration wafting off Cooper. His voice was tight as he spoke. "They were looking forward to their visit with you today, Gen."

Gen pouted her lower lip. "I was, too. But we'll get together again soon. Right, girls?"

Lily nodded, but Eva didn't respond. She looked from Gen to Cooper, then to me.

Then the giant rock on my finger must have caught Eva's sharp eye.

"Whoa! What is *that*?" Eva exclaimed, pointing at the diamond ring.

Gen noticed the ring for the first time. Her eyes went wide and her nostrils flared.

"Yes, Cooper. What *is* that?" Gen bit out tightly.

We were silent for a long, tense moment.

Sensing things were about to get ugly, Cooper turned to the girls. "Eva, Lily, why don't you say goodbye to your mother and go upstairs. I need to talk to her for a bit."

Lily gave Gen a hug. "Bye, Mommy."

"Bye," Eva said. She gave Gen a quick hug, then the two girls turned and climbed the stairs. Eva walked with her arm around Lily to comfort her.

When they were out of sight, Gen crossed her arms over her chest and glared at me, then Cooper.

"Engaged so soon, are we?" she hissed.

Cooper shrugged. "When you know, you know."

Gen narrowed her eyes. "What are you thinking, Cooper? You introduced my daughters to a woman without my consent. And you got engaged without even telling me you were in a relationship?"

Cooper laughed. "Didn't know I needed my ex-wife's permission to get married."

"It's just common courtesy to let the mother of your children know when you bring some"—she looked me up and down haughtily—"*girl* around the house."

"You're barely in Eva's and Lily's lives, Gen. I didn't think you'd care." He fixed an angry look on her. "You know, it hurts them when you cancel like this. Why did you come here if you're not going to spend the day with them?"

"I came to get my necklace," Gen huffed. "I must have misplaced it here when I moved out."

Cooper rolled his eyes. "Not this again. Gen, I don't have your emerald necklace. If I did, I'd gladly return it to you. You probably lost it on one of your cruises."

Gen flicked her eyes over at me, as if she'd find her necklace around my neck. She puckered her mouth and glared at Cooper. "You know what I think?"

Cooper raised an eyebrow.

"I think you're faking this whole engagement," she said.

"Do you now?" Cooper said, his previous anger replaced by a cool exterior.

"Yes," Gen huffed. "I think you just met this girl and hired her for this... ruse. You know your odds are terrible for keeping custody."

"How do you figure?" Cooper asked, poker face on.

"My attorney told me Judge Graves favors mothers. You know you'll lose this case, so you're grasping at straws. *Obviously.*"

She flicked her eyes up and down my body again.

Oh, really?

So she wanted to play dirty. I could play dirty.

I put my arm around Cooper's waist and cuddled my head against his chest, breathing in his masculine scent. I looked up at him, and he smiled at me. Then he wrapped both arms around my shoulders and pulled me closer.

Oh, God. I could die.

Was this really happening? Cooper Pierce was holding me in his arms. And it was amazing.

"Are we done, Gen? My fiancée and I would like some time alone now."

Gen huffed and spun on her heels, slamming the door behind her. We heard her storm down the front steps, start her car, and speed off.

Cooper and I stood glued together, looking at each other.

Okay, time to let go now.

But I didn't want to. I never wanted to let go.

His arms were so strong, and his chest so massive and muscular. He was warm, and I felt wonderful pressed against him.

Safe.

At home.

His eyes moved to my lips, and his breathing became faster. His chest pressed against my breasts, making my nipples hard.

"Felicity..." he murmured.

"Yes?" I whispered.

He moved his hands to my waist and grabbed me suddenly, holding me in place.

I gasped, breathless at the dominant way he handled me. I wanted nothing more than to submit to this man completely.

Slowly, he thrust his erection against my abdomen.

It was long, thick and hard as steel. Every inch of its length pressed against my soft belly. My panties were instantly drenched.

He moved his hand to my face, brushing his thumb against my cheek. Then he traced my bottom lip with his finger. He moved it to my open mouth and I closed my mouth around it, sucking on it.

He growled, his eyes moving hungrily over my face.

"I want you," he whispered. "No. I *need* you. You're all I can think about."

He reached down and grabbed my ass, pulling me closer. I whimpered.

Upstairs, a bedroom door made a loud noise as it swung open, followed by the sound of footsteps in the hall that led to the staircase.

Cooper and I both jumped back. He turned away, taking a few steps toward the living room as he adjusted himself.

My hands trembling, I straightened my blouse and my hair. Thank God the girls hadn't seen us standing like that.

"Daddy!" Eva shouted from upstairs, still out of sight. "Where are you?"

Cooper ran a hand through his hair and glanced at me, then looked away quickly. He drew a deep breath and let it out through his mouth. He'd managed to get rid of the tent in his pants.

"Downstairs," he called.

The two girls appeared at the top of the staircase. "Lily's crying," Eva said.

The girls descended the stairs, and Cooper met them at the landing. Lily was sobbing. Tears streamed down her red face. He picked Lily up and carried her to the living room. Eva, who looked concerned, walked beside me as we followed him.

"It's okay, Lily," Cooper soothed. He sat with her on the couch and held her. "Are you hurt?"

Lily sniffed and shook her head. "No. Just sad."

"Because you're not going to see Mommy today?" Cooper asked. Eva sat beside him, and I perched on the chair nearby.

Lily nodded. I spotted a box of tissues and handed one to Cooper, who wiped her face clean.

"I'm sorry, baby. I know you wanted to spend time with her today. It's okay to be sad."

Lily blew her nose and cuddled against her father. He pulled in Eva, who was tracing the seam on the couch cushion.

"Are you sad, too, Eva?" he asked.

She nodded.

"I'm sorry, girls." He held them for a long moment.

I felt useless, but I didn't know how I could help. I hated that Gen did this to these girls.

Why wouldn't she want to spend time with her precious daughters? What could be more important than them?

I chewed on my lip as I snuck glances at Cooper holding his girls. He was such a good dad. There was no doubt they should stay with him.

This fake engagement was the right thing to do.

After seeing the cold way Gen treated her kids—and hearing her confirm what Cooper had said about the judge—I was totally convinced.

But at the moment, I felt awkward. Maybe I was intruding on this family time.

Cooper glanced at me, then down at the girls. "Hey." He leaned back to look at Lily. "Who says we can't still go to the arcade?"

Lily blinked, pushing the hair out of her face.

"You'll take us?" Eva looked hopeful.

"Of course," Cooper said. "And maybe Felicity would like to go, too?"

Eva and Lily both looked at me, their blue eyes big and innocent.

"Oh, thank you, but I don't want to intrude," I said.

"It's no intrusion," Cooper said.

"Please?" Eva asked.

Lily looked at me hopefully.

"Okay." I grinned. "I'd love to."

9

COOPER

After several hours at the arcade, the girls were half asleep. Including Felicity.

I parked in the garage and we entered the house through the kitchen. I carried a drowsy Lily in one arm and the large teddy bear Eva had won in the other. Eva and Felicity followed me, yawning as they walked.

"Do you need help getting the girls upstairs?" Felicity asked sleepily.

"No, I got it." I laughed. "You're dead on your feet anyway."

She steadied herself on the counter. "I had no idea how much energy you need to keep up with little girls."

"Especially these two."

Felicity smiled at Eva, whose eyelids were so droopy she could barely keep them up. Eva and Lily had begged to eat dinner at the arcade. We had cheeseburgers, and after we ate, the excitement of the day caught up with them.

"I think I'll go rest on the couch for a minute," Felicity said.

"Good idea. Come on, Eva."

Upstairs, I helped the girls get ready for bed. Lily woke up enough to change into her pajamas and brush her teeth beside her sister.

"Okay, girls, let's get you tucked in. You've got school tomorrow, remember?"

"Will Felicity be here tomorrow?" Lily asked.

"Yes," I said. "She has to go to work like I do, but you'll see her in the evening."

"Can Felicity read to us tonight?" Eva propped her teddy bear on her nightstand before she climbed into bed.

"Maybe another time," I said. "She's pretty tired. And she's getting used to being here."

"I'm glad she's here," Lily said. She snuggled with her new stuffed animal in her own bed. She had won a stuffed rabbit with her tickets—and some help from Felicity and me.

I smiled. "Me, too. Ready for your story?"

"Yes," they said in unison.

I read their favorite, *The Little Red Hen*, and kissed them each goodnight.

Lily opened her heavy eyes to look at me. "Is Felicity going to love us like a mommy?"

Oh, God.

Her words hit like a shot in the heart, and I had to pause a moment so I wouldn't choke up. My poor daughters needed a mother so badly.

I wanted to promise that Felicity would love them. That she'd stay forever. But I couldn't.

I gave Lily a hug and brushed a strand of blonde hair out of her face. "Let's give it some time, okay, baby?"

"Okay."

"You girls are the light of my life. You know that, right?"

Lily nodded.

"I love you both to the moon and back," I said as I kissed Lily's head. "And I always will."

I went over to Eva's bed and gave her a kiss on the forehead. "I love you, Eva. Goodnight, silly goose."

"Night, Daddy."

I turned the light out and left the room, closing the door behind me. There was movement inside, and I opened the door a crack to see Lily climbing into bed next to Eva.

She'd started doing that recently. It worried me that Lily couldn't sleep alone. She was having trouble, and it killed me.

Lily was grieving the absence of a proper mother more than she was missing Gen. They both were, even if Eva acted tough and pretended she didn't care.

I didn't know how to fix it. And I would have given anything to fix the whole world for my daughters. They were seeing the best child therapist I could find, but that only went so far.

The best I could do was make sure they kept living with me. I could at least protect them while they were in this house and under my care.

And as long as this engagement with Felicity worked, I had a good chance at retaining custody.

I went downstairs, expecting to see Felicity crashed out on the sofa. Instead, she was sitting up. Her legs were curled up underneath a blanket.

I grinned. "I thought you'd be asleep by now."

"I had a cat nap. Hope you don't mind that I poured us some wine. I could really use a glass myself."

I sat on the sofa in front of the glass she'd poured for me. "I could, too." I was so close I could smell her floral scent.

She reached for her glass and took a sip. "Your daughters are hilarious, you know."

"Oh, I know. There's never a dull moment around here."

"Eva is so adventurous. She's a little risk-taker. She reminds me a little of myself as a kid. And Lily..." She pressed a hand to her heart. "Lily is just precious. She's so sweet and gentle." She smiled as she looked off in the distance. "They're great kids."

"Thanks." I took a sip of my wine. "They just told me they're glad to have you here."

She looked at me. "They did?"

I nodded. "They like you a lot."

"I like them, too." She beamed for a moment, then she shook her head sadly. "I just don't understand why Gen doesn't want to be in their lives."

"Yeah, me neither." I sighed.

"I'm sorry to bring up a sore subject."

"No, I'm fine talking about it." I shrugged. "It's just a shame the girls don't have a better mother. They deserve so much more."

"Absolutely."

I leaned back on the sofa, thinking of the past few years. "Gen and I were never meant to be. And she was never really cut out to be a mother."

"How long have you two been divorced?"

"A little over five years. Our marriage lasted four years. It was a mistake from the start."

"How so?"

"She's... not who I thought she was at first." I sipped my wine. "When we first met, it went well enough. We were dating for a few weeks."

Felicity looked down and shifted in her seat.

"And no, I'm not a womanizer. When I was younger, I had a bit of a wild streak. I dated a lot, but I gave all that up when I met Gen. And now that I have my daughters, a date is a rare event. She made that remark earlier about *my women* because she wanted to hurt me. And make things awkward for you."

She nodded, studying me.

"Anyway, after a few dates with Gen, I saw another side of her. Her true self. At first, I noticed the shitty way she treated waiters. Then I saw how she used people in her life. She'd betray friends or family members to get ahead. She's a social climber, and she wants a glamorous life without a day of work. So I broke it off. But she called me two weeks later and wanted to get back together. She was pregnant with Eva."

Felicity's eyes grew wide.

"She was excited to have the baby," I continued. "I wanted my kid to have a decent shot at life. Something told me it wasn't a good idea for a child to grow up with Gen alone. And I thought maybe Gen would change for the better." I laughed at that last part.

"So you did the right thing."

"Yeah. I married her." I ran my hand through my hair. "Neither of us were happy together. I told her I wanted a divorce, and she soon wound up pregnant with Lily."

Felicity's jaw dropped. "Wow."

"Don't get me wrong. My girls are the best thing that ever happened to me. I'd do it all over again for them."

"I know."

"Anyway, after Lily, I stopped sleeping with Gen. Obviously." I chuckled. "I asked Gen to move out when Lily was two. Gen was miserable being tied down, and she agreed. She never wanted to take the girls with her. The divorce was settled soon after that." I swirled the wine in my glass. "The girls have always lived here with me. Gen officially has joint custody, though she rarely wants to see them."

Felicity's jaw tightened. "So why is she filing for full custody now?"

"She spent her divorce settlement on cruises and clothes and whatever new man she was with at the moment." I shrugged. "She wants child support, so she filed for full custody."

"That's terrible."

"Her real name's Jennifer Bard, by the way," I added.

Felicity lifted her eyebrows. "Oh?"

"Yeah. She had it changed legally before I met her. That should've been my first clue she was fake. All she cared about was climbing the social ladder." I laughed bitterly. "I was such a fool to trust her."

"People make mistakes," Felicity said gently. "You're being hard on yourself."

"Well, in any case, I think it's obvious she just wants the money, not the girls."

"Yes, it's obvious to me."

"But maybe not to Judge Graves."

She put her hand on my shoulder. "It will be."

I met her hazel eyes, lost in the deep jewel tones of her irises.

"I can see the girls belong here with you," she said. "I'll do everything I can to help, Cooper."

"Thank you, Felicity."

She looked away quickly and removed her hand. I willed my cock not to wake up.

She took a sip from her glass. "I've had my own spectacular fail of a relationship, you know."

"Oh?"

"Yes. A professional skateboarder."

I raised my eyebrows. "For real?"

"Yes. Charlie the skater. When he wasn't skating, he was

playing video games. The guy didn't know how to operate a washing machine." She laughed so hard she set her wine glass on the table before she spilled it. "I felt more like his mom than his girlfriend."

"And you said you weren't good with children," I joked.

Felicity smiled into the distance. "Yeah, he really was just a boy. Not..." She swallowed. "Not a man."

She shifted her head sideways, letting her gaze trail up my body to meet my eyes.

She looked at me pointedly, her last words lingering in the air.

Felicity wanted to know what a real man could show her. And I was more than willing to oblige.

All hope of avoiding an erection was lost in the way she looked at me.

I set my wine glass on the coffee table.

"I guess we've both made some bad calls in the past," I said. I let my eyes move over her face, settling on her full mouth.

"How do we know we're not about to make another one?" she murmured.

I traced the collar of her pink blouse. "Would a bad call feel this amazing?"

She parted her lips. "No, it wouldn't."

This is it, Cooper. Your last chance to stop before you do something you'll regret forever.

Don't do it. This will make everything complicated.

But I was beyond listening to the voice of reason. I couldn't resist kissing Felicity another moment.

As she leaned in, her eyes closed, I pressed my mouth to hers.

Like a man crawling through the desert who spots water, I drank her in greedily.

She opened her mouth, letting me inside.

Fuck, she was so soft and sweet. I plunged my hand in her loose hair, holding the back of her head.

She put her delicate hand on my chest, then moved both hands behind my neck. I explored her mouth, pulling her petite body against mine.

She pulled away suddenly to look at me breathlessly. She looked shocked for a moment. Her features were flushed from the wine and the kiss.

Then she leaned in again.

Without a word, she moved into my arms, crawling into my lap and straddling me. I rose to my feet and lifted her by the waist.

She wrapped her legs and arms around me, and I carried her upstairs to my bedroom.

I couldn't care less about reason right now, or rules.

I only knew I had to relieve this raging hunger for her before it drove me crazy.

10

FELICITY

We were really doing this.

As Cooper carried me upstairs, I thought I was dreaming for a second.

But this was real. This was happening.

He brought me inside his bedroom and closed the door behind him. I was breathless and crazy with desire for him.

He carried me to the bed and laid me down. I sat up and kneeled before his massive frame. He lifted my shirt over my head, moving his hands over the cups of my lacy pink bra.

I reached for his shirt, and he helped me pull it over his head. I lifted my arms, moving my hands over his enormous, chiseled torso. He looked so much better with his shirt off. A patch of dark hair grew across his chest, and a treasure trail led below the waistband of his pants.

Cooper unfastened my bra and removed it, letting it fall to the floor. My breasts bounced free, and he moved his strong hands over them, kneading and massaging. The nipple stimulation made me wetter than I already was.

"Lie back," he commanded. I did as I was told and

watched as he unbuckled my jeans and pulled them off my legs. He tossed them and my socks to the floor.

Grabbing my hips, he pulled me to the edge of the bed. I was wearing matching pink lacy panties. Cooper slid his hands from my lower legs up to my thighs. He parted them and positioned himself between my legs.

I watched as he planted a line of kisses down each thigh, then blew warm air through the fabric of my panties. I shivered in anticipation. Slowly, he dragged his fingers over the crotch of my underwear. Bringing my legs together, he pulled at the waistband. Teasingly, he inched the fabric down my legs and dropped it to the floor.

He opened my legs again, placing one on each of his shoulders. He looked at the flesh between my legs for a moment, then up at my face.

"You're so beautiful," he murmured.

He moved his hands slowly over my belly and hips as he kissed the sensitive flesh of my inner thighs, moving gradually to the center.

Trailing a finger down my seam, he grinned at me. "You're so wet, Felicity."

I moaned in response. "That's what you do to me."

Finally, he kissed my clit. And that was all it took to become addicted to his mouth.

He began to lick my inner folds, first long, slow movements with his tongue and then rapid, shorter ones. I threw my head back and clenched the sheets in my fists.

He chuckled, the vibration sending shivers through my body. "You like that, don't you?"

"Mm-hmm." My core muscles tightened as the pleasure built in my body. "Please don't stop."

He sucked my clit as he inserted his middle finger inside

my opening. He curled it upward, somehow knowing exactly the right spot to touch.

"Oh, God," I moaned. "Yes, right there."

I braced myself as everything inside me contracted and released. My body writhed on the bed, bucking against his mouth.

"Fuck, yes," I gasped.

He kept sucking, pushing me over the edge completely. Warm pulses rolled through my body, and I felt myself go limp.

He gave me a few delicate kisses on my throbbing sex as I came down from my high.

Panting and dazed, I lifted my head to look at him. He smiled.

"You're even more beautiful when you come."

He stood up and looked down at me as he undid his jeans. He stepped out of them, then pulled down his boxers and tossed them to the side.

I propped myself up on my elbows to take in the glorious sight of Cooper Pierce's cock.

I'm pretty sure I gasped.

It was long, thick and fully erect. It bobbed in the air, pointing to the ceiling.

It was easily the largest cock I had ever seen. Suddenly I became worried it might even be *too* big.

"Um... are you sure you'll fit?"

He leaned over me and kissed my earlobe and neck. "I'm sure."

I ran a finger down the length of his shaft. It was warm and hard. My mouth watered.

"I want you inside me, Cooper."

He growled, then reached for the drawer in his nightstand. He retrieved a condom.

I put my hand on his. "I'm on birth control. And I was recently tested. You?"

A naughty grin spread over his face. "Just tested, too. All clear."

He tossed the condom behind him.

I giggled and lay back underneath him. He kissed me hungrily, conquering my mouth with his tongue. He lay over me, resting his weight on his elbows. His massive cock pressed against my abdomen.

I arched my body against his, and he moved down to suck on each nipple. Finally, he moved the head of his cock to my entrance.

His eyes closed. "You're so fucking tight."

As he kissed me, he worked the head of his cock inside me. I felt my muscles stretch around him. Slowly, he pushed himself in.

I gasped as he entered me.

"You okay?" he asked.

"Better than okay. Just getting used to you."

He sucked on my lower lip, moving his hands over each of my breasts and kissing my nipples. He pushed himself all the way in, pausing and studying my face.

I breathed and relaxed, wrapping my arms around his neck. "God. You feel so good, Cooper."

He kissed me again. "So do you."

He began to thrust inside me. I traced patterns down his hard, rippled back and wrapped my legs around his waist.

The sensation of being completely filled was incredible. His body took me over. All I could do was surrender and ride the waves.

Suddenly, he pulled out and rolled us both over so that I was on top. He lay back, grinning up at me. I braced myself with my hands on his chest. Slowly, I lowered myself onto his throbbing dick. At this angle, his length stimulated all my sensitive areas inside. I began to ride him. He cupped my breasts, letting them bounce in his hands.

"Let me see you touch yourself," he growled.

Closing my eyes, I let my fingers drift down to my clit, still sensitive after my first orgasm. I began to touch myself, moving in circles.

"Fuck, that's so hot," he said.

The intensity was rising. I bit my lip. My eyes opened and met his. Cooper's intense gaze focused on my face as I drew nearer to an orgasm. All my muscles contracted. I tossed my head back and moaned as the contractions began.

Quickly, he flipped us over again so that I was on my back and he was above me. He thrust himself in all the way, his cock hard as steel.

My orgasm had already started, and I let myself slip into the sweet current of ecstasy. He pushed himself in all the way a few times, then let out a primal noise.

His cock pulsated and throbbed as he emptied his seed into me. Warm wetness flooded me, and he moaned as he pumped his release deep inside.

It was the most erotic moment of my life.

I pushed him in deeper with my heels. I wanted to take him, and his essence, inside my deepest spaces.

"Holy shit." He propped himself up to look at me, then kissed my mouth long and deep.

I clung to him, with my arms clasped behind his neck and my legs around his hips. His cock was still inside me as we both caught our breath and came down from our high.

"That was... amazing." Words couldn't describe how I felt.

But did he feel the same way?

11

COOPER

Moving my eyes over her face, I committed every detail to memory. "It was."

I was still inside her, propped up over her delicate body.

I pulled out and looked down at her glorious pussy. I'd filled her up. My thick cum was slowly leaking out of her.

The sight made me start to go hard again, but I figured she'd like to clean up before anything else.

"Be right back," I said.

I walked naked to the bathroom where I grabbed a towel. Sitting at the edge of the bed, I wiped her clean, then myself. I lay back on the bed and reached for her. She cuddled up against me, her head in the crook of my arm.

I played with her hair lazily. Now that I'd been with Felicity, my mind was more at peace. My cock wanted more, but it wasn't torturing me like before.

But this blissful feeling was more than just post-sex satisfaction.

Having Felicity in my arms was amazing. It filled me with more contentment than I'd known in a very long time.

Sure, we'd broken our first rule. But maybe we didn't

The Fiancé Hoax

have to follow the rules. Maybe this fake engagement could work even while we had some fun.

Felicity suddenly pulled away.

From the troubled expression on her face, I could tell she was *not* thinking along the same lines.

"I'm sorry, Cooper. I didn't mean to start that." She sat up in bed. Her brow furrowed.

"What? Did I do something wrong?"

"No, of course not. You were great, Cooper. The sex... it was great, too." She turned her back to me. "It was incredible."

I reached for her, stroking her upper arm. "Then what's the problem?"

"We broke our first rule. It's my fault, really. I shouldn't have poured us that wine." She grabbed her bra off the floor and put it on quickly. "I don't want things to get complicated, you know?"

"Oh." I took my hand away. "Yeah. You're probably right."

She put on those sexy little pink panties and glanced at me. "We're business partners now. I worry that things could get messy if we... keep doing this."

I watched as she pulled on her jeans and her top. A lump was growing in my throat. I swallowed it down.

I rose to my feet and put my boxers on.

"Yeah, I guess I got carried away."

"We both did." She gave a smile that didn't reach her eyes.

I nodded. "It was a mistake under the circumstances. We should just forget about it."

She stood there motionless for a long moment. She watched in silence as I pulled my jeans and shirt on.

Finally, she looked away. With a shrug, she said, "It's just attraction and proximity. Now that we have it out of our system, we'll be fine."

"Absolutely."

She glanced at me. "Well, goodnight."

"Goodnight, Felicity."

She left the room, closing the door quietly behind her. I waited to hear the sound of her bedroom door opening and closing.

With a groan, I fell back on the bed.

Why did I have to make those stupid rules?

But deep down, I knew she was right.

There were so many reasons Felicity and I would never work out. She was sixteen years younger. She was my business associate. Marsh would find out sooner or later that I was investing in her business, and that she was helping me with the custody case. That would be enough to infuriate him already.

But if he found out I was sleeping with her? Not only would I lose my business attorney, but I would lose the only guy who gave a damn when I was going through the worst nightmare of my life.

Most of all, I had my daughters to consider.

Eva and Lily came first. Always.

This was already going to be difficult for them. They were already getting attached to her. And it would be hard for them to say goodbye in three months.

But if Felicity and I started getting closer to each other, it would make things worse for my daughters when she left.

If they saw Felicity and me growing closer, it would only hurt them. If they saw us flirting at breakfast or cuddling on the couch, they would become more hopeful that she would remain a permanent fixture in the house.

And Felicity and I both knew that wasn't going to happen.

Felicity had her whole life ahead of her. She didn't want to be saddled with a broken guy almost twenty years her senior with two kids.

Felicity was right. We had to keep our distance from each other.

I could handle heartache. I was used to it.

But I didn't want my daughters to lose any more than they already had.

12

FELICITY

The next morning, I felt like I had been hit by a truck.

It was bad enough that I had gone to bed with a heavy heart. I had to fight against everything inside me to pull away from Cooper. Being in his arms was the best feeling in the world. I never wanted to leave.

But I knew I had to.

As I lay there, I wondered how it would feel to sleep in his arms every night.

I had to shut down that kind of fantasy.

This wasn't a real relationship. This was a business arrangement.

And the sex was a momentary lapse in reason. Even if it was the best sex of my life. Even if Cooper was the lover from my dreams.

The worst part? Cooper thought it was a mistake, too.

Part of me had hoped he would fight me on it. That he'd say we could still have some fun while in our arrangement.

But he had been quick to pull away. Which just confirmed I needed to keep my distance.

On top of everything, I woke up feeling sicker than a dog.

In my bathroom, I washed my face and brushed my teeth. Wrapping a robe around myself, I dragged myself downstairs. Every step was painful.

In the living room, Eva and Lily were curled up under blankets on the sofa. They looked pale and fatigued. Cups of hot tea steamed from coasters on the coffee table.

"Oh, no," I gasped, my heart instantly constricting to see them suffering. "You're sick?"

Eva looked up at my sickly form. "You, too?"

I nodded and plopped into the chair next to the sofa. My entire body ached.

Male voices filtered in from the foyer. "Thanks, Samir," Cooper said. "I appreciate your stopping in."

"Anytime," said the other man, presumably Samir. "Let me know if you need anything."

"Will do."

The front door opened and closed. Outside, a car started. Cooper appeared in the living room. His eyes fell on me.

"So, you're all sick?"

"Uh-huh," I muttered. "What *is* this? Everything hurts."

"Dr. Sethi came by," Cooper said. "Friend of mine. He checked on the girls on his way to work. He says it's a stomach bug."

"Is that why my tummy hurts so much?" Lily asked.

Cooper sat down between the girls and felt Lily's forehead. "Yes, baby. And you both have a little fever. But you're going to be okay."

"How come you're not sick?" I asked Cooper.

He shrugged. "I never get sick."

I tucked my legs underneath me. "I'll have to close the store today. I can't go in like this."

Eva looked at her dad. "Do we have to go to school today?"

"No school today," Cooper said.

"Yay." Eva tried to cheer, but it came out weakly.

Cooper looked at me. "There's some ginger tea in the kitchen if you want it."

I gave him a smile. "Thank you."

He looked at his phone. "I'm staying home to take care of them. If you need to go upstairs and rest, feel free."

"Okay." I pushed myself to my feet. "I think I'll go get some tea first."

"Sounds good."

He was avoiding looking at me. It stung.

I trudged into the kitchen and poured myself a mug of the hot tea. While it cooled, I retrieved my phone from my robe pocket. Several notifications from Lauren popped up.

Lauren: Did you sleep with him yet?

Lauren: You did, didn't you?

Lauren: I need details, babe!

Lauren: Because I think he'd be really good in bed. But I need confirmation.

Lauren: Dammit, you know I live vicariously through you, Fel!

I chuckled and started typing.

Felicity: You have a sixth sense for anyone getting laid.

Lauren's response came back instantly.

Lauren: I knew it! You didn't even last twenty-four hours!

Felicity: You were right. And yes, it was amazing.

Lauren: And?? Tell me more.

Felicity: I promise to tell you every detail soon. Right

now I'm sick. Could you put up the Temporarily Closed sign in Moonstone?

The flower shop where Lauren worked was a short walk from my boutique. I knew she wouldn't mind stopping by my store to do this favor for me.

Lauren: No problem, F. Get better soon! And I expect to hear about everything.

Felicity: Thanks Lauren. <heart emoji>

I dropped my phone in my pocket and took a sip of the tea. It was warm and soothing... until it wasn't.

My stomach rumbled. Gripping my sides, I raced to the hallway bathroom and shut the door behind me. I kneeled before the toilet and vomited what little was in my stomach.

I stood up to wash my face and rinse my mouth out at the sink. I looked like a zombie in the mirror.

Not the look I'm going for around Cooper.

But by the detached way he was treating me today, he didn't seem very interested anyway.

It hurt that I apparently didn't mean more to him than just a hookup. But after all, we had agreed to not get attached.

I returned to the living room. The girls were watching a movie while Cooper stood behind the sofa, taking Eva's temperature.

"Mind if I join you?" I asked.

The girls both smiled up at me. Eva patted the cushion between them.

"What are you watching?"

"*The Little Mermaid*," Lily said.

"Oh, that's my favorite," I said, settling in between them.

"Mine too," Lily said.

Cooper gathered his things. "I'm going to be in my home office for a while. Let me know if you need anything."

"No, Daddy. Stay with us," Eva said.

"Just for a little while," Lily added.

Cooper glanced at me, then at the girls.

He set his stack of paperwork on the coffee table. "Okay, just for a bit."

He started to settle into the armchair, but Lily insisted he sit on the couch so she could sit in his lap. He sat next to me with Lily in his arms.

His presence oozed sexy masculinity. I just hoped I didn't smell like vomit.

"Daddy, why does Ariel want to be with the prince so bad?" Eva asked.

"I guess she likes him," Cooper said.

"Yeah, but enough to leave the ocean?" Eva frowned. "I don't get that."

Cooper chuckled, then he glanced at me. I smiled back.

"I guess she *really* likes him," Cooper said.

Eva shook her head. "I would never give up my mermaid tail for some dude."

Cooper and I laughed, and Eva and Lily broke out in giggles, too.

Even though my body ached, it felt good to be with Cooper and his girls. Really good.

Cooper ended up finishing the movie with us. At lunchtime, he made us chicken soup. I tried to help, but he insisted I rest.

I watched him as he cooked in the kitchen, talking to the girls as we ate at the table. He was unlike any man I'd ever known. Totally comfortable in his own skin. Confident. Take-charge. And his daughters were the apples of his eye.

It was incredibly sexy.

Part of me regretted running out of his bedroom the night before. A big part.

Couldn't I *not* follow the rules, just this once?

~

The kids and I spent the next three days at home watching movies, running to the bathroom to puke, and resting. Cooper took care of us in the mornings. He went to his office downtown to work when Inga arrived in the afternoons.

It was a good bonding opportunity. We watched countless kids' movies. I grew to love Eva's funny takes on the characters, as well as Lily's sweet, empathetic reactions.

By Wednesday, we were cuddled up together on the couch and laughing at the funny parts when our stomachs didn't hurt too much.

On Thursday, I woke up feeling much better. So did the girls. I went to work, and they went to school.

That morning, I parked my Plymouth in the employee parking area behind the boutique and unlocked the doors. Part of me was excited to get back to work.

The other part of me felt it was a lost cause.

The only emails and voicemails the store had gotten in my absence were from life insurance companies. I wondered if I would have had any customers even if the store had been open the past three days.

As I organized the retail section and my sewing materials in the back, I felt a nagging fear. What if Moonstone couldn't be saved? After two hours, I still hadn't seen a single customer.

The bell on the front door jingled, and I looked up hopefully. Instead of a customer, Lauren waltzed in. My shoulders slumped.

"Don't look so happy to see me," she said, clicking her tongue.

I met her by the cash register and gave her a hug. "I am happy to see you, Lauren. I'm sorry. I'm just throwing myself a pity party. I haven't had any customers this morning."

"Well, I'm sure that will all change as soon as Mr. Big Daddy works his magic." She winked. "I mean, his magic on the store. Not just on your lady parts."

I laughed. "That's not going to happen again, remember?"

I had already filled Lauren in on the awkwardness between Cooper and me after our time in his bedroom.

She scoffed. "I don't believe that for a second. From what I can tell, you two can't keep your hands off each other. Now that you're not puking your guts out every half hour, he'll be all over you again."

Secretly, I wished she was right. But I shook my head sadly. "That ship has sailed. I think I pushed him away for good." I shrugged, trying to sound cheerful. "It's for the best. I need to focus on my business anyway."

"Business, schmizness." She flipped her red hair over her shoulder. "I give you three days before that bad boy is making you see stars again."

"Lauren, you're incorrigible."

She gave me another hug, then turned to head toward the door. "I know, I know. Just keep me posted. I better get to the flower shop before Ernie gets there. He's always looking for some reason to fire me."

"Okay. Talk to you soon." I blew her a kiss as she walked out.

Returning to my laptop at the desk, I sighed. The numbers for this month's revenue weren't looking good. I just hoped Cooper was a miracle worker.

By lunch, I'd had two customers. One bought a shirt from the clearance rack, and another purchased a strapless dress from my summer collection. Both were thrilled with their purchases and promised to return. It gave me a little hope. Seeing people fall in love with items I had designed and created always made me feel like a million bucks.

Still, it wasn't enough. A few customers a week wouldn't keep my boutique doors open.

With a sigh, I opened the food delivery app on my phone. My appetite had returned, but my stomach still felt a little wobbly. Just then, the door opened. I looked up with surprise to see Cooper walk in.

My face opened into a big smile. Seeing him in my store filled me with excitement and pride.

"Welcome to Moonstone Boutique." I stood from my desk.

He took in the space, getting an overview of the store. "I thought you might like some soup." He lifted the bag he carried. The aroma of the chicken soup hit my nose, and my stomach growled.

"God, yes. I'm starving. I was going to order a sandwich, but soup sounds much better." I watched as he unpacked the containers on my desk. "Thanks, Cooper."

He grinned at me. "No problem. You were a big help with the girls the past few days, so it's the least I could do."

I shrugged. "I just watched movies with them. It was fun."

His blue eyes locked on mine, and his mouth curved into a smile. "Yeah, it was."

My stomach fluttered, and it wasn't from the stomach bug. Being close to Cooper was still so thrilling.

"What do you think of Moonstone?" I asked, gesturing to the store. It was his first time visiting.

He walked slowly through the main corridor, taking in the display racks, the cash register, and my sewing space at the back of the shop.

"It's a gorgeous store."

"Really?" I gushed.

He shifted some items on the rack, looking at the tunics and blouses. I expected him to be clueless about clothes. But to my surprise, he inspected the construction, looking at seams and checking the fabric like he knew what he was doing.

Then he crossed to the eveningwear section and lifted a blue dress off the rack. It was similar to the dress I wore the night I met him at my dad's party.

He glanced at me. "Felicity, you're really talented."

My face flushed warm. "Thank you, Cooper."

"And I'm not just saying that. I had a hunch from what I saw when we met that you had a knack for design. I wouldn't have agreed to invest in your business if I hadn't." He smiled. "My gut instinct is usually correct."

His eyes fell on me. Again, a rush of butterflies fluttered in my stomach.

"These past few days, I've been doing a deep dive into fashion design research," he said. "I have to know a little about whatever business I'm investing in."

"Makes sense." I nodded.

"And seeing your store and more of your designs in person, I'm certain I made the right choice."

He removed a sage green bohemian-styled dress from the rack. He brought it up to me, holding it under my chin. He squinted, as if to imagine what it might look like being worn.

With a nod, he returned it to the rack. I wiped my palms

on my skirt. Being around Cooper made me feel like my fever was returning.

"Please, eat," he said, gesturing to the food.

I cleared my stuff to make space on the desk and sat down. I began to devour the chicken noodle soup he'd brought, hungrier than I realized.

"Don't you want any?" I asked between bites.

"Nah, I already ate."

He was looking at some linen pants. Then he saw the price tag.

"What the hell?" he muttered.

"What?"

He checked the tags on the green dress and tunics. "I knew your prices were low, but this is ridiculous, Felicity."

"I know. I can increase them."

"Damn straight." He took a seat across from me at the desk. "I need to look at your financial records. You didn't send me your profit and loss statements."

I swallowed my bite of soup, then clicked on my laptop. "This is last month's bookkeeping." I turned the computer to face him.

He furrowed his brow, reading the spreadsheet and scrolling. I snuck a peek at his thick, tight forearms as he worked. His presence dominated the store—his huge frame and woodsy cologne seemed out of place in the girly boutique, but I loved having him here.

"The previous months are on the next page," I said.

He nodded and clicked around, studying my records. My heart pounded, suddenly feeling vulnerable as Cooper peered into my files. I finished my lunch and put the containers away.

Finally, he looked at me. "You need to increase your prices by eighty percent."

"Eighty? That's a lot."

"Then you're going to run a targeted ad campaign in some upscale magazines."

I held my hand up. "I don't have the budget for that. Do you know how much those ads cost?"

"That's what the investment check I gave you is for."

"Oh. Right," I said sheepishly.

Cooper had given me a large check after I signed his contract the other day.

"You haven't cashed it yet, have you?"

I cringed. "It's still in my purse."

He rolled his eyes, but he was smiling. "Do you want to turn this business around or not?"

"I do. I just... I was a little intimidated by all the zeros. It's a lot of money."

He shrugged. "To make money, you have to spend money."

I nodded, looking down at my lap. I was afraid I couldn't keep up my end of the bargain. What if I didn't do a good enough job as his fake fiancée and he didn't win custody of the girls?

There was so much riding on this arrangement. I didn't want to let Cooper or his daughters down.

"I'm here to help you, Felicity. You have to trust me."

I looked up at him, and his deep blue eyes bored into my soul.

"You do trust me, don't you?" he asked in a low voice.

"Y-yes," I stammered. I couldn't help it. When he talked to me in that deep voice, it did things to me. I got all flustered and sounded like an idiot. I bit my bottom lip, looking up at him.

"Good." He stood up and went to the cash register. "Now walk me through your procedure with customer service."

I followed and stood next to him, explaining my protocols for sales, packaging, and returns. Next, I gave him a rundown of my design and production area, pointing out the equipment I used and the fabrics I'd purchased.

Three hours later, he had given me a list of actionable items. I eagerly took notes on everything he said. I was a little embarrassed I didn't know any of this stuff, but I pushed my self-consciousness aside.

Mainly, I was excited to implement his suggestions. Cooper really did know how to run a business.

"I think that's enough for today," he said. "Are you ready to go home?"

I frowned. "But it's not closing time yet."

He raised an eyebrow. "You haven't had any customers all afternoon, Felicity. It might be a better use of your time to close early and focus on new strategies."

"As painful as it is to admit, I think you're right." I laughed as I gathered my things. "Let's go home."

I froze. We were talking like we were a couple. And I was thinking of Cooper's house as my home.

This was dangerous territory.

You can't think of this as real. His house is not your home. It's all temporary.

Keeping my head down, I packed my laptop and notebooks and turned out the lights. I walked with him to the front door so I could lock up behind him. Cooper's car was parked on the street.

"Need a ride?" he asked.

I shook my head. "No, I'm parked out back."

"Can you leave it here overnight?"

I hesitated.

"I don't think anyone's going to steal your Plymouth." He

smiled. "We can talk more business in my car. I'll drop you off here tomorrow on my way to work."

"Okay, sure," I said, trying not to sound too eager.

I stepped outside behind him, locking the front door and following him to his Bentley Bentayga. With a smile, he opened the passenger door for me. I climbed in, my heart aflutter. He sat behind the wheel looking like a male fashion model with his dark sunglasses on.

Cooper drove us to his house—my *temporary* home. As I rode, he gave me more advice. I scribbled down ideas in my notebook. He knew his stuff, and I wanted to get every word.

Most of all, I tried not to think about the future with him.

This was temporary, and I was just along for the ride.

13

COOPER

"So, can you, Daddy?"

I looked at Eva's expectant face. We were eating dinner, and I'd been distracted by Felicity sitting across from me. Those curves were enough to distract any red-blooded man.

I smiled at my daughter. "Sorry, Eva. What were you saying?"

Eva rolled her eyes. "Mrs. Denkins wants to know if you can chaperone our class trip to the museum in two weeks. Tamsen's and Olivia's moms are going. Clare's mom, too."

I opened the calendar app on my phone, then glanced at the date in the email from Eva's teacher.

"Okay. I can do it," I said.

"Yay!" Eva sprang to her feet and began to dance.

"No dancing at the table," I said. "Finish your chicken."

Felicity giggled, then winked at Eva as my eight-year-old plopped in her seat and ate a bite of potatoes.

"I'm glad to see you've all bounced back from that stomach bug," I said. "Lily, how was school today?"

"Fine. I have to make something for Mother's Day at school." Lily turned to Felicity. "Can you help me?"

"Sure," Felicity said. "What are you making?"

Lily shrugged. "It's a craft project. We're supposed to find out what our mommies like and make something for them."

I shifted in my seat. Mother's Day was always hard on the girls. School projects like this didn't make it easier.

Felicity glanced at me, then back at Lily. "Well, what does your mom like? We could make a list of her favorite things. Her favorite color, animal, food..."

Lily shook her head. "I don't want to make it for her. I want to make it for *you*."

Felicity paused for a long moment. My throat closed up, and I took a sip of water as I watched them.

Shit. What had I done? The girls were getting too attached to Felicity. I hadn't counted on that happening so quickly.

The last thing I wanted was to hurt them, and I was afraid this fake engagement would do exactly that.

But what could I do? It was too late to stop now.

Felicity reached across the table for Lily's hand and squeezed it. "That's really sweet you want to make it for me, Lily. But I don't want us to hurt your mom's feelings."

Lily looked down at her plate. "I don't think Mommy would care."

"Are you sure, Lily? You could make it for your mom and give it to her the next time you see her," I offered.

"She always cancels," Lily said. "I want to make it for Felicity."

Felicity and I exchanged a glance. I gave her a nod, ignoring the constriction in my chest.

"Okay. Well, I can tell you some of my favorite things."

The Fiancé Hoax

Felicity spoke cautiously. "I love chocolate. Purple tulips are my favorite flowers. And daffodils."

Lily nodded, trying to remember it all.

"What's your favorite animal?" Eva asked.

"Cats."

"What's your favorite color cat?" Lily asked with a serious look on her face.

Felicity thought for a second. "I like orange cats. Oh, and calico cats!"

"I *love* calico cats!" Eva declared. Then she shot me an annoyed look. "Daddy won't let us get a cat."

"He won't?" Felicity asked, her mouth curling into a smile.

"No, he won't," Lily said with a pout.

"Why not?" Felicity asked.

All three of them turned to me expectantly. My daughters were happy to have Felicity on their side.

I laughed. "I said we can get a pet someday. When you're both a little older so you can take care of it."

Eva harrumphed. "Like when I'm *fifteen*, probably."

"I can barely handle you two hooligans, much less a cat on top of everything."

The doorbell rang, and I heard Monica open the front door.

"Two more bites, please," I told Eva. I had a feeling the visitor we'd just received was about to put an end to dinner.

"Please, Mr. Hayes, they're having dinner," Monica's voice came through the hall.

Felicity's eyes widened as she looked at me.

"Lily, finish your potatoes," I said calmly.

Marsh Hayes blew into the dining room, his face red.

"There you are," he said angrily to Felicity.

Monica hustled in behind Marsh. "I'm sorry, Mr. Pierce. He wouldn't listen to me."

I waved her off. "It's fine, Monica. The girls were just finishing up." Monica nodded and left the room.

Felicity squirmed in her seat. "Dad, what are you doing here?"

"Well, I came to find out why you went against my request to stay away from my investors." His sharp eyes swept over the dinner table, taking in the cozy vibe. "But now I'm wondering what *you're* doing here. I expected to find you talking business, not having a family dinner."

I threw my napkin on the table. "Girls, time to go upstairs."

Eva sighed. "Man, we never get to hear anything good." She pushed away from the table and left the room with Lily behind her. I heard their footsteps as they raced upstairs to their bedroom.

When the girls were out of earshot, Marsh turned to me. "What the hell is going on here?"

I leaned back in my chair, refusing to take his bait. "Dinner."

"Damn it, Cooper, don't toy with me." His eyes flicked between Felicity and me. "Are you sleeping with my daughter?"

I paused. Marsh was pissed, and I had to tread delicately.

"Marsh, take a load off. Have a glass of wine. There's nothing devious going on. Felicity's here because she's helping me out in exchange for my help with her boutique."

Felicity nodded hopefully.

Marsh scoffed. "Felicity's helping with those girls?" He crossed his arms over his chest. "That's a crock. She hates kids."

Felicity cleared her throat and turned to me. "It's true I never liked kids that much. Until Eva and Lily."

Something warm flooded my heart, and I forced myself to look away from her.

Marsh shook his head. "I can't believe this."

He spun on his heels and began to pace through the dining room. While his back was turned, Felicity slipped off the engagement ring and put it in her pocket.

"I don't know what's going on here," Marsh said, turning to face Felicity again. "But I don't like it. I already forbade you from approaching my clients."

"I know. But this was important, Dad."

I stood up and pushed the chair out. "I needed a new project, Marsh. You know how stagnant things have been lately. Ever since the Sullivan brothers bailed out."

Marsh harrumphed. Exactly the response I wanted. "*You* bailed on them."

"They wanted eighty percent, Marsh. You and I both know I couldn't live with that. I'm not a charity." I crossed the room, gesturing for Marsh to follow me. "Come on, let's have a drink."

My strategy worked, and Marsh reluctantly went to my study with me.

Anything to get him away from that *family* dinner. My dining room suddenly felt like a crime scene.

"Whiskey?" I asked as I shut the door to the study behind us. Marsh nodded, and I poured us each a glass.

Marsh accepted the liquor and sat on the leather couch near the window. "If you hadn't reneged on the Sullivan deal, none of this would be happening."

I took a sip of my whiskey, considering my words carefully. "I'm going to help Felicity's business, Marsh."

Marsh sighed. "I'd rather you didn't."

I sat on the armchair in the corner. "Moonstone Boutique has potential. Felicity just needs some help for a while."

He scoffed. "No one should need help in business. If they do, they're not cut out for it."

"You and I both know that's not true."

"I didn't need help. And no kid of mine deserves a handout." He shook his head. "Handouts make you soft. Weak. I didn't make it to where I am now from Daddy's friends paying my bills."

"Well, not everyone is you, Marsh. Investing in businesses is *my* business. It's what I do. I don't tell you how to run your law firm, do I?"

Marsh tightened his jaw. I had him there.

"The forecast for high-end boutique clothing is good. Market shares are expected to increase rapidly in the next ten years," I said. "And your daughter's talented, Marsh. It would be stupid for me *not* to invest in Moonstone."

Marsh paused, then looked at me. "Well, I guess I can't force you to do the right thing, Cooper."

My gut twisted. "The right thing?"

"Let her go it alone."

I chuckled. "No, you're right. This one's out of your reach. You can't control everything, Marsh."

We were both quiet for a while. Finally, he drained his glass and stood up. "I'll talk to you later, Cooper."

I exhaled. He was leaving, and I was relieved he hadn't again questioned me about sleeping with his daughter.

I followed him out of the study, my whiskey glass in my hand. Felicity's voice wafted into the foyer from the living room.

"All right, Marsh," I said, hoping to usher him out the door.

The Fiancé Hoax

But Marsh turned and walked to the living room. Damn.

I was on his heels as he entered the space. Felicity and the girls were seated on the floor around the coffee table, coloring in notebooks and chatting happily.

"I thought I told you girls to go upstairs," I said.

Eva looked up. "It's too early for bed, Daddy. We were bored."

Marsh cleared his throat. "Felicity, do you need a ride home?"

Felicity straightened. "Um, no, thanks. I'll order a ride later."

My throat tightened as Marsh paused, taking in the scene one last time. God, he surely knew what was going on. He was drawing it out just to torture me.

"All right, then. Goodnight."

"Goodnight, Dad," Felicity said with a smile.

Marsh gave me a nod and trudged toward the front door. I heard Monica shut the door behind him.

With a heaving sigh, I plopped on the sofa.

Felicity looked up at me. She was clearly on edge, too. "Is everything okay?"

"Everything's fine." I peered at the girls' work. "What are you drawing?"

"Clothes!" Eva held up her notebook to reveal a sketch of a girl wearing a long, yellow coat.

With Felicity's help, Lily was working on a drawing of a purple dress.

"Hey, that's pretty good," I said. "I didn't know you two could draw like that."

"Felicity's teaching us," Lily said.

"Yeah, it's really fun." Eva bent back over her notebook to color furiously.

Lily nodded in agreement as she concentrated on her work.

"I wish we could make real clothes," Eva said.

Felicity paused. "You know, I could take you to my shop sometime and teach you how to sew."

Eva and Lily looked at her, their faces lit up. "Really?"

"Sure! If your dad agrees, of course."

"Please, Daddy." Eva clasped her hands together. "Please!"

"I think it's a great idea," I said.

"Yay!" Lily and Eva cheered and high-fived Felicity.

"I want to make some cool-looking shorts," Eva said. "Something to wear to the park so I can climb on the jungle gym but *not* look like a dork. And I want pockets like the boys get!"

"And I want to make a princess dress," Lily said.

Felicity giggled. "Well, we'll start with something simple like a tank top. I'll have to teach you the basics first. But then we can move on to princess dresses and shorts with pockets."

"Ooh, this is gonna be sweet!" Eva said. She turned the page in her notebook and began to draw the shorts she wanted, coloring them blue and purple.

Lily moved closer to Felicity and rested her hand on her shoulder as Felicity added some details to Lily's dress.

I smiled. It had been a long time since I'd seen the girls like this, cozying up to anyone other than me or Inga.

They're getting too close to her. This will end in disaster.

But I told that nagging voice to shut up. My daughters loved this time with Felicity, and I did, too.

It would hurt like hell when it ended.

All I could do was enjoy it while it lasted.

14

FELICITY

The next afternoon, I smiled to myself as I hemmed a pair of wide-leg pants.

Eva and Lily were such a hoot. My heart felt lighter remembering the fun we had the evening before.

We were starting to feel like a family. And I couldn't help but love it.

The bell on the door chimed, and I looked up.

My heart jumped into my throat. I rose to my feet so quickly my chair fell behind me.

It was the last person I ever expected to see in Moonstone Boutique.

"Dad?"

My father's imposing frame paused in the door, as if he was having second thoughts.

Finally, he stepped inside the space and looked around. Silently, he approached a rack of blouses near the entrance. He grasped the price tag and shook his head.

"This is priced too low," he announced gruffly.

My words seemed to escape me as I stared at him. It took me a moment to speak.

"I know. I'm going to adjust the prices on everything tomorrow." I swallowed.

I shut my machine off and crossed the space toward him while he took everything in. He still hadn't looked at *me*, though.

"What are you doing here, Dad?"

"Just thought I'd see what kind of place you have."

I shook my head, amazed. "You've never set foot in the store before."

He shrugged. "First time for everything."

He swept his gaze over the walls and ceilings, and looked at a couple more racks. Then he headed toward the back.

"Here, let me show you my workspace. I cut all the fabric here." I gestured to the bolts of material and the large table I used to cut pieces. He nodded, then glanced at my small collection of sewing machines and sergers. "And I make all the clothes here." I held up the wide-leg pants I'd just finished. "Hot off the press."

Dad frowned. "Why are you doing that today? I thought you'd be working on managing the business, not making more clothes."

"I wanted to finish the garments I was working on before..." I shifted my weight. "Before Cooper gave me his recommendations. I can't stand leaving a project unfinished."

Dad grunted noncommittally.

I clipped the pants on a wooden hanger and hung it on the rack in my workspace. "Actually, that was the last item for my new summer line. Now I'm free to focus on the prices and marketing."

He came to a stop in front of my oldest machine, a vintage Singer. Slowly, he reached out and ran a finger over the top of the machine. "This was your mother's, wasn't it?"

I nodded. "Yeah. Good memory."

After a pause, he walked toward the large window in the back of the store. "Lots of windows in here."

"Yes, that was what convinced me to rent this space. I need natural light to work."

With a nod, he turned and walked a few steps toward the middle of the store. He went to the sales counter where I had the cash register and some small items for sale.

He pointed at a small bowl full of pearly white stones. "Are those moonstones?"

"Yes." I smiled. "Mom's favorite."

A slight smile pulled at his lips as he picked up one of the stones. "That's right." He got a faraway look for a moment, then replaced the stone in the bowl with a sigh.

Finally, he turned to face me.

Here it comes.

I clenched my teeth and braced myself for his criticism of the boutique. Or maybe he'd scold me for mooching off Cooper.

Instead, he gave me the surprise of the century.

"You've got a good setup."

I beamed. A weight lifted from my shoulders. "Thanks, Dad. I've worked really hard on this place. And the clothes, of course."

"It shows."

He held the sleeve of a flowy dress on a display rack, inspecting the design.

"There's still so much to do," I said. "There's so much I wasn't aware of when it comes to running a business. Cooper's been helping with that." I fidgeted. "Hopefully, it will be a thriving store soon."

He looked at me. "You could have done that yourself, Felicity."

I opened my mouth to protest but stopped myself. It was his way of giving me a compliment.

"You have so much of your mother in you," he said quietly, glancing at her old sewing machine. "She was such a fighter. She never let anything stop her. Not even cancer... Well, until she couldn't fight that anymore."

I swallowed the lump in my throat. "I know, Dad."

I was almost speechless. He never talked to me about Mom.

He looked down at the sleeve he held, then let it go. "Well, I better head out. I'm bringing some work home from the office tonight."

"Thanks for stopping by, Dad. I'm... I'm glad you came to see the store."

"Yeah, I guess I should have come by sooner."

"Come back anytime."

He gave me a nod, then headed toward the door. I followed behind him. Just before he reached the entrance, he turned to me.

"You know, Cooper used to have quite the reputation before he married Gen. He was known as a ladies' man."

Shit.

"Oh, really?" I croaked.

"Yes. And you would have been just the type of girl he'd go after."

My heart pounded in my chest. "Oh."

"*If* you weren't my daughter and so much younger than he is."

My throat was as dry as the desert. I managed to make a noise that approached a chuckle. "Right."

"Okay, see you, Felicity."

"Bye, Dad."

I shut the door behind him and leaned against it, my

eyes closed. Breathing out, I released the tension in my shoulders.

He was suspicious about me and Cooper. That made me nervous.

It was all the more reason to stay out of Cooper's bed.

I still dreamed of our night together, but I had to stay strong. It was better for everyone this way.

Besides, my dad had come to visit the store for the first time ever. I decided to count that as a victory.

It was time for me to close the store, so I packed up my laptop and books, locked the doors, and turned off the lights.

Cooper and the girls would be back at the house, and I was eager to see them.

⁓

"You're finally home!"

Seconds after I knocked on the front door of Cooper's house, it flew open. Eva and Lily gave me hugs.

Eva took my hand. "Come on! We've been waiting *forever* for you to get here."

"Where are we going?" I set my work bag down on the long table in the entry.

Lily took my other hand. "Upstairs. Daddy's waiting for you up there."

"Yeah, he's been acting really weird. He's been in a spare room with some people for hours."

I blinked. "Oh. Are you sure we should interrupt?"

Eva tugged harder on my hand. "He told us to bring you up there, silly!"

I laughed and let them lead me. "Okay."

"Why are you knocking on the front door, anyway?" Eva asked as we climbed the stairs. I had to hustle to keep up with them. "Don't you have a key?"

"Yeah, your dad gave me one. But I figure you guys are still getting used to having someone new in the house."

"You live here now," Lily said seriously.

I chewed my bottom lip. The girls were attached to me, and the feeling was mutual.

They led me down the long hallway past several rooms I'd never been in before. Cooper's house was huge. I grew nervous as we walked.

What if Cooper was with some woman? Or two or three women? I had no idea what kind of crazy stuff the man got up to.

Dad *had* said he had a reputation.

I stopped in my tracks, my mouth dry. "Girls, we shouldn't bother your dad. Maybe he's busy."

Eva and Lily ran to a shut door a few feet down the hall.

"He's busy with some big surprise," Eva said. "And I'm not waiting one second longer to find out what it is!"

She pounded on the door.

"Is Felicity here?" Cooper asked from inside the room.

"Yes, I'm here," I said.

The door swung open. "Come in," Cooper said. "We were just finishing up."

The girls darted ahead of me. I entered behind them and gasped.

Cooper had converted the room into a sewing studio—for me and the girls.

The walls were covered with reams of fabric and sewing tools. A cutting station, complete with child and adult tools, stood in the corner. In the center of the room were three sewing stations.

"I want this one!" Eva called, descending upon a bright purple child's sewing machine.

Cooper laughed. "Yes, that machine's for you, Eva. And this one's for Lily."

Lily smiled as she looked at a tiny pink sewing machine, made just for a girl her size.

Behind them, the workers gathered up their tools. There were two woodworkers who had apparently built the racks and shelves. A prim older woman smiled as she watched the girls flutter around the room.

I clamped my hands over my mouth as I stopped in front of the adult sewing machine. "Is that a Sailrite Deluxe?"

"Yes, dear," the woman said, walking up to me in her designer suit. "Your fiancé spared no expense. He told me he wanted the best of everything." She flashed me a smile and extended her hand. "Julia Harrison, sewing consultant."

"Felicity Hayes," I murmured, feeling woozy. "Lovely to meet you."

I looked from her to the machine, to Cooper. I'd always dreamed of a Sailrite, but had never been able to afford such a top-of-the-line sewing machine.

"Oh, my God, Cooper," I breathed. "Thank you."

He smiled at me before turning to his daughters.

"Now, safety comes first, girls," he said. "You have a lot to learn before you'll use these machines."

But the girls had already moved to the fabric.

"Can I make my shorts out of this?" Eva cried, pointing at some yellow cotton.

Lily gazed up at some pink tulle longingly.

"I think someone has already picked out the fabric for her princess dress," the woman said with a smile. "Let me know if you need anything else, Mr. Pierce."

"I will, Ms. Harrison. Thanks for all your help on such short notice. Monica will show you out downstairs."

The woman winked at me with a smile before she left, carrying a Chanel handbag and a tablet.

"A sewing consultant?" I asked. "Cooper, when did you arrange all this?"

Cooper shrugged. "Last night. I didn't know sewing consultants existed until my assistant found her for me. I needed someone to tell me what equipment to buy."

The workmen gave Cooper some paperwork and took their leave as well.

Cooper and I watched as the girls chattered excitedly, pointing to the fabrics and the tools hanging on the wall out of their reach. His masculine, woodsy cologne reached my head, making me feel even more woozy.

No, it wasn't just his cologne. It was everything about him. Just being in the man's presence was mesmerizing.

"Don't feel like you have to teach Eva and Lily," Cooper said. "I know you're busy with your store. Ms. Harrison can hook me up with teachers who'll come here."

I smiled. "Are you kidding? I'd love to teach them."

"Okay, but don't let it pull you away from those marketing campaigns." He winked.

"I wouldn't dream of it."

"This room is for you as much as it is for them, you know. If you ever need equipment to work on your designs, you can use what's here at home."

I looked at him, and his gorgeous eyes locked on mine.

"I took the liberty of looking at your purchasing records. I ordered the fabrics you seem to stock up on the most."

My eyes bulged as I saw where he was pointing. "Oh, wow, Cooper. You got all my favorites. And then some."

He'd even bought the high-end linen and silk I'd never been able to afford.

"I also got a few items from your wish list," he said, watching me run a finger along a bolt of silk.

I looked at the beautiful space and blinked back tears. "This studio is amazing. Thank you so much for all this, Cooper."

"Don't mention it. Thank you for spending this time with the girls."

Eva ran up to Cooper. "Thank you, Daddy! This is the coolest place ever."

He bent down so Eva and Lily could wrap their arms around his neck.

"Thanks, Daddy," Lily said. "We really like it."

"Felicity, can you start teaching us now?" Eva asked.

"Of course." I took a steadying breath, trying to compose myself after the studio reveal—and the proximity to Cooper. I pulled my hair into a bun and secured it with a pencil. "But where to start?"

I thought back to my first sewing lessons with my mother. I was six, the same age as Lily.

I walked over to the section of felt squares, located on a shelf within reach of the girls. I turned back to Cooper. "Ms. Harrison really thought of everything."

He laughed. "Best in the business."

I grabbed several pieces of felt, two pairs of children's scissors and a pair for me. I selected some thick thread and large needles, perfect for beginners.

"Come on, Eva and Lily. Let's start from the beginning."

Three hours and several miniature felt heart pillows later, the girls and I had lost track of time.

We'd gone over the basics of hand sewing and cutting fabric. Now I was showing them the ropes of the sewing machines. I was glad the kids' machines had lots of safety measures built in.

Cooper had spent most of the time watching us, but he'd disappeared twenty minutes earlier. The girls and I were so focused on our lessons that we hardly noticed until the smell of pepperoni wafted into the space.

"Who wants pizza?"

Cooper stood in the doorway with three pizza boxes and a bottle of soda.

"Me!" Lily exclaimed.

"Me, too!" Eva shouted. "Can we eat in here please?"

"Sure," Cooper said.

I stood up and began to clear off the table we were working at.

"I guess I am pretty hungry," I said. "I kind of lost track of time."

Monica brought up some plates, napkins, and glasses. Cooper thanked her and dismissed her for the evening so she could get home.

"How's it going, girls? Looks like you're already making some stuff."

"Heart pillows, Daddy," Eva corrected. "And Felicity's teaching us how to use the machines now."

Cooper put a slice of cheese pizza on a plate for Lily while Eva plated some pepperoni for herself.

"Having fun?" Cooper asked before biting into his own slice.

"It's the best!" Eva cried.

"I wanna be a seamstress like Felicity," Lily said.

I laughed as I added parmesan to my slice. "You girls are naturals. You'll be fashion designers before you know it."

The girls chattered to their dad as they ate, filling him in on everything they'd learned and the bags, pillows and clothes they wanted to sew. They'd definitely caught the sewing bug. They reminded me of myself at that age.

As we ate, I felt myself getting comfortable with them. How was it possible that I'd just met the Pierces a week ago?

Being with them felt so natural, so right. It almost felt more real than my previous life.

It was hard to remember this was all pretense.

After we ate, I carried the dishes and pizza boxes downstairs while Cooper got the girls ready for bed. They were tired after the excitement with the sewing room, and their chattering wasn't as fast-paced as it normally was.

I put the dishes in the dishwasher and wiped the counter. Even though Monica had left it spotless, I wanted something to keep my hands busy. I thought about pouring a glass of wine but thought against it.

You're trying to stay out of Cooper Pierce's bed, remember?

Instead, I made a cup of chamomile tea. Right after I poured the water into the mug to steep the tea, Lily called down from the top of the stairs.

"Felicity?"

I went to the bottom of the staircase. She was standing in bumblebee pajamas, looking adorable and holding her stuffed rabbit.

"Yes, Lily?"

"Will you read us a bedtime story?"

My heart melted. "Of course."

Upstairs, I sat in the chair between the two beds. Cooper

tucked them both in and sat in the chair in the corner and handed me a copy of *The Princess and the Pea*.

As I read to the girls, that comfortable feeling settled over me again. I loved to see the girls' reaction to the story—their giggles and smiles—and their heavy eyelids as the story came to a close.

I stood as Cooper kissed them each goodnight, and we left the room and headed downstairs together.

I followed him to the kitchen, where I grabbed my cup of tea. He busied himself collecting the girls' schoolwork and putting it in their backpacks. Then he turned to me, his eyes smoldering and intense.

"Thanks, Felicity. For everything."

"Thank you, Cooper. It's been nice being here."

My eyes shifted away from his. I didn't know where to look. If I lost myself in his gaze, I knew I wouldn't be able to resist him.

I covered my mouth as I yawned. "Those kids wear me out. I think I'll hit the sack, too."

He nodded. "Yeah, another busy day tomorrow. I'll be in my office if you need anything."

Yes, I do need something, Cooper. I need your hands all over me, now.

"Okay. Goodnight, Cooper."

"Goodnight, Felicity."

I left him in the kitchen, forcing myself not to turn back for one last look.

15

COOPER

"Antoine's?" Felicity raised an eyebrow as I pulled my car up to the valet area of the restaurant. "Color me impressed."

I chuckled as I got out and jogged around the car to open her door.

"Nothing but the best," I said as I held out my hand to help her out of the vehicle.

Her diamond sparkled on her finger. It was big and gaudy—just what I wanted. I needed a big flashing sign that screamed, *Engaged*. And that rock on her finger was as close as I could get.

Antoine's was the current hot restaurant where all the well-connected dined in LA. I hardly ever came here without running into someone I knew. Businesspeople, investors, attorneys, even celebrities were regulars. I wouldn't be surprised if Judge Graves ate here.

Luckily, Marsh hated the place.

Felicity looped her hand around my bent arm, and we walked in.

This was our first public appearance in a high-profile

place since Felicity had moved in. And she had dressed for the part. Her long emerald green dress with a slit up to her upper thigh made her look stunning. She wore her rich brown hair up to showcase her shoulders and neck, left bare by her sleeveless dress.

Several heads turned as we moved through the restaurant, following the hostess to our table. Felicity was so close I could breathe in her scent, and it made me want her all the more.

Once we were seated and had ordered our drinks, she perused the menu. I tried to keep my eyes off the hint of cleavage revealed by her gown.

She glanced up at me. "Do you already know what you're getting?"

"I always get the steak," I said.

"Always the same thing?"

I nodded.

"Why am I not surprised?" She smiled.

I lifted a shoulder. "If something works, why change it?"

"Good point." She chewed her lip as she studied the menu. "Okay, I'll get the steak, too. That sounds perfect, actually."

She closed the menu and looked around the room. I made myself look away from her beautiful face. It was refreshing to see a woman eat more than a salad.

She leaned in and lowered her voice. "You really think coming here together and wearing this ring will help your custody case?"

"I do. LA's a big city, but the circles I run in are small. People talk. They'll notice us together, and they'll definitely notice that ring."

She giggled. "How could they not?"

I spotted an investor I knew a few tables down. I held my glass of wine up to him and nodded.

"See what I mean?" I muttered under my breath to Felicity.

"I do," she said, looking a little nervous.

"You're doing great," I reassured her. "Tell me about your day."

"Well, I changed the price on everything in the store," she said.

"You *increased* the prices, I hope?"

She gave me a dubious look. "Of course. I followed all your recommendations."

"Good." I sipped my wine.

"Oh, and the web developer I hired launched my new website, and I just got my first online sale!" She beamed, giddy with excitement.

"Wonderful. Here's to many more." I raised my glass and clinked it against hers.

"Thanks. And tomorrow, I'll work on new advertisements to try to get more people into the store."

I nodded. "Advertising will be a game-changer for you, Felicity."

"I hope so." She played with her dangling earring, looking off into the distance. "It does feel like things are about to really change with the boutique. And... I still can't get over my dad visiting my store yesterday."

"It was high time he did." I shook my head. "I can't believe he took so long."

"He's stubborn. He hated the fact that I went into fashion design. He was never supportive of my decision to open the store because he thought it would fail." She looked down at the table, sadness on her face.

I reached over and took her hand in mine. Not because I

wanted people to see us, but because I wanted to comfort her. She looked at my hand on hers, then up at me.

"He was wrong about your business. You're going to prove it to him."

Her eyes brightened. "I hope you're right, Cooper." She smiled. "And maybe he's starting to come around. His visit to the store felt really big. Like he was finally starting to accept me and my life choices."

I smiled at her, glad to see the sadness in her face gone.

"Either that or he's trying to snoop," she said. "Maybe he's suspicious something's up between you and me."

"It could be a little of both," I said quietly. "Now that we're going out in public like this, he's bound to find out about the engagement sooner or later."

"Yeah." She shuddered. "That won't be fun."

"As long as he understands it's just temporary, and it's just a contract, he'll learn to accept it."

I withdrew my hand and cleared my throat.

That meant we couldn't sleep together again. If Marsh found out about that, all bets were off.

She nodded. "So, how was your day?"

"Nothing eventful. Everything's going well at my company. I'm reviewing investment opportunities."

"Any good leads?" she asked.

I nodded. "There are a couple I'm considering."

I left it at that. I loved my work, but it didn't make for the most stimulating conversation for people who didn't deal in my world. Investing in Felicity's business was the best move I'd made lately, and I hadn't regretted it.

"You know, now that we're engaged," she said, her eyes twinkling, "I should really know more about your background."

I set my wine glass down. "Well, you know I grew up in

The Fiancé Hoax

Philadelphia." Eva had told Felicity about our annual visits to the East Coast to see my brother, Rhys, and my parents.

"Right. And you moved to LA for college. Why so far away?"

"My school had a good business program. And it was about as far away from my family as I could get."

She studied me. "You didn't get along with your family?"

"I got along with them well enough, I suppose. But there wasn't always the best dynamic in my house growing up."

She tilted her head. "How so?"

"Well, my dad was a drunk."

She sucked in air through her teeth. "Oh. I'm so sorry."

"It wasn't as bad as it could have been," I said. "He never got violent with my mother or my brother or me. And he's been sober for ten years now."

"I'm glad. Are your parents still together?"

"Yes. But there was a lot of crazy shit in my house growing up. My dad had a stressful job running a small business. He couldn't cope with it, and he just checked out by getting wasted. My mom made excuses and tried to cover up the messes he made. As the older kid, I had to pick up the slack." I swirled the wine in my glass. "I guess I had a lot of anger back then."

She gave me a sympathetic look. "That sounds hard, Cooper."

I lifted a shoulder. "I guess most people have some sob story. That's mine—my dad was an alcoholic, and my mom enabled him." I took a sip of wine. "That's why I wanted to get away from them, back when he was passing out on the couch and my mom was pretending everything was perfect."

"I can understand that."

"I never wanted to be like him," I said, thinking back. "I

never wanted to be unavailable to my kids. The type of guy to run and hide in a bottle instead of facing shit."

She gave me a warm smile. "You're not like that at all. I can't imagine a better father than you."

"I do what I can for my daughters. It's not always easy, but they deserve someone who's there for them. They sure don't have that in their mother."

Felicity nodded. "Sadly, they don't."

"I'm so glad to have Eva and Lily." I smiled. "But... two kids is it for me. I couldn't handle any more."

She looked up at me. "You don't think you'd want any more if you met the right woman?"

I shook my head firmly. "No." Lowering my voice, I added, "And I definitely don't want to get married again."

She blinked at me, and something like surprise flickered across her face. "Never?"

"No. I'm not making that mistake again."

Felicity looked away and became silent, leaving me to my thoughts.

What I didn't mention was that I didn't *trust* myself to fall in love again.

Gen had taught me that lesson. It was too easy to get trapped in a bad situation.

I couldn't let myself fall for that again.

Our food arrived, and I was glad when the topic of conversation shifted to something lighter.

Felicity told me some details of her own childhood. She skirted around what were obviously painful memories of her dad's emotional unavailability.

Instead, she focused on her mother, who had been a loving parent to her. Her mom, like her father, had come from humble roots. I got the sense Felicity's mother never

The Fiancé Hoax

quite fit in with the new upper-class society Marsh had expected her to thrive in after he made it big.

And like her mother, Felicity had stayed down-to-earth. She'd grown up in a fancy house, but she was still humble.

Listening to Felicity, I began to appreciate her even more. She'd been through a lot, especially with losing her mom at age eighteen.

Though she didn't say it, I could tell that she'd turned to her dad for support in her grief, but he'd withdrawn.

As the night carried on, I felt a sense of protectiveness rising inside me. I wanted to be that support Felicity needed. I wanted to keep her safe, to tell her that everything would be all right.

And then I wanted to carry her to my bed and make her writhe in pleasure until she came over and over.

But none of that would be possible. There were so many reasons it would never work with us.

All I could do was enjoy the company of this remarkable woman while she was here.

16

COOPER

"Woo-hoo!"

Felicity cheered beside me as Eva sauntered down the "catwalk" wearing her new fashions.

Two weeks after Felicity started to teach the girls to sew, they were already showing off their creations in a fashion show at home.

Of course, Felicity had given them a lot of help. In fact, some of the things they were wearing she had made on her own. But I was amazed at how much my daughters had learned in a short period of time.

Eva struck a pose at the end of the catwalk we had created by rearranging the furniture in the living room. Then she turned and exited the room. Inga was waiting in the hallway to help her change into the next outfit.

Felicity and I clapped and cheered when Lily stepped out wearing a pink dress. The little girl was beaming as she shyly walked through the room and twirled around.

"Beautiful, Lily!" Felicity shouted above the booming music filtering through the speakers.

"I can't believe how much progress they've made in two weeks," I said.

"They're naturals at this." Felicity shrugged. "I'm just glad they're having fun. And I am too, honestly. I had no idea designing for children would be such a blast."

Eva appeared in her next outfit: a purple sleeveless top with bright yellow shorts. The color combination was outrageous and bold, but it suited her perfectly.

After Lily's next appearance in a lavender skirt and white top, the show was over. The girls entered the living room for their final bows.

"Nice work, girls!" I said as we applauded. Inga joined us in the living room to cheer them on. "I'm so proud of you both."

"I am, too," Felicity said. "You've both been working so hard."

They really had been. Most evenings after Felicity got home from Moonstone, she and the girls would put in a few hours in the sewing studio. It seemed the girls loved spending time with Felicity even more than they loved making clothes.

Lily stood close to Felicity, who put her arm around her and gently squeezed her little shoulders.

"Thanks for teaching us how to sew," Eva said. "It's our new favorite thing."

Felicity laughed. "It's been my pleasure."

I turned the music off and looked at my watch. "It's almost time for your dance lessons, girls."

"Come on, you two. Let's get you ready for dance class," Inga said. She gathered up all the outfits and hustled the girls toward the staircase.

The girls ran upstairs with Inga following them.

I started to move the couch back to its proper place, and

Felicity helped by grabbing one corner. "You've really outdone yourself, Felicity. Those designs were amazing."

Felicity set her end of the couch down. "To be honest, I don't know anything about kids' fashions. I was just winging it."

I scoffed as I moved the coffee table. "You know plenty about kids' fashions. The show just now made that obvious. I'm no fashion expert, but I know you can't find unique clothes like that in department stores."

She laughed. "I was just having fun."

"Maybe you should think about expanding your line into children's wear." I picked up the armchair and set it down by the coffee table.

Felicity blinked. "Really?"

"Absolutely. You have a knack for it, Felicity."

"Well, it *was* really fun working on these little outfits." She beamed. "But selling kids' clothes? I never thought about that before."

I turned to face her, taking a step closer. "Well, you should think about it now." My voice came out lower than I intended. Suddenly the conversation felt... intimate.

Her eyes locked on mine, and we froze in place. I breathed in her floral perfume, becoming acutely aware of how close we were standing. She looked up at me, those deep doe eyes innocent and mesmerizing.

Fuck, I wanted her.

It had been torture being in the same house with her the past few weeks without touching her. Right now, it was excruciating. Everything about this woman turned me on.

"Daddy, we want Felicity to take us to dance class!" Eva announced as they raced down the stairs.

Felicity and I took a step back from each other just before the girls ran into the living room.

Inga was behind them, and she grabbed her purse from the entertainment center. It was the end of her Friday afternoon shift, and I usually took the girls to dance class.

"Are you heading off now, Inga?" I turned my attention to her, keeping Felicity out of my sight. I needed a chance to cool off after our heated moment alone.

"Yes, that's all for today. Have a good evening, everyone," Inga said with a smile. She gave the girls a hug, and they told her goodnight.

"Bye, Inga. Thanks for your help," I said.

When she was gone, the girls turned back to me.

"Please, Daddy," Lily begged. "Can't Felicity take us today?"

I shook my head. "No, Felicity has things to do. I'll take you to dance class like I always do."

"It's okay," Felicity said. "I don't mind. Really."

"Yay!" Eva and Lily high-fived.

I turned to Felicity. "Are you sure? I know you have a lot on your plate with the boutique."

"I'm positive. This will be a nice break from working on ad campaigns." She laughed.

"Okay." I rubbed my jaw. "I could catch up on some work while you're gone and then meet you guys at the diner afterward."

"Sounds like a plan." Felicity fished her keys out of her purse as the girls pulled her toward the front door. I grabbed the girls' dance bags and walked with them to Felicity's car.

"Did you notice we're wearing the stuff we made to class?" Eva asked, tugging on my hand.

"I did notice," I said. "You two look awesome."

Eva was wearing her purple and yellow outfit to her hip-hop dance class. Lily took ballet, and she wore a leotard with the pink skirt Felicity had helped her create. A fairy skirt, I had been informed.

I had already bought child car seats to keep in Felicity's car, and I watched as she carefully strapped them in.

I had offered to buy her a new vehicle, but she'd refused. So I'd insisted on taking the Plymouth to my mechanic to make sure it wouldn't break down on the highway.

"Bye, Daddy!"

"Bye, girls. Be on your best behavior for Felicity."

She smiled at me and got in the driver's seat. "See you soon."

I watched as she drove down the driveway. For the thousandth time that week, my heart flipped over.

I made my way upstairs to my office, smiling to myself as I walked. Felicity was making the girls' lives better. There was no doubt about that.

But we were getting really deep into this thing. Eva and Lily were getting more attached to her all the time. And it had only been three weeks since she moved in.

It was easy to think the four of us would go on like this forever. Having Felicity with us in the house felt so normal, so natural.

But this was all based on a little white lie. Or a big one, depending on how you looked at it.

Either way, Felicity and I were not in a real relationship. I had to keep reminding myself she wasn't always going to be a part of our lives.

The guilt about how it might affect the girls was overwhelming. Maybe I was setting the girls up for heartbreak. But it was too late to change things now.

I had just over two months until the custody hearing. The girls and I could get through a few more weeks. Maybe we wouldn't get through unscathed, but at least we'd be together in the end.

Without Felicity.

I swallowed the lump in my throat and sat down at my desk. Pushing away my worries, I threw myself into my work.

An hour later, I walked into our favorite diner. I spotted Felicity and the girls at a table in the back, chatting excitedly.

"Daddy!" Eva exclaimed as I sat next to her in the booth. Felicity and Lily sat across from us.

"Hey, girls. How was dance class?" I asked, ruffling her hair. I picked up the menu.

"Awesome!" Eva said. "My teacher taught us this really cool new move. Here, I'll show you."

She popped up to stand in the booth.

Before she could show us the move, I shook my head. "Show us after dinner, okay, silly goose?"

"Okay." She plopped back down in the booth. "And we got Felicity a new customer."

I looked at Felicity. She grinned.

"Yeah, one of the moms at the dance studio really liked the clothes Eva and Lily were wearing. I gave her my card, and she said she'd come by soon to check out the boutique."

"Really? That's great."

Felicity nodded, her face lit up with excitement. She was beautiful, and her enthusiasm was contagious. "And the best part is that she works for *LA Now Magazine*."

I dropped the menu. "She does?"

"Yeah, she's a writer... for the *fashion section*."

She danced her feet with glee under the table, then reached across the menu and squeezed my hand. Her touch was sweet and warm, and I never wanted her to let go.

"Cooper, do you think she might write a review of my store?"

"She might. What's her name? I may have heard of her."

"Hold on. She gave me her card."

Felicity let go of my hand to rummage in her purse. I cursed myself silently for asking the question. I instantly missed her skin on mine.

"Here it is." She handed me the card. "Dana Berceli."

I looked at the card, then handed it back to her. "I don't know her, but I think this is a very good sign, Felicity. You should put some of the clothes you designed for the girls on display in your store. And you could advertise a custom design service for little girls."

Felicity smiled. "I do like the idea. It just seems like a big change. I've never designed for children."

"Until us!" Eva interjected.

Felicity grinned at her. "Right. Until you two."

"I should have thought of this in the beginning," I said. "Expanding your market to children. People in high financial brackets will pay top dollar for custom, one-of-a-kind clothes for their kids."

Felicity played with a strand of her hair, looking off into the distance. "I'll have to think about it. But it's very exciting."

The waitress came to take our orders, and we spent the rest of the meal talking with the girls. I did my best to keep my eyes off Felicity. But she was so gorgeous it was hard not to stare at her.

Back home, Felicity helped me put the girls to bed. It was quickly becoming a routine for her to read to them at night, and I sat in the room to listen and tuck the girls in.

By the time she finished the story, both Eva and Lily

were out cold. We turned the lights out and left the room, closing the door behind us.

In the hallway, I turned to her. Her chocolate brown hair fell down her shoulders. Her full mouth pulled up at the corners. Those gorgeous eyes sparkled as she looked up at me.

She was perfect, and I didn't want to pretend anymore.

I couldn't hold myself back any longer.

"You're so beautiful, Felicity."

Her eyes widened slightly.

I didn't wait for her to respond. Bending toward her, I grasped the back of her head with my hand and plunged my fingers into that silky hair. I pressed my mouth against hers, and she sighed against me, parting her lips and kissing me back.

It was like wildfire erupting.

She pressed herself against me, making contact with my rock-hard dick. I thrust the length against her soft belly, and she whimpered in my mouth. I lifted her up by her hips and she wrapped her legs around me. I carried her to the nearest room, which was her bedroom.

I couldn't wait another second to be inside her. I needed her like I'd never needed anything in my life.

I laid her down on the bed and stood above her. She gazed up at me, panting.

I smiled down at her and started to unbutton my shirt.

But my fingers froze on the first button.

What the fuck was I doing?

My mouth turned dry, and I forced myself to look away.

I was screwing everything up. We'd gotten carried away, lost in the moment. If we went through with this, we'd regret it.

After all, she was the one who said we shouldn't have a repeat of our first night together.

"I'm sorry, Felicity," I took a steadying breath, willing my cock to back off. "I shouldn't have done that. We agreed that night would be a one-time thing."

I headed toward the door.

"Goodnight," I said.

I left, closing the door behind me. I couldn't look back at her. If I did, I knew I wouldn't be able to stop myself.

17

FELICITY

What the hell just happened?

One second Cooper was all hot and ready for me. The next he left me high and dry.

Or soaking wet, as the case may be.

And suddenly, I was angry about it.

I didn't appreciate him getting me all worked up and then running out of the room. If he was doing this because of our agreement to no longer have sex after the first time, then it was up to me to set the record straight.

I no longer cared about that agreement. I just wanted to be with Cooper.

I couldn't hide how I felt anymore.

I sprang to my feet and charged out of the room, crossing the hallway quickly. I knocked on the door, then opened it. I was going to give him a piece of my mind, and I didn't want to wait around for him to give me the go-ahead.

"Listen, Cooper," I said as I walked inside and closed the door behind me. "I don't care about…"

I froze.

I'd walked in on him undressing. He was unbuttoning

the last button of his shirt and removing it from his shoulders. We stared at each other for a second.

Then he tossed the shirt on the floor and came to me, crossing the distance with large steps.

He pushed me backwards against the wall and crushed his mouth against mine. He was already breathing heavily, pulling at the hem of my shirt and lifting it over my head.

"Oh, God," I whimpered.

All the times I'd wanted him, fantasized about him touching me like this once more... It was finally happening.

As I moved my hands over his taut, muscled chest and shoulders, he grabbed me by the ass and squeezed me firmly, making me yelp. He unbuttoned my jeans and pulled them roughly down my hips and legs. I stepped out of them and stood before him in my bra and panties.

A noise that sounded like a growl escaped his throat as he stood above me. He kissed me on the mouth, even more deeply and forcefully than before. Reaching behind me, he unhooked my bra and removed it from my body. His hands moved over my breasts and hard nipples, and he bent down to suckle one, then the other.

I plunged my hands into his hair, grasping his head. Every muscle in my body was tight with need for him.

"Oh, fuck," he moaned as he unzipped his pants, opened his boxers, and brought his long, hard cock out. It pointed straight at me. "I need you now."

He clenched my ass in one hand, pulling me against his erection. I wrapped my arms around his neck and lifted one leg over his hip. Roughly, he pulled the crotch of my panties to the side and pressed his dick against my entrance.

"Yes, please," I begged. I couldn't stand the anticipation one second more. I needed to be filled up by him.

He still wore his pants. Removing them would take

precious seconds, and I knew he was just as impatient as I was.

He pushed the head inside, and I gasped at his sheer girth. With one strong thrust, he pushed his way inside me, all the way to his balls. We groaned together.

"Oh my God," I moaned. "That feels so good."

I was so wet and ready for him, and he thrust inside me several times. He lifted my other leg, and I wrapped them around his hips. He was supporting my full weight now, fucking me against the wall.

I leaned my head back, biting my lip and closing my eyes for a moment. I arched my back, pressing my breasts against his hard chest. When I opened my eyes again, he was looking straight at me, his gaze fixed on me.

"Oh, Cooper," I whimpered. "Don't stop. Please don't stop."

My muscles began to contract around his cock. He moved one hand to my breast and rolled the nipple between his thumb and forefinger. His touch set my nerves on fire.

I squeezed my legs around him, drawing him nearer to me. I wanted him closer. I couldn't get him close enough.

He thrust into me again and again, finally pushing me over the edge.

"I'm coming," I whispered.

I held on to his shoulders for dear life as I sank into the warm oblivion of my orgasm. My sex clenched around his cock rhythmically, milking him.

He released a deep, low grunt as he pushed himself inside all the way and stayed still. His cock pulsated, sending his warm release deep inside me.

We stayed like that for a long moment, with his cock still inside me, throbbing and pulsing.

Slowly, he released me and set me back on the floor. His dick slipped out of me.

I felt weak on my feet, still reeling from my orgasm. He led me to the bed, pulled the covers back, and helped me lie down. Then he disappeared into the bathroom and returned a moment later with a towel. He carefully cleaned up between my legs and wiped himself off, removing his pants and boxers in the process. Then he crawled into bed beside me, his naked body pressed against mine.

I turned to look at him and we both burst out laughing.

His blue eyes sparkled as he laughed. He pulled me closer, snaking his arm underneath my head. I closed my eyes, breathing in his scent and relishing the feeling of being in his arms.

I looked up at him. "What are you laughing at?"

"I'm not sure. All of it, I guess. The way you charged in here. You looked like you were going to chew me out."

"I was." I laughed. "But then I got distracted."

He smiled. "What are *you* laughing at?"

I moved my hand along the side of his body, tracing the rippling muscles on his back and abdomen. "Most people take their clothes off before sex, not after."

He grinned. "We're not most people."

"That's for sure."

He kissed me on the forehead and looked in my eyes. "What were you going to say when you came in here?"

"That I don't care about that agreement we made to not have a repeat of our first... sexual encounter."

He raised his eyebrows. "Is that so?"

"Yes, that's so."

"So the one time wasn't enough to get it out of your system?"

I bit my lip. "Apparently not."

"Good."

"Cooper, you're all I could think about the past few weeks." I swallowed. That sounded way too intimate. "I mean, sex with you was all I could think about," I quickly added.

"Same here."

"And I don't think this second time will be enough, either."

He kissed me on the mouth, his tongue probing my depths. Then he pulled back to look at me. "Not nearly enough."

"So should we amend the rules?"

"Definitely."

"So, sex is okay? We can do this as much as we want?" I asked. "I mean, as long as this fake relationship thing continues."

"I can agree to that."

I nodded. "We *are* two adults, after all. We can have a mature physical relationship."

"Absolutely." He trailed a finger over my nipple, which grew pebbled under his touch.

"We should still keep this just between you and me, though. I definitely don't want my father finding out we have something like this going on."

"He's the last person who should find out. He'd take the news of the fake engagement better than finding out we're sleeping together."

"Yeah. He certainly would."

"And we shouldn't change things in front of Eva and Lily. This is already too confusing for them. Eva pretty much knows it's all for the custody hearing. But Lily..." He swallowed. "Well, it's better if they don't see us cuddling on the couch."

"Right. I'm sorry this is confusing for them."

"Yeah. I hate to bring more changes into their lives. But it was my only choice to keep custody of them."

I nodded. "Yeah. I know it's going to be hard for them, but I agree—it's for the best."

He was quiet.

"If you want, I could still come see Lily and Eva sometimes. After this is all over."

My throat formed a lump as I said the words. I didn't want it to end.

He kissed my forehead. "Thanks, Felicity. I'd appreciate that."

We were quiet for a while, and I snuggled closer to his chest.

His breathing grew more shallow, and he moved his palm over my hip and bottom. His hips pressed against me, and I gasped.

His cock was erect again, and he thrust the length against my abdomen.

"You're already hard again?" I asked.

His eyes moved over my lips. "I've been that way for a while. How could I not be? I'm lying next to the most beautiful woman I've ever seen."

My face turned warm, and I knew I was blushing. He kissed me, then pulled me on top of his body as he rolled onto his back.

I straddled his waist. He supported my back with one strong arm as he trailed the other hand over my breasts and belly.

"I'm not just saying that, you know," he whispered.

He grabbed my rear and lifted his hips, pushing his cock against my back.

I moaned, already craving the feeling of his cock filling

my body.

"I need you," I murmured.

He lifted me and moved me back slightly, positioning my entrance over his eager cock. I sank down his length, taking him inside me slowly, inch by inch.

"Is that what you needed?"

I nodded, biting my lip as he thrust upward.

God, yes.

Cooper Pierce was *exactly* what I needed.

⁓

"Felicity's awake!"

Lily announced my presence with glee as I entered the kitchen the next morning, which was Saturday.

After Cooper made me see stars for the third time last night, I left him in his room. Back in my own bedroom, I texted Lauren the update.

She was glad to know I was planning to regularly hook up with Cooper. I needed to, as she put it, *ride that bad boy* as much as possible.

I didn't tell her everything, though. Like how sad I was to return to my own room. Alone.

Cooper and I had both agreed it would be better if we slept in our separate bedrooms. That way, it wouldn't confuse the girls even more if they noticed.

We didn't say this part out loud, but we both knew sleeping separately served another purpose as well: to avoid getting our own emotions mixed up in the sex.

Even though I longed to sleep in his arms.

And I was pretty sure I was *way* past the point of getting my emotions involved.

Now, I stood in my pajamas and bathrobe in the kitchen.

Both girls and Cooper were seated at the kitchen table waiting for me.

Eva jumped up and pulled me toward the table. "Just in time, sleepyhead."

"We made breakfast!" Lily said. "Just Eva and me."

"You did? Wow, this looks amazing, girls!" Eva pulled me down into the chair across from Cooper. I sat obediently.

Cooper smiled at me. "Hungry?"

"Very hungry."

I blushed and quickly looked down at the table. We had both worked up an appetite last night, but we weren't going to talk about it now.

"Let's eat!" Lily grabbed her spoon and dug into her bowl of mixed berries.

"Yum, this is perfect," I said, putting the cloth napkin in my lap. "Could you pass the butter?" Eva pushed the dish in my direction, and I added a pat to the breakfast waffle on the plate before me. "I didn't know you girls could cook waffles."

"Yeah, it's easy," Eva said between mouthfuls. "Monica taught us how to use the toaster."

I smiled. Right. Toaster waffles. I felt a little silly, thinking they knew how to cook regular waffles from batter. I still had a lot to learn about kids, I supposed.

Still, the girls had gone all out. They had set four places perfectly, made the waffles, and filled the bowls with berries. Pretty impressive.

I took a sip of orange juice.

"Daddy helped us pour the juice," Lily said. "But we did everything else."

"Well, I'm very proud of you both," Cooper said. "It was a really nice thought to surprise us with breakfast today."

Eva cleared her throat theatrically.

"Wouldn't it be nice if we had breakfast like this together every day?" She looked between me and Cooper. "Forever?"

My eyes met Cooper's.

He shifted in his seat. "Yes, having breakfast together is a nice treat. It's a little hard to pull off on weekdays, though. You girls have school and I have to get to work."

I swallowed a bite of waffle without a word. Cooper always knew how to answer diplomatically.

"Well, there's dinner, too. We could have dinner together. Every single day. The four of us." Eva lifted her eyebrows expectantly.

Cooper gave her a smile meant to acknowledge her, but he didn't say anything. And soon, the topic of conversation changed as the girls babbled excitedly about their weekend activities.

I snuck a few glances at Cooper. He did the same, and our eyes lingered on each other.

Our new plan to maintain a sexual relationship thrilled me.

But I agreed with Eva. Sharing a meal with the Pierces everyday sounded just about perfect.

18

COOPER

I stood in the hallway of my kids' elementary school wearing a goofy grin on my face.

That happened a lot lately. I couldn't help it. Felicity had that effect on me.

Nearby, Eva was chatting excitedly with her friends. I was one of the adult chaperones for her class museum trip, and her teacher was running late in getting everything ready for us to leave.

Normally, the delay would irritate me. But not today. I had a surprisingly good attitude about it. After all, what was the rush?

It was four days after Felicity and I had agreed to a physical relationship, and I was already feeling more content. Each night since then, after we put the girls to bed, Felicity and I had amazing sex in my bed. Usually multiple times.

It would be easy to get used to this.

Of course, we had to sleep in separate beds. But I would've preferred to have her sleep in my arms all night. Every time I had to say goodbye to Felicity, it hurt a little.

Down the hall, I caught a glimpse of a woman with long

brown hair wearing a flowery dress as she walked toward the first-grade area. My heart picked up speed.

"Felicity?"

She turned around at the sound of her name. A smile brightened her face as she saw me, and I approached her at the end of the hall.

"What are you doing here?" I asked, grinning at the pleasant surprise.

Felicity's eyes sparkled. "Lily's showing her Mother's Day art today. She asked me to be here."

"Oh, right. I forgot that was today."

Felicity watched as several women filed inside the first-grade classroom after the students. They were the kids' mothers, no doubt.

"I think it's starting now," Felicity said. "I better get in there. Are you about to leave for the field trip?"

"Eva's teacher said it would be another half hour, so I have time. I'll go in with you to watch."

"Great!"

I held the door to the classroom open for her, and we entered.

The kids sat at their desks. When Lily saw us, she smiled and waved excitedly. At the front of the classroom, the student art projects were on display. At the back of the room, several mothers and a few dads sat in chairs that were lined up in rows.

"Let's take those two over there," Felicity said. She pointed at the only two empty seats that were together. Then her hand fell and she took a step backward in surprise. "Oh, I didn't know..."

Gen sat right next to the empty seats. When she saw us, she plastered a saccharine smile on her face and patted the empty seat beside her.

Why the hell was she here? She *never* came to class events for the girls. I was surprised she even knew which school they attended.

With a sigh, I took the seat beside Gen. Felicity sat in the chair on my other side.

Lily's teacher, Mrs. Goldstein, cleared her throat at the front of the classroom.

"Welcome, parents, to this very special art show, brought to you by our first-grade class!"

As the parents politely applauded, I spoke in a low voice to Gen. "Surprised to see you here. Why did you bother showing up?"

Gen sniffed. "I'm Lily's *mother*, Cooper." She flicked her eyes toward Felicity. "I wouldn't miss this for the world."

I snorted. "I bet your attorney advised you to come here and play the part, didn't he?"

Gen ignored the question and focused on the first child to display his art—a rather misshapen ashtray. His mother, who I figured was not a smoker, looked thrilled.

I put my arm around Felicity's chair, and she moved a bit closer toward me. Gen rolled her eyes.

We listened as the next few kids said a few words about their art projects. Finally, it was Lily's turn, and she walked to the front of the classroom to stand beside her project. I could tell she was nervous. I tried to meet her eyes to give her strength and encouragement.

"Tell us what you made, Lily," the teacher prompted.

"I made a picture...a *collage*," Lily said in a clear voice. "I cut up magazine pictures to make it. It's of a calico cat sniffing a flower."

Everyone applauded, and Lily smiled at us as she returned to her seat. She had spent a lot of time on her project, flipping through endless magazines to find the perfect images of a cat, a daffodil, a sun, and a blue sky.

My chest filled with pride. Not just because of her art project, but because she spoke up in front of a large crowd. I knew that was difficult for her. Beside me, Felicity beamed.

Gen crossed her arms in a huff. I could practically feel the anger emanating from her. I just hoped she wouldn't make a scene.

The next three children displayed their artwork, and the teacher wrapped up the presentation. The parents stood up and approached their kids to congratulate them.

"Don't make this difficult, Gen," I said under my breath.

She ignored me and crossed the room to Lily. Felicity and I followed close behind her.

"Awesome job, sweet pea," I said to Lily. "I'm so proud of—"

"Lily, darling, you know I hate cats," Gen interrupted. She looked down at Lily with a frown. "Why would you make that picture of a cat for me?"

"Gen, this is not the place," I muttered under my breath. "We can talk about this later."

Lily blinked up at us. "I made it..." Her voice trailed off in the last few words, and she fidgeted with the bow on her dress.

"What's that, dear?" Gen asked.

"I made it for Felicity," Lily said. She looked at the floor.

I put my hand on her shoulder. "You did a great job, Lily. It's a beautiful picture, and you did so well speaking up in front of everyone."

Gen was fuming. She turned to me. "I suppose this was your idea, Cooper?"

I ignored Gen.

"Lily, I'll see you later, okay? I'll pick you up from school this afternoon." She nodded. I bent down to give her a hug. "I'm so proud of you, kiddo."

I turned to Felicity. "Will you stay here with Lily while I talk to Gen for a couple minutes?"

"Sure," Felicity said. She gathered her long skirt and kneeled to be at Lily's eye level.

Gen opened her mouth to say something, but I surreptitiously grabbed her elbow to steer her away before she could.

I wouldn't allow her to make a scene in my daughter's classroom. Lily had gone through enough without her parents arguing in front of her teacher and friends.

"Bye, Lily," Gen called over her shoulder.

I glanced back to see Felicity hugging Lily. Silently, I led Gen out the door to the hallway. She yanked free of my hand and scowled at me.

"What the hell, Cooper? Keep your hands off me."

"Gladly," I said. "But I wasn't going to let you ruin Lily's day like that."

"I'm the girls' mother, Cooper. Not *her*!"

"But you've never acted like it, Gen. In fact, this is the first school event of Eva's or Lily's you've ever attended." I kept my voice low and calm. "Why should Lily make a picture for you? You're never around."

Gen rolled her eyes. "I won't be judged by you, Cooper. And I'm not fooled by"—she waved her hands through the air—"your little act. You're just playing house with that girl."

"It's up to the judge to decide."

"Yes, it is," she hissed. "And I'm going to make sure I get the money."

My eyes widened as her words hung in the air.

When she realized what she'd said, she quickly

corrected her slip of the tongue. "I mean, the *girls*! I'm going to get custody of the girls."

I chuckled to myself and took a step closer so I could speak under my breath. "You know, my offer still stands. I can just give you a lump sum. We both know the money is all you want."

She sniffed. "That's ridiculous. I'm their mother, and they deserve to be with me."

I shook my head. This wasn't the first time she'd refused my offer to pay her off. She wanted ongoing income, and she wouldn't drop the charade.

The classroom door opened, and some of the other parents began to walk out, hurrying toward the parking lot so they could get to work.

Gen leveled me with one final glare. "See you in court."

She stalked off, and my shoulders slumped.

Gen had played dirty as long as I'd known her. It was a shame her pride had to get in the way now when she could just take the money and be done with it.

I looked up as Felicity walked out of the classroom and stood beside me with a concerned look on her face.

"Is everything okay?" she asked.

"It is now that Gen left." I smiled. "Are you okay?"

Her face brightened. "I'm amazing." She lifted the collage Lily made for her. "I get to keep this."

I wrapped my arm around her shoulders and pulled her in close as we looked at the picture together.

"Thank you for being here for Lily."

She looked up at me. "Of course. I wouldn't have missed it. I'm sorry if I caused trouble with you and Gen."

"That trouble has been here for a long time. You had nothing to do with it." I smiled. "It meant a lot to Lily that you came."

She looked at the picture again. "You know, I never thought of myself as overly maternal. But now, with Eva and Lily, I'm starting to think..." Her voice trailed off.

She blinked at me, and her eyes grew watery.

"Are you okay, Felicity?"

She nodded, looking down. "I'm fine. I... I'm being silly, I guess. I should get to work," she said hastily, digging in her purse for something. "It's time to open the shop. That *LA Now* writer is supposed to show up later."

I took her hand in mine. "Good luck today. See you at home this evening?"

She smiled and gave my hand a squeeze. "Absolutely."

I watched as she walked down the hallway, that goofy grin back on my face again. As I headed toward Eva's classroom, I couldn't help but notice the hope welling up inside me.

Maybe Felicity would find a reason to make our relationship real.

I froze in the middle of the hall. Realization dawned on me.

That was exactly what *I* wanted. To make things with Felicity real.

I didn't just want sex. I wanted to be with her.

The thought felt good. No, more than that—it felt *right*. Like the way things were supposed to be.

But there was another part of me that rebelled against that feeling.

How could I go with what felt good? How could I trust my instincts?

Once upon a time, in the early days with Gen, *that* had felt right, too.

I shook my head and began to walk toward Eva's class.

No, I couldn't follow my instincts. I had to trust my brain.

Logic. That was what always worked out for me in the end.

My gut instinct had never let me down in business. I invested in companies I had a good feeling about. And my success proved it was a good strategy.

But love was a different story.

When it came to romance, I couldn't trust my heart.

That had been my mistake with Gen. I'd ignored the red flags popping up in my head. I'd followed my heart like a damn fool.

As perfect as it felt to be with Felicity, I couldn't make that mistake again.

I had to pull back before everyone got hurt.

19

FELICITY

"Oh, my goodness! This place is just darling!"

Dana Berceli, the fashion writer, walked into Moonstone Boutique at eleven o'clock on the dot.

I'd spent the previous few days working around the clock—arranging the store, increasing the prices and implementing Cooper's strategies. Things were really starting to come together for the boutique.

Now I just needed more customers.

Judging from Dana's response, at least the store looked good.

She grabbed a pair of wide-leg linen shorts off the rack and shrieked. "These are gorgeous! The details, the stitching!" She looked at me. "Girl, you're a hidden gem!"

I beamed. "Thank you. That's my new summer line. Fresh off the sewing machine. Sleeveless shirts, shorts, and dresses," I said, pointing at the various racks as Dana walked through the space.

"Mind if I take some pictures?" She produced a fancy camera from her bag.

"Not at all. Go right ahead."

I suppressed a squeal of excitement. When Dana called me the other day to set up this appointment, she hadn't said she would interview me. She'd said she wanted to see the store. But now that she was taking pictures, an interview seemed likely.

"And you make everything right here in the store?" she asked, moving toward my studio space beyond the sales racks.

"Yep, this is where the magic happens." I blushed, feeling like a nerd. But Dana didn't seem to think the same. She gushed over the layout of the space.

I was glad I'd recently added some potted plants to several corners of the store. The lush greenery really made the store come alive. The ample natural light gave it a vibrant feeling, especially when paired with the lavender and dusty pink color scheme. The boutique had never looked better.

"Felicity, I'm loving everything I see here," she said, looking through my collection of bohemian dresses. "You've got quite the unique style. California boho meets sustainable classics."

"Yes," I nodded, thrilled she'd picked up on my branding. "That's exactly what I'm going for."

"Now." She clapped her hands together. "Show me your adorable children's line."

I gulped. This was the section I was most uncertain about.

I'd just started to dip my toes into kids' wear, but I'd been able to sew a few pieces in the past week. Despite my relative inexperience in this area, I was proud of what I'd created. I led her to the small section off to the side.

She shrieked again. "Oh, have mercy! These are just to die for!"

She picked up a green and yellow playsuit, inspired by Eva's bold color combinations. Then she fawned over a rainbow tulle dress I'd designed with Lily in mind.

"How precious! I love them all!"

"Thank you."

"Felicity, your store is just precious. But children's clothing is where you really shine." She removed a handheld recorder from her bag. "As you know, I'm a writer at *LA Now Magazine*. I'd love to interview you about your children's section. What do you say?"

I swallowed. Oh, God. This was really happening.

It was exactly what I wanted, but I was also nervous. I put on a confident front and nodded.

"Of course, Dana. That would be wonderful."

Dana smiled and started recording with her device.

"So, Felicity, how did you get your start in fashion design?"

I took a deep breath.

"My mom taught me. She had a hobby of designing clothes since I was a little girl. She never went to school for it. But she loved to work on her sewing machine, and she always made dresses and outfits for me growing up. When I got a little older, she taught me to sew, and soon I was designing for both of us... and all my friends."

Dana smiled and nodded, encouraging me to continue.

"I went to UCLA for fashion design. And it was always my dream to have a store where I sold my own creations. Three years ago, I opened Moonstone Boutique. I named it in honor of my mother, who loved moonstones and those flower-print dresses the hippie girls wore. She always said if she had been born earlier, she would have run off to San Francisco with flowers in her hair."

Dana laughed. "And how did you get interested in children's clothing?"

I tucked my hair behind my ear.

"That's a recent development. I was inspired by the two young daughters of... someone I've been spending time with lately."

Dana grinned. "How cute! There's nothing like falling in love to set us on a new path."

I nodded, remembering that I was supposed to be Cooper's loving fiancée.

"How would you describe your children's line?"

"Well, I tried to capture the magic and wonder of childhood for Moonstone Girls. I'm focusing on girls' fashion for now, though I plan to expand to boys' clothing in the future. I wanted to give girls some fun, colorful pieces. And hopefully take away some of the frustration in getting dressed in the morning."

Dana looked at the racks. "I see you have quite a variety of girls' fashions. Not just pink dresses."

"Right. I do have some frilly pink dresses to choose from. I also wanted to have some active fashions for girls. Who says being a girl is restricted to looking pretty in a pink dress? Lots of girls like to climb trees or build forts, and I wanted to give them options as well. Just like adults, children are three-dimensional. They have individual personalities, and lots of interests. I want to offer them clothing that suits all of their needs."

That came out better than I'd hoped. I was on a roll.

"Perfect. And what does the future look like for Moonstone Girls?"

"In addition to the off-the-rack fashions I sell in the store, I'll also offer custom-made fashions for girls twelve and under. They will be one-of-a-kind pieces created just for the special girl in your life."

I blinked, surprised at my own words.

"How fabulous!" Dana exclaimed. "I'm sure there are lots of parents in the city who would love to get their hands on one of your bespoke creations."

I smiled, pushing my panic down. Did I really just say I was offering custom-made fashion for children?

Cooper had suggested the idea to me the other day, but I'd never decided to offer bespoke fashion for kids. Until now, apparently.

It had been a major commitment just to design the girls' clothes I was selling on the rack. Now I'd have an entirely new addition to my business.

Dana grinned and turned off her recorder. "That's perfect, Felicity. This will give me enough to write a short piece for the magazine. Now I *must* buy that cute little jumper for my Amelia. It looks like just her size."

"Of course." I beamed as I removed the jumper from the rack and carried it to the sales counter. My first, and likely only, sale of the day.

She handed me her credit card and looked around the empty store once more. There hadn't been a single customer the entire half hour she'd been here. "I guess this is a slow shopping day."

"Yeah, very slow."

"Well, not to worry. You'll have hordes of LA parents looking for upscale children's clothing beating down your door once this goes to press."

I laughed. "I'll be ready for them."

I handed her the bag with her purchase. Dana shook my hand and gave me a warm smile. "Thanks again, Felicity. I appreciate your time."

"Thank you, Dana. It was so nice to talk to you."

"Let's talk again soon!" She walked to the front door and gave me a wave before she left.

I walked toward the entrance and looked out on the street. Shoppers streamed in and out of the stores surrounding Moonstone. Apparently it wasn't a slow day for them. Just me.

The reality of what I just said in the interview sank in. I began to pace through the center aisle of the store.

Had I gotten in over my head? Was I really prepared to offer custom-made clothing for children?

For so long, I'd wanted Moonstone to be a thriving business. Now that I had this opportunity laid before me, I was a nervous wreck.

And what would Cooper say when he read the article? Would he think I was just using him to further my business?

"Babe, are you doing some new exercise routine you haven't told me about?"

I whipped around to see Lauren standing by the front door. I had been so caught up in my worry, I hadn't heard the door chime when she walked in.

"Lauren!" I exclaimed, rushing to her and wrapping her in a hug. "I'm so glad to see you."

"It's good to see you, too. But it's only been a couple days. Look, I brought lunch." She carried it to the sales counter and unpacked some takeout sandwiches from the sub shop down the street.

"Thanks."

She looked at me. "Hey, are you okay? Did you do that interview?"

"Yes, the writer just left. And I'm fine. I just bit off more than I can chew."

"What happened?"

"I told her I was offering custom-made fashions for little girls."

"That's awesome!" Lauren grinned. "I love the direction you're taking with the store now. That bad boy has been a good influence on you. I knew it all along."

I pulled my hair up into a bun and secured it with a pencil from the sales counter. "I'm happy about these changes. But I'm worried I won't be able to keep up with it all."

"Aren't you teaching Cooper's daughters how to sew?"

"Yes. They still have a lot to learn, but they've made excellent progress for their age."

"There you go. Put *them* to work making the clothes. Two more pairs of hands."

I laughed. "You've been here two minutes, and you're already trying to get me to break child labor laws."

She giggled. "Don't worry, Felicity. You'll figure it out. And you better do it soon, because you're going to be in high demand as soon as that article is published."

I clasped my hands together. "I know! It's so exciting. And nerve-racking. But exciting!"

"What I want to know is what's up with you and Mr. Bad Boy?" Lauren sat on the stool behind the cash register. She unwrapped her chicken salad sandwich and took a bite.

I felt my face grow warm. "It's going well."

"Just well?"

My fingers went to his engagement ring, and I smiled. "It's going great, Lauren. I really like him. He's sweet and caring. And you should see how adorable he is with his daughters. They have him wrapped around their fingers."

"Don't forget the most important part," Lauren said, swallowing a bite. "He's amazing in bed, right?"

"Yes. He *is* amazing in bed. Mind-blowing." I pulled a

chair up to the sales counter with a smile. "And I love living at his house. I really feel like I'm part of the family."

"So what's the problem?"

I started to unwrap my sub, my heart constricting a little. "It's all pretend."

"It doesn't sound that way to me," she said. "It sounds like he cares for you."

"I don't know. The sex is incredible, but he hasn't expressed any interest in a relationship."

"Is that what you want?"

I looked at her. "Yes. It is what I want. I really like him." It was the first time I'd admitted it to anyone, including myself.

Lauren shrugged and talked around her bite of food. "Why don't you tell him that?"

"Because… I don't think he feels the same way. He would have said something by now."

"What if you're wrong, though? Maybe he wants more than just sex, too."

I shook my head. "I don't know, Lauren. He hasn't dropped any hints that he wants anything serious. That was one of his rules in the beginning—no catching feelings."

"You broke the rule about sex, though," Lauren pointed out.

"This rule feels different." I swallowed a lump in my throat. "And if I tell him I'm into him and he rejects me, it would make things awkward." I shuddered at the thought. "At least this way, I get to enjoy the time I have with him."

"I don't know. I think you should be up front with him. He might surprise you."

I nodded and took a bite of my sandwich, but I wasn't convinced.

He had the upper hand in this situation—I was living in

his house, and we were in this fake engagement for his kids. If he wanted to make it real, he should be the one to say so first. Otherwise, if I confessed my feelings and he didn't reciprocate, I'd lose everything.

There'd be no chance at being with Cooper. I wouldn't even get to enjoy our wild nights in his bed anymore.

It wasn't a good idea to make any drastic moves yet.

We ate our lunch, and the conversation shifted to Lauren's latest conflict with her boss. I did my best to push aside my disappointment over what I was sure was Cooper's lack of interest, but it was nagging at me.

After Lauren left, I took an hour to sketch some new designs for my children's line. It helped to channel some of my nervous energy into the sketches. I always felt better once I had a good plan.

As I drew new designs for my girls' collection, I found new confidence that I would be able to handle the changes coming to Moonstone Boutique.

Next, I went to my laptop and began to order some materials. I would need some new fabrics in bright colors for children.

The chime on the door rang and I looked up to see my father walk in.

I smiled, delighted that he had stopped by to visit me again.

"Dad!" I rose to my feet.

"Hi, Felicity."

"Is everything okay?"

"Yeah, everything's fine. I spoke to Cooper on the phone this morning, and he mentioned you were selling kids' clothes now. Thought I'd come by and see it."

I led him over to the kids' section. "Here it is." I grinned, on cloud nine that my father was showing interest in my work. "I never thought I would be designing clothes for little girls, but it's been really fun. Cooper came up with the idea."

Dad rubbed his jaw sheepishly. "These look nice, Felicity."

"Thanks. And guess what, Dad? A fashion writer from *LA Now* just did an interview with me this morning! She's going to run an article about the boutique."

He lifted his eyebrows. "Really? That's great news."

"Yeah. It's a lot of change in a short period of time. But hopefully they're all good changes."

My chest tightened to see the frown forming on his face.

"What the hell is that?" he asked, pointing straight at Cooper's engagement ring.

I looked down at the rock on my finger, and my mouth went dry.

"Dad, I can explain," I stammered.

"Felicity, it was bad enough that you went behind my back to ask for help from one of my business associates. Now you're engaged to the guy?"

"Dad—"

He spun on his heels and began to pace angrily across the floor. "This is outrageous. I thought I raised you better than this, Felicity. He's way too old for you. And he has two kids, for God's sake! Just when I thought you were finally being responsible and mature, you go and pull a stunt like this. What's the matter with you?"

His words stung me to the core. I blinked at him, paralyzed for a moment, then finally found my voice.

"We're not really engaged, Dad. It's all fake."

"What do you mean, fake?"

"We're pretending to be engaged so he can keep custody of his daughters."

He shook his head, trying to make sense of the new information. Then he turned to me with disgust.

"So you're lying?"

"Well, yes. But for a good cause."

"I'm shocked at you, Felicity. This is dishonest."

"I know, but the judge handling the custody case is extremely difficult. He almost never grants custody to a single father in the cases he presides over. Cooper's custody lawyer told him he'd be more likely to win the case if he wasn't a bachelor."

He paused. "So that time I caught you at his house... have you been living with him all this time?"

I nodded. "Yes. For about a month."

My shoulders slumped. I hated disappointing my father. Just five minutes ago, he had actually looked proud of me. It was the first time in years.

He crossed his arms over his chest. "This is appalling, Felicity. And you know it."

"Dad, you've met Gen, haven't you?"

"Of course I have. Cooper and I go way back."

"Did you ever see her act like a loving mother to her daughters?"

Dad thought for a moment. "No, I haven't. I know how much those girls mean to Cooper. But Gen..." He shook his head. "She's a piece of work."

"Yeah, from what I've seen, she wants very little to do with the girls. She's just after money."

Dad snorted. "That doesn't surprise me."

"And those little girls deserve to be with someone who treasures them. They deserve to be with Cooper."

"Yeah. They do."

"So don't you think Cooper deserves all the help he can get?"

Dad heaved a big sigh. "I suppose so. But I hate the idea of you getting mixed up in this... ruse." He said the word with disdain.

"I know you don't approve. But..." I took a deep breath. "Will you keep this secret? If this gets out, Cooper will lose custody for sure."

He heaved a sigh. "Yeah, I'll keep my mouth shut about it."

I exhaled in relief.

"But this has to end soon, Felicity."

"Yeah, I know. And it will. After the custody trial in a few weeks."

I swallowed the lump in my throat. I hated to think of the ticking clock over my head. Soon, I would no longer be a part of Cooper's and the girls' lives.

~

"Daddy, can we watch a movie tonight?"

Eva brought her plate to the sink and looked up at her father. "Lily and I can go brush our teeth and change into our pajamas. Right, Lily?"

Lily nodded. "Yeah. And we'll go straight to bed as soon as the movie's over."

Cooper looked at his watch. "Sure, why not? It's still early. But it'll have to be a short movie."

"Yay!" The girls cheered and ran out of the room.

"Be right back!" Eva shouted from the staircase.

Cooper and I exchanged a smile. He rinsed the plates off and began to put them in the dishwasher. "So the interview with Dana went well today?"

I told him a little about it earlier, but this was the first time we'd been alone tonight.

"Very well. Except for the part where I said I designed custom-made fashion for children. Talk about jumping in head-first."

He grinned. "I think that was a wise business decision. I bet you won't regret it."

I cleared the table and brought the remaining dishes to the sink. "Let's hope not." I leaned against the counter and took a deep breath. "After Dana left, Lauren brought lunch over."

Cooper smiled. "That was nice of her."

"Yeah. And then I had one last visitor this afternoon."

"Oh, yeah? Who?"

"My dad. He said he wanted to check out the children's clothes."

Cooper looked at me with surprise. "That's the second time he's visited you in three weeks. He's really coming around, isn't he?"

I rubbed the back of my neck. "Well, he *was*. But then he saw something today that really set him off."

Cooper turned the water off and glanced at me. "What?"

"My engagement ring."

Cooper tossed the dish towel into the sink. "Damn."

"Yeah, he flipped his lid for a minute. I had to come clean and tell him we've been faking an engagement for the custody trial."

Cooper sighed. "Well, it was just a matter of time until he figured that part out, anyway. What did he say?"

"He scolded me for being dishonest." I shrugged. "It'll just go down as another time I disappointed Marshall Hayes."

"I'm sorry your dad is so hard on you."

"Thanks. I did manage to get him to see why it was important. I explained about the judge siding with mothers

The Fiancé Hoax

in custody trials. Dad was able to admit that you should have the girls and not Gen."

"So he agreed to be discreet about the fake engagement?"

"Yes. And I believe him. He doesn't want to ruin things for you."

"Okay, well, that part's good, at least." He ran a hand through his hair.

"I told him the engagement thing was temporary. I said I'd be moving out of your house after the trial."

My chest tightened as I said the words. I glanced at Cooper, trying to read his reaction.

Was that as painful for him to hear as it was for me to say?

But his face was neutral as he leaned against the counter. "Okay."

My mouth was suddenly dry. "I don't think he suspects we're messing around or anything."

Cooper nodded. "Good. But I don't like sneaking around behind his back."

"I don't, either."

I faced him, my breath catching in my lungs.

Was he going to say what I wanted to hear—that he wanted more than just sex? That he wanted to make the relationship real?

No, he wasn't.

Instead of saying the words I desperately craved, he turned to close the dishwasher and start its cycle.

I looked away quickly and began to wipe down the counter. "Did your day go okay?" I asked, trying to hide the disappointment in my voice.

"Yeah, Eva's field trip went well. I was relieved to see that she could use her indoor voice in the museum."

I laughed. "She's making progress."

"She certainly is. After I picked up the girls from school, I came back to get some work done in the home office while Inga was here."

"That's good."

"Hey. Come here." He took me in his arms and pulled me close.

I looked in his intense blue eyes, searching for any sign that he wanted more. That he was interested in a serious relationship with me.

He kissed me on the mouth, then pulled away to look at me. "I'm proud of you for doing that interview. I think this will change things for your store."

I smiled. "Thanks, Cooper. I really hope so."

His eyes moved over my lips, and his deep voice made my nipples hard. "Want to celebrate later in my room?"

I closed my eyes, already feeling a flood between my legs. "Absolutely," I whispered.

"Okay! We're done getting ready!" Eva shouted as they ran down the stairs.

Cooper took a step back and turned away quickly. I shook off the daze that had fallen over me in Cooper's arms. He always had that effect on me.

The girls appeared in the kitchen wearing their pajamas.

"We're in charge of getting the snacks," Eva announced. "You two go pick out a movie, okay?"

"Since when do you want *me* to pick out the movie?" Cooper asked.

"Since today," Eva said confidently. She shooed us away. "Go on."

Cooper and I followed her orders and went to the living room. As I settled on the couch, he flipped through a kids' streaming channel. The microwave roared from the kitchen.

Soon, the girls joined us in the living room. Lily carried two plastic kids' cups and Eva carried a large bowl of popcorn. She set it on the coffee table. "I have to get one more thing!"

Eva ran off to the kitchen, then returned a moment later carrying a bottle of wine and a corkscrew. She concentrated as she walked slowly, careful not to drop it.

Cooper laughed. "You two thought of everything, didn't you? But what are you girls going to drink?"

Eva stretched her arms overhead and faked an exaggerated yawn. She elbowed Lily, who followed suit.

"Boy, I sure am sleepy," Eva said in a loud voice that didn't at all sound sleepy.

"Yeah. Me too," Lily agreed.

"We're too tired to watch the movie, Daddy. I think we'll go upstairs and go to bed now."

Cooper raised an eyebrow. "It's not even your bedtime yet."

"Yeah, but it's been a long day with the field trip and Lily's art show and everything."

Cooper smiled. "Okay. Well, do you need me to tuck you in?"

Eva waved him off. "No, we're fine. You two stay here and enjoy your date."

She gave us a big grin before she led Lily out of the room.

Once we were alone again, Cooper and I looked at each other and burst out laughing.

"That was adorable," I said. "They planned that all along."

"I especially enjoyed the fake yawning." Cooper sat next to me on the couch, and I snuggled against him.

"They never fail to amaze me," I said. "They really are smart."

"Sometimes too much for their own good."

"Will they be okay up there alone?"

"Yeah, they'll probably play in their room. I'll go upstairs in a while and tuck them in."

He grabbed the remote control and gave me a lopsided smile. "Do you still want to watch *Princess Pia Saves the Day*?"

I chuckled. "No. But a movie does sound nice."

He reached for the corkscrew and opened the bottle of wine. "I'll go get some wine glasses. Unless you want to drink your merlot out of a sippy cup?"

"I'd love a wine glass," I laughed. "I'll look for a movie."

He handed me the remote and went to the kitchen, then returned with two glasses.

Soon, we were snuggled together on the couch, sipping wine and watching a comedy. He had his arm around me, and I rested my head against his shoulder. We fit perfectly like this.

There was just one problem.

Cooper didn't seem to mind that I would be leaving soon.

20

COOPER

"Cooper!"

I had just parked my car in the garage at my company office the next morning. The sound of my own name made me stop in my tracks.

I turned to see Marsh glaring at me from where he leaned against his Porsche. He'd parked diagonally, taking up three spaces.

"What the hell did you get my daughter mixed up in?"

"Good morning to you, too, Marsh. Interesting parking job."

"Cut the shit, Cooper. I can't believe you're using my daughter like this."

We were standing near the sidewalk at the front entrance of the parking garage. Two of my employees walked past, sneaking peeks at the scene Marsh was creating.

"Why don't you come inside and we can talk about this in my office?"

"No. Right here." He pointed at the asphalt, his face twisted in anger.

"Okay, fine. I laid it all out for Felicity as part of our business agreement. She knew what she was getting into. She's an adult and she can make her own decisions."

"But you're asking her to lie in court, Cooper."

"No, I'm most certainly not. She hasn't been summoned to speak in the trial. And my custody lawyer said he doesn't expect her to be. A simple declaration that I am engaged to be married, and her showing up in court, will be enough to get the message across."

He crossed his arms over his chest. That placated Marsh slightly, but he was still too upset to speak.

"I'd never ask her to lie in court, Marsh."

"No. You just asked her to tell your lies everywhere else."

"I didn't want to do it this way, Marsh. But you know how Gen is. And you know how some of these judges can be. They don't always see reason."

Marsh scoffed. "You're talking to a seasoned attorney. I know exactly how judges can be."

"Then try to understand. I can't lose my little girls." I raked a hand through my hair, feeling uneasy at the very thought. "Gen is not a good mother to them. And who knows where she would drag them to. She might run off to Europe with a new boyfriend for all I know. She might bring shady guys around. I just can't let that happen, Marsh. Everything I've done has been for Eva and Lily. I can't lose them."

Marsh let his arms fall at his sides.

"Fine. I won't say anything if she doesn't have to testify. But if she's at risk of committing perjury, I'll put a stop to this whole thing."

"I can agree to that."

Marsh squared his shoulders and opened his car door. "I've got to get to work."

"See you, Marsh."

He ignored me, slammed the door behind him, and sped off out of the garage.

Shit. Now my closest friend was pissed at me.

I stepped out of the garage and into the sun to head toward the office once more. But as I turned my head before crossing the street, a movement in the corner of the garage caught my eye.

Trying to be subtle, I shifted my eyes to get a glimpse of a man wearing a black jacket and baseball cap. He walked stealthily around a parked car.

Why did he look familiar?

I didn't break my stride, but something was off about this. And I was pretty sure I had seen him driving behind me on the way to work.

At the next block, there was a loading alley just before my building. At the last second, I made a quick detour. Ducking behind the corner where I would be out of sight, I waited for him to appear.

Seconds later, he passed in front of the alley. I emerged from my hiding place, startling him. I got right up in his face, and he took a step back until he was cornered against the wall.

"You want to tell me why the fuck you're following me?"

His eyes went big for a second, then he concealed his surprise. "I don't know what you're talking about, man. I'm not following anybody."

He had pasty skin and shifty, beady little eyes. A real slimeball. The guy couldn't be any more suspicious.

"Why were you driving behind me? And why were you hiding in the garage?"

He raised his hands. "I don't know you."

He started to walk off, but I took a step toward him and grabbed him by the collar.

"Stop fucking around. What are you after?" I demanded.

His face contorted in fear. "Let me go, man. Let me go!"

I tightened my grip on his shirt. "Not until you tell me."

"Okay, okay! Gen hired me."

"To do what?"

"To keep an eye on you. Now let me go, okay?"

He looked so pathetic and scared, I let go of his shirt. I didn't back up, though.

"What's she trying to get on me?"

But instead of answering me, he twisted away and ran off toward the parking garage.

Fucking hell.

I thought about chasing after him, but what was the point? He couldn't tell me anything that would be of use. With a sigh, I entered the building and headed straight for my office, fumbling with my phone as I walked.

My divorce attorney answered my call just as I closed my office door behind me.

"Nick, I've got a situation," I muttered. I told him about the sleazeball following me.

"Sounds like a private investigator," Nick said. "Just be vigilant. Don't do anything that would jeopardize the custody case."

"So keep doing what I'm doing."

"Felicity needs to be vigilant, too."

"Okay." I looked out the window behind my desk.

"It might be a good idea to hire a PI for our side, too, you know."

I clenched my jaw. "Is that necessary?"

"It couldn't hurt."

I sighed. "Fine. Got any contacts? I'm not exactly up to speed with the PI market these days."

Nick assured me he would take care of it, and we hung up. I shook my head, staring out the window. Gen was not making this easy.

~

"A real private eye? Like in the movies?"

Later that evening, after we had put the girls to bed, I sat at a table in Felicity's sewing studio. I told her about the unsavory character following me. And about the run-in with her father.

She took the news in stride. Or maybe she was too focused on her work to care that much.

"Yeah, it's nuts. I never would have thought Gen would stoop this low."

Felicity cut some green fabric from a bolt and began to position a pattern over it.

When she didn't say anything, I went on. "I mean, if she has the money to hire a private investigator, why does she need more from me?"

"I have no idea," Felicity mumbled.

"Anyway, we have to be perfect in public. There's no room for mistakes now that this guy will be watching us."

Felicity's brow furrowed as she cut out what looked to be the front piece of a kid's shirt. She began to pin it to another piece, holding several pins in between her teeth.

"Okay," she said between her clenched teeth.

Something about the way she hardly looked up from her work bothered me.

"One little slip-up could mean the end of my custody case."

Felicity didn't respond. She bent over her work so that I could no longer see her face. Maybe it was the stress of the whole situation, but I was starting to get irritated.

"Felicity, are you listening to me?"

She looked up. "Of course I'm listening." She looked back down and finished pinning the shirt.

"Because you seem a little distracted," I said with a sarcastic edge to my voice. "I'm telling you this is really important for the custody case. And you don't seem to be taking it very seriously."

She stared at me for a long moment, taken aback by the anger in my voice. "Cooper, I *am* taking it seriously. I'm just stressed out about all this work I have to do for the new children's line. But I can work and listen at the same time. I heard every word you said."

I looked away. "Okay. I just hope you understand the gravity of all this."

She took a step toward me and reached for my hand. "I completely understand how serious it is."

"Felicity, if this guy finds out that we faked our engagement, it's all over. I'll lose the custody case." I drove a hand through my hair. "I'll lose the girls."

"Don't worry," she assured me, looking me in the eyes. "He won't find anything. I'll make sure my Is are dotted and my Ts are crossed."

The tension in my shoulders loosened a bit. "Okay. Thanks. That's all I want."

"Of course."

I nodded. "I'll let you get back to work."

She gave me a smile, then returned to the garment she was pinning. She was working around the clock now, and I hoped that she wasn't pushing herself too hard.

Downstairs in my study, I paced back and forth. My

nerves were on edge. Finally, I poured myself a whiskey and sat at my desk, staring into the amber liquid.

It was just the type of thing my dad would have done. When the going got tough, he withdrew and poured himself a drink.

I never wanted to turn into my father. He'd always been quick to anger, then he'd go off alone and drink.

But dammit, what other option did I have? I couldn't face the prospect of losing any of them. Not my daughters, and not Felicity.

All I could do was focus on the burn of the whiskey going down.

The next evening, I got home from work to Eva and Lily greeting me at the garage entrance.

"You have to be quiet, Daddy," Eva said.

"Felicity's sleeping on the couch," Lily said.

"We should let her sleep," Eva said. "She came home *sooo* tired from work."

"Like a zombie!"

"Okay," I said, setting my briefcase on the kitchen island.

Inga and Monica appeared in the kitchen, having finished their duties. After making sure I didn't need anything else, they both left for the day.

I walked into the living room to find Felicity asleep on the sofa, her brown hair splayed out around her. A blanket had been draped over her body.

She looked so beautiful lying there, and something turned over in my chest.

But I didn't have time to pay much attention to it, so I

returned to the kitchen where the girls were coloring at the table.

"We put the blanket on her," Lily said.

"That was nice of you, girls." I washed my hands at the sink.

I opened the refrigerator to pull out the chopped chicken and vegetables Monica had prepared. "Can you girls set the table? Everything but the plates for now."

"Okay," Lily said. She joined me at the kitchen sink, and Eva followed.

"We have to wash our hands first, Lily," Eva instructed.

As the girls stood on the stool in front of the sink to wash their hands, I started to sauté some onions and garlic. After a couple of minutes, I added marinated chicken strips.

"What did Felicity say when she got home?"

"Nothing. She just passed out on the couch," Eva said. She pantomimed the scene, pretending to collapse onto the sofa.

I didn't like the sound of that. I'd already been worried about her pushing herself too hard.

I added red bell pepper and zucchini to the skillet as the girls made several trips from the cupboards to the table. Then they carried the bowls of grated cheese, sour cream, and chopped lettuce and tomatoes to the table. As the stir fry sizzled, I heated up another skillet to warm some tortillas.

"That smells delicious."

I looked over my shoulder to see Felicity standing in the doorway, yawning.

"You're awake!" Eva exclaimed. She ran over to grab Felicity's hand and guide her to her usual spot at the kitchen table.

"We're having tacos," Lily announced. "It's our favorite."

"I'm sorry I fell asleep like that," Felicity said.

I began to serve up the stir fry onto the plates, accompanied by warm tortillas. The girls carried the plates of food carefully, one by one, to the table.

"You've really been burning the candle at both ends," I said.

"You can say that again," Felicity said as the girls sat at the table. "Launching this kids' collection before that magazine article is published is a major endeavor."

I brought my plate over to the table and sat down. "You shouldn't overwork yourself, Felicity."

She shrugged. "I know, but it has to get done."

"Maybe you should hire help."

She shook her head as she assembled her tacos. "I don't think I'm ready for that step."

"Okay," I said, deciding to drop it for the time being.

The girls were eager to talk about their upcoming summer vacation. They attended year-round school, and their summer break was a month long. This year, they were going to day camp.

I smiled at my daughters as they discussed their excitement over riding horses and swimming at camp.

But I couldn't help being worried—about Felicity, the custody battle, and anything Gen's PI might unearth.

21

FELICITY

Over the next few weeks, sales started to pick up at the boutique.

The advertisements I'd bought began to gradually drive traffic into the store. And my online sales steadily increased.

For the first time ever, I was busy with customers. Plus, I had new responsibilities to juggle. I used every spare moment to prepare my children's line before the magazine interview came out.

I was expanding the girls' collection as well as preparing for the bespoke offering. New fabrics and supplies had to be ordered. A shipment of shelves and display racks would arrive soon. Then I'd have to rearrange the entire store to make room for the expanding children's section.

I was exhausted.

I worked long hours at the store, and I worked even more in the studio at Cooper's house. I was barely eating, and when I did, I felt sick to my stomach.

The stress was mounting with each day. I was a nervous wreck.

The Fiancé Hoax

Despite the increase in sales, the future of Moonstone Boutique was riding on this children's line. I'd invested so much into the kids' section. If I couldn't handle the demand—or worse, if there was no demand—I might have to close the shop.

So I had to get this right. And that meant working around the clock.

I missed spending entire evenings and weekends with Cooper and the girls, but I couldn't spare the energy to worry about it. I could only hope they would understand. Still, being apart from them hurt.

At least I could still join them for dinner every night. And most nights, Cooper and I found comfort in each other's arms in his bed.

But I couldn't shake the feeling that something had shifted between us.

I kept telling myself it was because we were both busy. He was worried about the trial, and I had to renovate my store.

No matter what excuses I told myself, Cooper felt more and more distant with each day.

For a while, things had been great between us. I'd started to wonder if he wanted to have a real relationship with me. We'd gone out for drinks with Lauren a couple of times, and he'd taken me on a couples' date with his work friend and his wife.

And of course, our time together with Eva and Lily was fantastic. With the girls, it was easy to feel like we were a family.

We seemed to fit perfectly into each other's lives.

But lately, he felt so far away. Like he was counting the days until I was gone.

I longed to feel close to Cooper again.

But what could I do? I couldn't make him feel the way I did.

It was the middle of the afternoon—another busy day at Moonstone. I'd just finished designing a new dress in toddler sizes when the door chime sounded.

"Welcome to Moonstone Boutique," I said cheerfully, pushing away my worries.

I was a little surprised to see a man standing there. But I shrugged it off. Guys sometimes came in to buy something for their wives or girlfriends. Now that I was selling children's clothes, I would probably get even more dads shopping for their daughters.

I wrapped my tape measure around the back of my neck and approached him. "Is there anything in particular you're looking for today?"

He turned toward a rack of dresses and began to sort through them. "No, just seeing what you have."

I smiled. "Okay. Let me know if you need any help."

I moved to the sales counter where I had left my laptop and began to scroll through my bookkeeping for the week. Cooper's lessons about staying on top of my financial records had sunk in. He was right—I hadn't been paying enough attention to the flow of money.

Suddenly, I noticed the guy was looking at me. Something about him gave me the creeps.

"You been in this location for long?" he asked.

"Three years," I said.

He looked at the racks I had pushed to the side to make room for the children's section. "Are you moving things around in here?"

I walked around the sales counter and approached the kids' section. "Yeah, I'm expanding the girls' section. I had to make room for it."

"What made you decide to do that all of a sudden?"

I looked at him. Why was he asking all these questions?

I swallowed, suddenly wishing I wasn't alone in the store. "Just turning over a new leaf." I put my hand on the rack and fidgeted with a hanger.

Suddenly, it all clicked.

This guy was the private eye.

And my engagement ring was *off* my finger. I had taken it off because the diamond had a tendency to snag the fine linen and silk I was working with today.

His eyes darted to my left hand. I quickly hid my hands behind my back, where I clasped them together.

The guy noticed my movement and gave me a smile. He had seen everything.

"I didn't catch your name," I said, keeping the panic out of my voice. I took a step toward the door.

He looked at me. "The name's Drew."

"Lovely to meet you, Drew. I'm afraid that I'm closing early today. Sorry about that." I crossed the space toward the front door. I opened it, waiting expectantly for him to leave.

He grinned at me as he breezed past. "No worries. I'll stop by another time."

I slammed the door behind him and locked it.

Shit. Shit. Shit.

I raced to the cash register, my heart pounding. I retrieved the engagement ring from the drawer and returned it to my ring finger. *Cooper's going to kill me.*

I grabbed my phone and dialed his number as my pulse raced.

"Hey, what's up?" he answered.

"Cooper, I have to tell you something. Something really bad." I winced.

He drew in a sharp breath. "Okay. Just tell me."

"I'm pretty sure that private investigator was just here at Moonstone. It was some creepy guy I've never seen before, and he started asking me a bunch of questions."

"Did he have beady eyes that were too close together?"

"Yes, exactly."

"Fuck. That's him." He paused for a second. "Well, I guess it was bound to happen. It's not that terrible if he just stopped by to check out your store."

I swallowed. "No, the terrible part is that I wasn't wearing my engagement ring when he came by."

"What?"

"I just took it off for the afternoon because it snags the fabric I was working with today."

"Are you fucking kidding me right now?"

My stomach twisted. "I'm sorry, Cooper. I just needed to take it off for a few hours. I didn't know that guy was going to come to the store."

"Jesus, Felicity. This is exactly what I warned you about. We have to put up a perfect front in public now that this guy is following us."

"I know. I'm sorry."

There was a sinking feeling in my core. My dad yelled at me for wearing the ring. Now Cooper was angry with me for taking it off.

He scoffed. "I don't think you're taking this engagement seriously, Felicity."

"Please don't start with this again, Cooper. I promise I'm taking this seriously. You know how much I care about those girls." *And you,* I silently added. "Besides, it's not like he took a picture. It would just be his word against mine."

The last part I blurted out quickly, hoping it would help, but knowing it probably wouldn't.

"You don't know if he took a picture or not," Cooper said.

"I'm sure he has some hidden camera. He may be a bargain basement private investigator, but I'm sure he at least has some cheapo camera you didn't see."

Tears pressed against my eyes. I didn't want to mess up Cooper's custody case. And I hated to disappoint him like this.

"What can I do to fix this, Cooper?"

He was quiet on the other end for a while. "I don't know," he said flatly. "I don't know if it *can* be fixed."

I fought back the tears. I couldn't believe this was happening. "I'm sorry, Cooper."

"I know. Listen, I've got to go. I'll see you tonight."

Before I could say goodbye, he hung up.

Defeated, I set my phone on the sales counter and returned to my chair at my sewing machine.

I didn't know what had changed between Cooper and me, but something had. It wasn't just Drew seeing my empty ring finger. It wasn't only because I was working long hours. It was more than that.

Cooper had withdrawn, turned colder. And I wanted more than anything to return to the closeness we shared before.

But instead of getting closer, I'd driven a bigger wedge between us. I had screwed everything up.

Not only was he furious with me, but I might have cost him the custody case. If this Drew guy took a picture of my hand without an engagement ring, it might be enough to sway the judge. Especially since Judge Graves was already looking for a reason to grant custody to Gen.

If Gen's attorney could make a convincing argument that we faked the engagement... Well, Cooper would be right. Everything would be lost.

All because of me.

I buried my face in my hands and let a sob rack my body. The front door was locked, and no one looking in through the front windows could see me where I was sitting.

I gave up my strong front for the moment. Finally, I let the tears flow.

Twenty minutes later, I'd cried all the tears that had built up inside me for two weeks. I went to the bathroom to clean up the eye makeup that had run down my cheeks. I looked in the mirror.

"It's going to be okay," I said to my reflection. "Everything's not lost yet."

But I wasn't sure I believed my own words.

In the front of the store, I unlocked the door in case a customer appeared. Then I returned to my design space.

I had planned to design and sew two more pieces today. Taking a clearing breath, I sat at my sketch book, my pencil poised against the white page.

I stared at that white page for a long time. Nothing was coming to me.

Was it really possible for Cooper to lose his custody case because I wasn't wearing my ring?

Yes, it was possible. It might be the final piece of evidence in the case Gen's attorney was mounting against Cooper.

My stomach twisted in knots. Cooper couldn't lose custody of his daughters. That was unthinkable.

Eva and Lily mattered most in all of this. And Cooper losing custody would hurt them the worst.

They had all but given up on having a relationship with their mother. Even at ages six and eight, they knew she wasn't a good influence in their lives.

My heart went out to them. I had been fortunate to have a loving mother who was always there for me. I couldn't imagine if Mom had been cold, heartless, and aloof. If she had never made an effort to be part of my life. Never shown any interest in my achievements or who I was as a kid.

Well, I *could* sort of imagine it. Because my father had been like that.

But my mother had made up for the cold way my dad treated me. And Eva and Lily had Cooper, who I was sure was the best dad in the world.

They couldn't be torn from the only loving parent they had. It would be a disaster for the girls to move in with Gen.

And it would destroy Cooper to lose his daughters. They were the light of his life. I shuddered to think who he would become if they were ripped from his care.

Gen would disappear with them. He would rarely be able to see the girls, if at all.

It would crush his spirit.

And I would never be able to forgive myself.

Surely there was something we could do.

Looking down at the white page, I realized my hand was shaking. I closed my sketchbook and put my drawing supplies away. I wasn't going to get any more work done today.

I locked the doors and left through the front entrance. I longed to call Lauren and spill my guts to her. But she was visiting her parents in Seattle for a week. She'd just arrived there today. I didn't want to intrude on her family time.

I walked on the sidewalk slowly, the late afternoon sun beating down. My favorite sandwich shop was two blocks away. A dry turkey sandwich was about the only food I had an appetite for at the moment. I decided to pick up sandwiches for Cooper and the girls, then head home. It might be nice to have an easy meal so we could focus on damage control the rest of the evening.

Cooper and I could brainstorm ideas to deal with Drew noticing the ring off my finger. Surely, we could come up with something to avert disaster.

There had to be some hope left.

On the next block, I passed a French restaurant. Normally, I loved the food from that place. But today, the rich, buttery aroma made me feel sick.

Really sick. My stomach churned, and a wave of nausea rose through my body.

I gripped my stomach and hurried to a trash can on the street. Lifting the lid, I bent over and vomited.

What the hell is happening to me?

I stood up, feeling woozy. Humiliated and hoping no one had seen me, I replaced the lid on the trash can, which was thankfully lined with a sturdy trash bag. I hurried down the street, wanting to escape.

When I reached the sandwich shop, I went straight to the restroom to rinse my mouth out. My heart was still pounding, and I felt light-headed.

I bought a soda and sat at a table to sip it slowly. The carbonation helped to settle my stomach a bit. But I could hardly think straight. My mind and emotions were caught in a whirlwind.

Was that stomach bug coming back? The one that had made me and the girls so sick?

But it wasn't just today that I had felt weird. For a few weeks, I had felt nauseous off and on. I had lost my appetite.

I kept thinking it was stress. After all, there had been so many big changes. Getting closer to Cooper and the girls, the magazine interview, changing almost everything in my store. And with the custody trial coming up in two weeks, it made sense that I had an upset stomach.

But is that enough to make me miss a period?

I gulped at the sudden awareness. I hadn't had a period in months. Life had gotten so busy that I hadn't given it a second thought.

But it had been a *really* long time. In fact, I couldn't remember having a period since moving into Cooper's house.

Shit.

The longer I sat in that sandwich shop, the stranger I began to feel.

I rushed out of the store and crossed the street. I could come back later and buy the sandwiches. Right now, I urgently needed to get to a pharmacy.

My hand shaking more than ever, I paid for a pack of pregnancy tests. I hurried back to my boutique, unlocked the door, and went to the bathroom.

As I peed on the stick, I scolded myself for being silly.

Of course I wasn't pregnant. I was on birth control. This was just a moment of panic.

I set the stick on the counter and set the timer on my phone for two minutes.

In just a couple minutes, this would all be over. Then I could go back to dealing with all the other emergencies in my life. I certainly didn't need a pregnancy on top of everything.

I looked at myself in the mirror, noting the dark circles under my eyes. I wasn't getting enough sleep.

Once I finished launching the expanded children's section, things would calm down. We'd find a way for Cooper to keep custody, and all our lives would go on as normal. The way they had been before.

Which meant I would leave Cooper's house.

"You're getting ahead of yourself," I muttered to my

reflection. "First things first. Make sure you are *not* knocked up."

The timer went off, startling me. I grabbed the test stick and held it in front of my face. Then I jumped back, dropping the stick to the floor.

A big fat plus sign.

My stomach rolled, and for a second I thought I was going to be sick again. But I breathed through it and calmed myself down. Tearing open the package of another test stick, I repeated the process.

And was met with another pink plus sign.

I didn't bother to take the third test. I knew the first two tests were right. There was no sense in trying to deny it any longer.

I was pregnant by Cooper Pierce.

In shock, I threw away the evidence, washed my hands, and left the bathroom. Wrapping my arms around my waist, I squinted in the bright light coming in through the window.

How did this happen? And what will I do?

I sat in my chair and stared at the empty store for a while. My eyes didn't really fix on anything, and I just sat there blinking.

Rising to my feet, I walked to the front door and stepped out on the street. Thankfully, I had enough sense to lock the door behind me.

I turned right this time instead of left, trudging slowly down the sidewalk. I was in a daze.

I'm pregnant.

How did it happen when I was on birth control the whole time?

Then I thought back to the stomach bug I'd had soon after moving into Cooper's house. The girls and I had gotten that virus immediately after my first time with Cooper. I had puked my guts out for three days. Maybe that was enough to make the contraception ineffective.

Why didn't I think of that before?

I shook my head, eyes on the sidewalk as I moved in a kind of stupor.

I'd always been on the fence about having kids. Like I told Cooper outside Lily's classroom, I'd never thought of myself as having much of a maternal streak.

But after spending time with Eva and Lily, I felt so many things I'd never experienced before.

I loved those little girls. I loved making them happy and seeing them smile. A protective streak rose inside me every time I thought of them. They were so sweet and innocent. I wanted to keep them safe.

Now that I had a life growing inside me, I recognized that protective streak again. I felt a new sense of hope, despite my panic about how I'd make it work.

I was going to be a mother. And I would love this baby forever.

I looked up to see I had walked several blocks. And on the next block stood a birth center.

I had driven past it a thousand times and barely noticed it. But today, the sage green sign out front looked warm and welcoming. I opened the front door and stepped inside to make a prenatal appointment.

The receptionist was friendly. She seemed to sense my anxiety, and her soothing manner calmed my nerves a little. I walked out holding an appointment card. A doctor would see me tomorrow, which was a relief.

Outside, the sun was low in the sky and cast long shadows on the sidewalk. But I wasn't ready to go home yet —if I could still call Cooper's house *home*.

I wasn't ready to face him. He was angry with me about the ring, and I understood why. But every time I disappointed him, it caused me pain.

What will he say when I tell him? Will this be one more disappointment for him?

He'd already told me he didn't want any more children. His two daughters were enough.

This was the worst possible timing with the custody trial two weeks away. How could I tell Cooper when he had so much to worry about already?

If only Lauren was around. I suddenly felt so alone, and I missed my mother more than ever.

I shook my head, trying to push all the uncertainty and fear out of my mind.

As I walked, I noticed it was starting to get dark. Suddenly, I realized I was late getting to Cooper's house.

We had planned to discuss the appearance of the PI. Now Cooper would probably think I was flaking out on him. Or worse, he would be worried about me. And I had left my phone back at Moonstone, so I couldn't let him know I'd be late.

I turned around and headed toward the store. It took me a while to walk back, and then I had to go inside and grab my purse and laptop. My phone was dead, so I couldn't text him. By the time I was in my car and driving toward his house, it was almost the girls' bedtime.

He would be worried, or angry, or both. But if I told him why I was so late, that would be one more thing for him to worry about. And not just a minor worry, either. This was a bombshell.

I would have to wait a few days to tell him this news. I just hoped he would be able to understand when I did.

22

COOPER

The girls were almost as worried about Felicity as I was.

As I got them ready for bed and read their bedtime story, they kept asking where she was and if she was coming back. All I could say was that she was busy with work and she would be home soon.

But after I closed their door and headed downstairs, my mind got carried away.

I texted her yet again, but there was no response.

Damn it. What kind of game was she playing?

She knew how tense I was with the custody trial and this sleazeball following us. And now, he had likely gotten photographic evidence that she wasn't wearing her engagement ring. No doubt Gen's attorney would use it to argue that the engagement was a big ploy to keep custody of my children.

I'd been upset with Felicity on the phone earlier. But I knew taking her ring off at work had been an honest mistake. It was a mistake that could cost us dearly, but she couldn't put her life on hold for me.

Once the initial shock had worn off, my anger had, too.

I was disappointed and worried out of my mind about the court case, but I wasn't planning to yell at her tonight. What was done was done. Now we just had to focus on damage control.

If only she would come home.

Where the hell was she? The past few weeks, she had arrived home a little later from her store than usual, but she rarely missed dinner with me and the girls. And if she did, she always called to let me know.

She'd never been home this late.

Why the hell wasn't she answering her phone?

I paced back and forth through the living room, glancing out the dark windows and hoping to see her headlights.

What if she had been in an accident? What if she was lying on the side of the road?

If she wasn't home in the next five minutes, I would start making calls. Police, hospitals, whatever it took. It wasn't like her to disappear without a word.

Despite my initial impression of her as flighty and a little reckless, I had come to know Felicity for the responsible, mature person she was. She'd never go MIA like this. Especially when she knew what we were facing with the custody trial.

Headlights turned into the front driveway, and I breathed a sigh of relief.

I opened the front door and went out to greet her as she emerged from her car.

"Are you okay? I was worried sick about you, Felicity." I took her laptop bag from her shoulder, and we walked inside the house together.

"I'm fine," she said sheepishly. "I'm sorry I didn't call or

The Fiancé Hoax

text. I didn't have my phone with me when I was out, and when I went back to the store to pick it up, it was dead."

I put her bag down on the foyer table, and she followed me into the living room.

"So you weren't at Moonstone? Where were you?"

She sat on the sofa and curled her legs underneath her. Her gaze rested on the floor. "I was out walking."

My relief at seeing her safe and sound instantly gave way to anger. I froze, standing in the middle of the living room.

"Walking?"

She nodded, avoiding my eyes. "Yeah. I went for a walk through the neighborhood around Moonstone."

I raked a hand through my hair, the frustration building in my chest. "After everything that's happened, after my ex-wife's private investigator got a picture of your hand without the engagement ring... You decided that would be a nice time for a stroll?"

She chewed on her bottom lip. "I just needed some time to collect my thoughts. I guess I wasn't thinking clearly. I'm sorry I'm so late."

I turned away for a moment, trying to calm myself.

Anger was mounting quickly. And jealousy.

I looked at Felicity, searching her face for something.

"Were you with a man, Felicity?"

She finally looked at me. "What? No. I wasn't with anyone. I was walking alone."

I narrowed my eyes at her, expecting to find some clue in her expression that would give her away.

Felicity looked nervous, her brow furrowed as she looked up at me. She opened her mouth to speak.

I held my hand up to stop her. "Save it. I don't believe you."

She frowned. "What do you mean, you don't *believe* me?"

I folded my arms across my chest. "I think you're lying." The words tumbled from my mouth, hot and angry. "Your body language gives away your dishonesty. Why else would you lie to me, unless you were messing around with some guy?"

"Cooper, you're being a jerk right now. Look, you got so upset with me when I told you about the ring... I needed some time to process all this."

"I got upset because you're not taking this seriously."

Her mouth tightened. "I *am* taking it seriously. And I don't appreciate being accused of lying, Cooper. Maybe you shouldn't fly off the handle at me for an honest mistake. Any seamstress would take off a ring if it was snagging the fabric."

"I'm done listening." I looked at her, consumed by jealousy. The thought of another man touching her made me sick to my stomach. "Do you remember our agreement? We agreed to not date anyone else for the length of the engagement."

She swallowed, her throat rolling. "Yes, of course I remember that. And I didn't break the terms of that agreement."

"I don't believe you. It's bad enough that PI weasel saw your ring off your finger. Now he may have evidence of you with some other guy. I'm sure he followed you after you left the boutique."

Felicity's eyes grew round, and her face turned white at my words.

Her shock at realizing she might have been caught was all the confirmation I needed.

I turned away and began to storm out of the living room.

I was certain she was lying. She had hurt me to my core, and I wanted her to know how it felt. I stopped just before reaching the hallway and turned to say one last thing.

"You know, you wouldn't have a shot of success with Moonstone if it hadn't been for my help."

She gasped, her hand going to her chest.

"You're not holding up your end of the bargain," I said angrily. "You got what you wanted from me, and now you're flaking out on our agreement two weeks early."

She stared at me with her mouth open in shock. Then she sprang to her feet and rushed past me. She grabbed her purse and laptop bag in the foyer and stormed out the front door, leaving it wide open.

I leaned against the wall, listening to the sound of her car starting and driving off.

Fuck. What had I done?

I shouldn't have said that she owed her success all to me. Not only was it untrue, but it was a shitty, cruel thing to say.

I felt awful for losing my temper with her. But did she really expect me to believe that she had been walking aimlessly for hours?

She was headed back to her apartment, no doubt. I was too upset to go after her or try to reach her on the phone.

Instead, I shut the front door, went upstairs, and lay in bed for hours. Felicity didn't come home.

When sleep finally arrived, it was fitful and restless.

∼

The next day, I parked my car in the company garage. As I walked toward my building, I looked around for that piece-of-shit PI. I'd grown used to looking for him. And though I hadn't seen him since that first day, I knew he was probably following me.

Sure enough, he appeared as I emerged onto the sidewalk. He was just a few steps behind me, not even trying to hide. It was like he *wanted* me to see him.

I was not in the mood for this.

I spun on my heels and faced him head on.

"You've got to be the shittiest private eye in the city. You're *supposed* to stay out of sight when you're tracking people. Where did Gen find you, a comic book convention?"

He smirked. "I'm doing my job just fine. You ought to worry about yourself, Cooper."

I took a step toward him. "Is that so?"

He nodded. "That's so. I have evidence to show your engagement is a lie. You're about to lose your fake family."

That was the last straw. I grabbed the guy and pushed him against the wall of my building. My fists were just itching to slam into his face.

He cowered in fear, but he couldn't control his tongue. "Go ahead and hit me, Cooper. I'm sure Judge Graves would love to see photographic evidence of your out-of-control anger."

I stepped back, knowing he was right. I'd lose the case for sure if I hit him. He'd been taunting me all along.

"Get out of here before I change my mind. And stay the fuck away from my fiancée."

He ran off and I stood there, watching him scurry away. Then I walked into my building, hoping none of my employees had witnessed the scene.

I got on the elevator, my breath still rapid. I'd come close to punching that guy, and it would've been a disaster.

"Good morning, Mr. Pierce." My executive assistant, Rebecca, greeted me with a warm smile as I stepped off the elevator on the top floor.

"I need to cancel my appointments this morning," I muttered before retreating to my office.

"Sure thing, Mr. Pierce."

I shut the door behind me and slumped in my office chair. How had everything fallen apart so quickly?

I threw myself into my work, grateful for the distraction brought by my quarterly prospectus. But my mind kept returning to Felicity.

I checked my phone yet again. Still nothing from her. But then, I hadn't reached out since she stormed off last night, either.

I had no idea where we stood. Was she calling off the pretend engagement? Was I ever going to see her again?

As the hours passed, I felt more and more ashamed of my behavior last night.

I had been on a hair trigger, and with everything that had happened the day before, I lost it. When she told me she had been out walking, it seemed such a vague and unlikely answer that I couldn't believe it.

By the light of day, it *still* struck me as odd that she had disappeared for hours with her only explanation being that she had gone for a stroll.

But on the other hand, Felicity wasn't the type to mess around like that. Even though we weren't technically in an exclusive relationship, she had signed the contract and agreed to not date anyone else. If nothing else, she wouldn't sabotage the engagement for the sake of Eva and Lily.

Still, though, her behavior was strange. My mind swam with confusion.

I worked through lunch. Rebecca brought me a sandwich, which I ignored, and a cup of strong coffee, which I gulped down.

Soon, Rebecca buzzed my line and told me there was someone here to see me.

"Reschedule," I said.

"But it's your fiancée."

Felicity. The dark cloud over my head began to lift. "Send her in, please."

A moment later, there was a soft knock at my door.

"Come in," I said.

Felicity walked in, looking as radiant as ever in a long black skirt that hugged her curves and a white blouse. God, she was beautiful.

"Hi," she said. Her face was tense, but she gave me a tentative smile.

"Hi." I stood up and walked around my desk, gesturing toward the leather sofa near the window. She sat down, looking uncertain. I eased into the armchair at her side.

She took a breath and looked up at me.

"I want to apologize for storming out last night," she said. "And for disappearing without a word before that. I know you were worried about me, and I should have sent a text."

"I'm the one who needs to apologize," I said. "I'm sorry for being a dick last night. It wasn't true what I said about you owing your success to me." I shook my head. "I was just upset and hurt. I guess I was jealous at the thought of you being with someone else."

She blinked at me. "You were jealous?"

"Yeah. It wasn't just about the custody case and the PI following us. I care about you, Felicity. I don't want you to be with another man. And I don't want to be with another woman."

Her eyes lit up. "I don't want to be with another man either, Cooper. And I wasn't."

I searched her face again. And this time, I knew she was being honest.

She leaned forward to grab my hand. "The truth is, I was feeling overwhelmed last night. I went for a walk to clear my mind, and I lost track of time. I was alone the whole time."

I squeezed her hand. "I believe you, Felicity. I was an idiot last night for accusing you of that."

"It's okay. We're both under a lot of stress right now."

I started to lean in to kiss her, but I stopped. She looked like she wanted to say something else.

Felicity drew a big breath that filled her chest. She opened her mouth to speak.

Then her phone rang in her purse. She frowned as she retrieved it. When she saw the screen, she gave me an apologetic smile.

"I'm sorry, I have to take this. It's the furniture delivery company."

"No problem."

I watched her as she took the call. The sunlight from the window fell on her brown hair. She seemed to glow in the warm light. Once again, I was mesmerized by her beauty.

She ended the call, dropping her phone in her purse and looking sheepishly at me as she stood.

"I have to be at the store in ten minutes to receive the delivery. They weren't supposed to come this early. I'm sorry, Cooper."

I waved her off. "No big deal. We can talk later."

"Should I come to the house this evening?"

"Yes. I'd like that."

"Okay. See you tonight." She gave me a smile before hurrying out of the office.

I watched her go, feeling a little better. At least we were talking now. Maybe we could get through this rough patch.

But then what?

I wanted her to stay forever, but Felicity was planning to move out after the custody decision was made.

The pain in my chest felt like someone had driven a knife through it.

How would I ever be able to say goodbye to Felicity?

Maybe she was open to a genuine relationship. She'd said she didn't want to be with anyone else, either.

Did that mean she wanted more from me?

I was being stupid. I just needed to tell her how I felt. Talk it through.

That's why I'd gotten so upset last night. I didn't know where we stood.

I wanted more from her than just sex. More than a fake relationship. I wanted to make this real.

I turned my computer off and stood up. I should go to her boutique to help her move the furniture, anyway.

Then, I'd tell her the truth.

23

FELICITY

The furniture delivery couldn't have come at a worse time.

I was just about to tell Cooper I was pregnant. Now I'd have to keep this bombshell to myself a little longer.

But still, we'd made progress. Cooper had said he didn't want to be with anyone else.

Did that mean we were exclusive? I was confused, and I needed to talk to him about it.

I rushed back to Moonstone Boutique to unlock the doors, my emotions nearly overwhelming me. The deliverymen arrived at the rear entrance of the store soon after I did.

The two guys quickly unloaded the furniture, racks, and stands for the bespoke children's section. I needed the new pieces to display a small variety of fabrics for customers to choose from, as well as information about how the process worked. Some of the furniture would be used for my off-the-rack girls' section, too.

As they worked, I consulted my order form, comparing it to the items they delivered. The temperature in the store suddenly felt stifling. I tied my hair into a bun and fanned myself with the paperwork.

"Everything looks good," I said. I watched as they moved the last piece to the front of the store.

"Great," the older of the two men said. "We just need your signature, and we'll be on our way."

"Of course." I followed the guys to the parking area in the back and waited for them to get the tablet from their van.

Outside, the bright sun made me feel dizzy. A fresh wave of nausea rose in my stomach.

Great. Not this again.

But this time, I felt unsteady on my feet. I braced myself against the doorframe and shut my eyes, willing myself not to faint.

"Whoa," the younger guy said. He grabbed me just before I lost my balance. "Let's get you inside."

He helped me through the door. The world was spinning, and I held on to his arm to steady myself. He pulled a chair over and I sat down, glad to be off my feet.

"Ma'am, are you okay?"

He looked at me, worried.

"I... I think I'm okay," I said. But I wasn't certain. I felt disoriented and scared.

I blew out a shuddering sigh, trying to collect myself.

The older man approached me with a bottle of cool water he'd retrieved from his van. He twisted the cap open and handed it to me.

"Thank you." I smiled at him gratefully. The water revived me, and I took a few sips.

"No problem," he said, giving me a smile. "My wife had terrible morning sickness her whole first trimester. Not just in the morning, either. All day long."

I blinked up at him. "How... how did you know?"

He lifted a shoulder. "You have that same look she did. I guess they call it a glow."

A clatter from the front of the store startled me.

I looked up to see my father standing near the front entrance.

He had knocked over one of the new display cases. Apparently, he had entered from the front, overheard the man's words, and reacted out of surprise.

Dad stood there glaring at me.

I squeezed my eyes shut in frustration. I was fed up with being scrutinized.

My head had stopped swimming, and I wanted to finish up with the deliverymen before my father flipped out.

"I can sign that form now," I said. The younger man handed me the tablet. I scrawled my signature on the screen, thanked them again, and they left.

I took another sip of water and rose to face my dad.

"Felicity, are you pregnant?" he asked.

"Dad, Gen already has a private eye following Cooper and me. I don't need you spying on me, too."

"I wasn't spying on you. I came by to see if you needed help with your delivery."

"How did you know I had a delivery?"

"I saw you mentioned it on Moonstone's social media," he answered irritatedly.

Despite the tense situation, I felt a tug of joy at his interest in my store. His furious expression quickly stamped it out, though.

"Answer the question," he pressed.

I paused, unsure of what to say. I couldn't tell my dad the news before I told Cooper. That didn't feel right.

"I'd rather not say until I have a chance to discuss it with the father first."

"So it's true." He shook his head in disappointment and anger. Disgust, even.

"Dad..."

"It's bad enough you agreed to pretend to be Cooper's fiancée. But now you're sleeping with him? And having his... *baby*? Jesus, Felicity."

His face turned red and his nostrils flared. I braced myself for a lecture. But this time, he was too angry to say much.

And I didn't know what to say at all.

"You know, maybe I should blow open this entire farce for your own good," he said. "Maybe it's time the truth came out."

"No, Dad. Wait."

But I was too late. He flung the front door open with so much force I was afraid he would break it. Then he stormed out.

I leaned against the wall and let myself slide down to the floor.

This was the last straw in a series of disasters, and just when I had started to gain my dad's approval. He looked so angry, I couldn't imagine he would ever forgive me.

And worse, he'd threatened to expose the engagement as a fake, which would destroy Cooper's chances at the custody trial.

I buried my face in my hands as the tears streamed down my face. Cooper and his daughters were the best things to ever happen to me. And I was on the brink of losing them all.

Just as my sobbing began to calm down, a new worry entered my mind.

I'd nearly fainted. I wasn't sure if that was a normal pregnancy symptom—I'd never heard of it happening to anyone I knew. What if something was wrong? My stomach twisted on itself as I worried about my baby.

My shoulders shook as I let myself wallow in misery. It felt like my world was coming apart at the seams.

I wasn't sure how long I stayed like that, but at some point, the front door opened. Dread moved through me. Now a customer would see me completely undone, crying on the floor of my store.

But Cooper's soothing presence washed over me instead.

Without a word, he sat beside me on the floor and wrapped his arm around my back. I curled against him and sobbed.

"It's going to be okay, Felicity. Whatever it is, it's going to be okay."

I looked up at him. His blue eyes met mine, and for a second I almost believed him. I wanted so badly to lose myself in those eyes. I wanted to trust that as long as we were together, everything would work out.

But everything had fallen apart. I wasn't even sure that Cooper could fix this.

"No, it isn't. My dad figured it all out."

His jaw tightened. "He knows we're sleeping together?"

I sniffed. "Yes. And he said he might blow open the farce of our engagement."

There was so much more I needed to tell him. Like *how* my father had figured it out.

I wanted desperately to tell Cooper I was pregnant, but I just couldn't bring myself to admit it yet. I knew he would get upset and maybe even accuse me of doing it on purpose. I still felt woozy and overwhelmed, and I just couldn't handle any more stress. I'd tell him about the baby soon. Just not right now.

"He threatened to tell the judge we're lying?" Cooper asked, his voice tight.

I nodded. "He didn't say those exact words, but that's what he meant."

Cooper's free hand clenched into a fist. He gazed off into the distance, his eyes becoming hard.

"I know this is the last thing we need right now," I said. "I tried to stop him, but he just stormed out."

"Shit."

Cooper lifted his arm, removing it from its place around my back. He stood up and helped me to my feet. "I have to go talk to him before he does something crazy."

I nodded, wiping the tears off my face.

"Are you going to be okay here alone?" he asked. "I came over to help you with the furniture delivery." He looked at the furniture the guys had unloaded. "I don't want you moving all that by yourself."

I gave him the best smile I could manage. "I'll be fine. I won't be moving any of it today. It can wait."

"Okay. I'll see you back at the house later."

He turned and rushed out of the store, hopping in his car that was parked out front and speeding off.

What a mess. Now that my father knew everything, he was going to use it against me. I just hoped he had the decency to not tell Cooper about the pregnancy. I'd made it clear I wanted to tell Cooper myself.

But Dad had never been one for respecting boundaries.

My stomach growled, and I realized I'd skipped lunch. I dug in my bag, finding a protein bar, an apple, and a bag of dried fruit. I devoured it all, washing it down with some milk from the mini fridge. Then I washed my face in the bathroom.

I wanted nothing more than to crawl under the covers and hide from the world, but I didn't have that luxury at the moment.

I had a prenatal appointment to get to.

～

I sat on the exam table at the birth clinic. I had just gotten an ultrasound with the technician, and I was waiting for the obstetrician to talk to me.

It was amazing to hear the heartbeat and see the little blur on the screen. I was still early in the pregnancy—ten weeks—but it was thrilling to think I would be a mother in a few months.

But when I thought of how I had almost fainted, panic welled inside me. I had only discovered my pregnancy a few days ago, and already I was so attached to the life growing inside me.

The door swung open, and the obstetrician, a woman with beautiful silver hair and a warm smile, entered the room. She introduced herself as Dr. Temple, and I nervously shook her hand.

"Good news, Felicity," she said. "Your ultrasound looks great."

I closed my eyes and exhaled. "Thank God. I was so worried after what happened earlier this afternoon."

She nodded. "I understand your concern, but it sounds like a case of dehydration and low blood sugar. How have your stress levels been?"

I fidgeted with the paper gown I was wearing. "Pretty bad. I'm going through some major changes with my small business. And, well, a lot of changes in my personal life, too."

Dr. Temple gave me a sympathetic look. "That sounds like a lot to deal with. I encourage you to do what you can to manage your stress. Reach out to the people who care for you for support. Try to rest as much as you can. And you may find that frequent, small meals help maintain your energy levels."

I bit my lip. Keeping stress levels down would be tricky. "I'll do my best."

She patted my knee. "Good to hear. You'll be fine, Felicity. The baby and all your vitals are perfectly normal."

"The tech said it's too early to know the sex?"

"Right. But at your next ultrasound, we should be able to tell. By the way, this is for you."

She handed me a copy of the ultrasound image. Gazing at the black and white image of my baby, I felt tears pressing against my eyes once more.

Dr. Temple said goodbye and left me to change into my regular clothes. Recalling the earlier incident with my father, I moved quickly.

I grabbed my purse and checked out at the front desk. If I hurried, maybe I could get to Cooper before Dad broke the news of my pregnancy.

24

COOPER

I parked outside Marsh's law firm, my ears ringing and my heart pounding.

But Marsh's car wasn't here. I pounded my steering wheel in frustration. My phone pinged with a text.

Marsh: Where the hell are you?
Cooper: At your office. Where are you?
Marsh: At your house.
Cooper: Monica will let you in. Wait in my home office. I'll be there in fifteen.

Thirteen minutes of white-knuckle driving later, I pulled into my driveway.

Felicity had just texted me asking if I'd found her dad. I fired off a response that we were both at my house before I hurried inside.

Marsh stood in my study, his face red and furious.

"What the fuck, Cooper? I trusted you. And now you're screwing around with my daughter."

It wasn't a question. It was an accusation. Betrayal was written all over his face.

"Marsh, just keep calm here, okay?"

"She's not one of those women you used to pick up at bars, Cooper. She's my *daughter*. And she's twenty years younger than you!"

I rubbed the back of my neck. "Sixteen, to be precise."

But that only made his nostrils flare more.

"I don't give a rat's ass."

"Are you going to tell the judge the engagement is a pretense?"

"I haven't decided yet." He narrowed his eyes at me.

"That wouldn't help Felicity, you know. It would be bad timing with her interview about to go to print. Bad publicity is the last thing she needs right now."

"What do you know about what my daughter needs?" he scoffed.

"I know what her business needs. And I know she deserves success."

"Don't talk to me about what she deserves, Cooper. Felicity *deserves* to be with someone her own age." He leveled me with a defiant look. "Someone who loves her for who she is."

"I *do* love her for who she is."

I froze. It was the first time I had admitted I loved Felicity. I'd never even admitted it to myself before now.

But it was true. And it felt damn good to finally say it.

But my declaration just made Marsh angrier. He glared at me and took a step forward.

"You're selfish, Cooper. You're trying to tie down my twenty-six-year-old daughter when she's in a completely different phase of life from you. This isn't about love. You just want to give your kids a ready-made mother and make your own life easier."

My mouth fell open. I was stunned at his accusations. "No, that's not it at all."

"If you really loved Felicity, you wouldn't treat her this way. You wouldn't use her to keep your kids. You would give her freedom to live her life on her own terms. You just want to tie her down."

I stood there staring at him. I was speechless.

I knew I loved Felicity. I didn't doubt my feelings for her. I cared for her as she was. I wasn't interested in her just because she would make a good mother for my children.

I was in love with her. I'd fought against it all this time, but I couldn't deny it anymore.

But maybe Marsh was partly right. Perhaps I was doing the wrong thing by trying to tie her down.

Maybe she deserved to start a family of her own with someone her age.

More to the point, maybe *I* didn't deserve someone like Felicity.

Marsh and I stared at each other, each waiting for the other to make the next move.

Finally Marsh spoke. "But I guess it's too late for all this, anyway."

I frowned. "What do you mean?"

He drew a breath, as if reluctant to tell me something more. We both looked up to see Felicity walk in the room.

"Dad, I think it's time for you to leave."

Marsh looked between her and me. He seemed to want to say something more, but he clamped his mouth shut.

With one last glare at me, he stalked out of the room. Moments later, I heard Monica close the front door behind him.

I crossed the space to take Felicity into my arms. I held her for a long moment, and she rested her head against my chest.

"Is he going to expose us to the judge?" she asked.

"He hasn't made up his mind yet."

She sighed. "I guess he's going to do some *careful consideration*," she said sarcastically.

"Yeah. It sounds like he could go either way."

After a moment, she looked up at me.

"I'm sorry my father is butting into our business."

I gave her a wan smile. "Marsh has always been a control freak."

She chuckled. "You should have seen him in his thirties. He had to micromanage everything in the house when I was a kid." She looked down, sadness crossing her face. "I don't know how Mom put up with it."

I caressed her cheek. "Maybe his redeeming qualities made up for it."

She nodded slowly. "I guess so. As much as he drives me crazy, he does have a caring side. He just doesn't show it much."

"I know. He does want the best for you, Felicity. He cares about you. He just... has a strange way of showing it."

"Yeah. Like trying to control who I spend my time with."

I nodded. Felicity hadn't told me the details of how Marsh had figured it out. But I didn't bother asking. The guy was a master at reading the room. His sharp eye picked up on everything. He'd probably seen the way Felicity looked at me or heard the way my voice changed when I talked about her. He was good at putting two and two together.

"Are you okay with your father knowing about us?"

She lifted a shoulder. "I guess it doesn't matter, since it's done now. I just hope he doesn't say anything to the judge."

"Me too."

"Thanks for coming to the store earlier," she said. "It... helped. Having you there."

She gazed up at me, and once again I was made speechless by her beauty. She pressed herself against my torso and parted her lips, making my cock punch up in my pants.

Maybe it was fucked up to be turned on at a time like this, but I didn't care. I needed her.

My hands moved down to cup her voluptuous ass, pulling her roughly against me. She gasped as I thrust my erection on her soft belly.

With my mouth pressed against hers, I kissed her long and deep. She melted against me, her body warm and soft. It felt like home.

I moved her hair off her shoulder, exposing her long neck.

"You're so fucking gorgeous," I said, kissing her silky skin. She moaned.

"I want you, Cooper."

"Stay right there," I growled, letting go of her long enough to close my study door and lock it.

I was back at her side a second later, lifting the shirt she wore over her head and moving my hands over her round breasts, showcased in a white lacy bra. I unhooked it and removed it from her arms, letting it fall to the floor.

Her perky tits bounced free, and I moved my hands over them. I bent down, sucking one nipple into my mouth, then the other. She plunged her hands into my hair and tossed her head back, moaning in pleasure.

Impatient and needing to touch her bare skin, I yanked her long skirt down. Then I pulled her panties down her legs. Holding on to my shoulders, she stepped out of them.

I dove between her legs, kneeling before her and burying my face between her thighs.

She was already so wet, and I lapped at her delicate folds hungrily, sucking all her nectar onto my tongue.

"Fuck, that feels so good." She bucked her pelvis against me.

I could barely breathe, and I didn't mind one bit.

I didn't need air. I only needed her, this perfect woman standing before me.

As I flicked my tongue over her clit, I slipped one finger inside her, hooking it forward. I knew it would drive her crazy. And it did.

She dug her nails into my back and her muscles began to contract around my finger as she whimpered.

"That's it, baby," I murmured against her skin. "Come for me like a good girl."

I sucked her flesh and she closed her eyes, losing herself as she surrendered to the orgasm. She braced herself against me, her legs gone wobbly.

When she came down from her peak, I stood. Sweeping her into my arms, I carried her to the leather sofa.

She was still recovering from her climax. I watched her catch her breath as I removed my clothes.

I shrugged off my shirt, but as I began to unfasten my belt, she moved her hands to mine.

She looked up at me with a naughty smile. "Allow me."

Tucking her legs underneath her, she perched on the edge of the sofa as she undid my belt and pants.

She pulled them slowly over my hips, and the wait was agony. I wanted to be inside her already.

Teasingly, Felicity tugged the boxers down. I stepped out of the clothing and stood before her, my dick hard and bobbing in front of her face. She licked her lips then wrapped them around the head of my cock.

"Fuck," I moaned as she took my length in slowly, inch by inch.

As she swallowed down as much of my shaft as she could, her eyes moved upward to meet mine.

The sight of her looking at me with my dick in her mouth nearly made me blow my load right then. But I managed to hold back.

I drove my hand into her hair, holding her head in place. If she moved much more, I'd lose it.

As I released my grip, she wrapped her hand around the base and moved her mouth to the head. I was breathless, and I took a step back, letting my cock slip out of her hot, wet mouth.

I sat beside her on the sofa and moved her into my lap. She straddled me, wrapping her arms around my neck. Grabbing her curvy hips, I thrust my erection against the dripping folds between her legs. She arched her back, pushing her perfect breasts in my face, and I took one of her nipples gently between my teeth.

I guided her to my cock and pushed my hips upward, entering her tight little pussy. Her eyes were big as she looked at me, her eyebrows knitted in concentration.

"Does that feel good?" I whispered.

"Uh-huh." She bit her lip, and I pushed all the way in, making a loud moan escape her throat.

She began to ride me, her tits bouncing against my face as I held her close.

But I needed to be deeper. I took over the movement, and she held on to me as I thrust inside her over and over.

I couldn't get enough of her. I wanted to be as deep inside her as I could.

With a swift movement, I lifted her off my cock and placed her on her back on the leather. She looked up at me, her mouth curling into a smile, as I positioned myself over her delicate body.

I pumped inside her folds, and she squeezed her eyes shut for a moment. As I began to thrust deep inside her, she opened her eyes again to look at me.

My hands roamed over her breasts and stomach, her face and neck. I committed every detail of Felicity to memory.

Her legs wrapped around my waist, pulling me closer and allowing me deeper access. I didn't stop. I couldn't stop until I filled her up completely.

Her mouth opened in a circle as she fell over the edge into orgasm once more. I watched her face as she came, knowing I'd never see anything as beautiful as this in my life.

Her pussy muscles began to milk my cock, and I couldn't hold back any longer. I groaned as I came, too, shooting my warm release inside her walls.

Panting for air, I rested my head against her chest. Her heart beat against my ear. My dick was still inside her, and she caressed my head, running her fingers through my hair.

I never wanted this moment to end.

But before long, she squirmed underneath me. "I can't breathe," she said with a smile.

"Oh. Sorry."

I got up and gave her a hand to help her sit up, which she accepted. I handed her a box of tissues, and she cleaned up.

She stood and reached for her bra. I snuck peeks at her as we both dressed, sad to see her gorgeous flesh being covered up once more. She was quiet, and I wondered what she was thinking.

When we were both dressed, I stood before her.

"Are you okay?" I asked.

She nodded and gave me a small smile. "Yeah. I'm just worried about my dad blabbing to the judge."

"Same here. I'll call my lawyer and see what he advises."

"Okay." She looked up at me. "You have to win this case, Cooper. Gen can't win. Those girls belong with you."

I brushed her hair out of her face and moved it behind her shoulders. "I know. I'm worried about it, but I have faith that we can figure this out. There's got to be some way to still win this."

"Yeah. Let me know if I can help in any way. I mean that."

"Thanks. I will."

"Well, I'm going to get some work done in the studio upstairs," she said. "I don't feel like going back to the boutique today."

"Okay. I'll try to get some work done, too. Inga will be here soon after she picks up the girls from school."

Felicity stood on her tiptoes to give me a quick peck on the cheek. "See you later."

"Bye."

I watched her walk out, my throat tight.

I wanted to tell her the truth—that I loved her. That I wanted to be with her for real.

But I just couldn't bring myself to say the words. Not after what Marsh had said about tying her down.

With a heaviness in my chest, I straightened the cushions on the sofa, then I ran upstairs for a quick shower to clean up. Soon, I was back in my study.

Alone with my thoughts for the first time since my conversation with Marsh, a dark feeling sank in.

Pouring myself a glass of whiskey, I pondered my situation.

There was no way to know what decision Marsh would

make. If he decided to tell the judge, it would be disastrous. Was he really that petty? Would he want to sabotage my custody case just because I was sleeping with his daughter?

Sadly, I could see him doing it. He had no problems hurting people he thought had hurt him.

As I sipped the liquor, Marsh's words rang in my ears.

Felicity deserves to be with someone closer to her own age.

What if he was right?

I'd planned to tell her the truth of how I felt, to profess my love for her and ask if she wanted to try this for real.

But maybe it was wrong to tie her down.

A tightness took hold of my chest and wouldn't let go.

I must have lost track of time at some point, because the girls' voices roused me from my thoughts.

"Daddy!"

The girls ran in, all hopped up from their afterschool snack.

"Daddy, we didn't know you were home," Lily said.

"Felicity is asleep again," Eva announced. "She's sleeping at her sewing table upstairs."

"That's okay. We'll let her rest."

Eva pouted. "But we wanted to work on our sewing projects with her."

"I know, girls. But you have to remember that Felicity is very busy now with her store. She's been working a lot lately, and she's tired."

Lily blinked her long lashes up at me. "We miss playing with her."

"I know, Lily. I'm sorry."

I ran my hand over her head, smoothing her blonde hair.

"Why don't you two see if Inga can play with you outside

in the backyard? I'm going to get some work done, and then we'll have dinner together. Deal?"

"Deal!" Eva said. Lily nodded, but she was disappointed. They ran out of the room, calling for Inga.

I slumped in my office chair. Tension mounted in my gut.

Marsh's angry face appeared in my mind's eye, his words haunting me.

If you really loved Felicity, you would give her freedom to live her life on her own terms. You just want to tie her down.

Fuck.

He was right.

Her business was starting to take off. I'd helped her with Moonstone just as I'd promised. And she had almost completed her end of the deal by pretending to be engaged the past few months.

In two weeks, she'd go to the custody trial at my side. After Judge Graves' decision, her part of the deal would be over.

I couldn't expect any more from her. Asking her to stay with me and be my girlfriend would complicate her life. It would mean she'd be tied down to a guy in a different stage of life.

It could mean she might become a maternal figure to my daughters—permanently. She'd have to take on a lot of responsibility.

Felicity deserved a big white wedding. Judging by the way her face lit up whenever the topic was mentioned, that was what she wanted.

She'd probably want kids, too. Though she'd said she was on the fence about becoming a mother, I saw how she acted around my girls. She would want children of her own when the time was right.

And I couldn't give her what she wanted. Ever.

After Gen, I just couldn't take the risk. I couldn't trust myself enough to commit to someone long-term. And I couldn't have more kids just to worry about them being ripped away from me.

She would never be satisfied with what I could offer her. And she shouldn't have to settle.

I couldn't ask that of Felicity. I couldn't let her put her life on hold for me and my daughters.

I couldn't bear to watch her grow to resent me over the years because I was a chickenshit. Because I was afraid of commitment after my divorce.

No matter how much I loved Felicity, I couldn't ask her to stay.

I loved her too much to let her make that decision.

Didn't they say if you love someone, set them free?

I loved Felicity more than I'd loved any other woman. More than I thought possible.

I had to set her free.

25

FELICITY

The interview in *LA Now* changed everything.

The article was published three days after my dad found out about Cooper and me. And the very next morning, there were people lined up to get into Moonstone Boutique when I arrived to open the store.

Suddenly, I was swamped with customers.

I was working long hours before, but that had been a walk in the park compared to my new life after the interview. Out of nowhere, my store was flooded with parents ordering bespoke fashions for their little girls.

The adult clothing started to sell more, too. Once mothers stopped in the store to shop for their daughters, they often found something for themselves.

Three days after the interview was published, I had a large list of custom orders to make. I worked on designing and sewing in every free moment I had at the store. But it was hard to finish the pieces. Nearly every time I sat down at my sewing machine, another customer came through the door.

I barely saw Cooper and the girls. I was working around

the clock, trying to do everything. I missed them, and I hated letting them down, but the boutique needed me now more than ever.

Wednesday night, I got home after the girls were in bed. When I walked in the front door, Cooper was coming down the staircase after tucking them in.

"Hey, stranger," he said, his face neutral. None of the old warmth was there.

"Hey." I set my bags on the front table.

"I saved you some dinner. It's in the microwave if you want it."

"Thanks," I said. "I haven't eaten since breakfast." I kicked my shoes off.

"The girls were asking about you. They hardly see you anymore," Cooper said.

"I know, and I hate that I've been getting home so late. It's just a lot to manage with all the new customers at the shop."

"The trial is on Monday, you know."

I swallowed the lump in my throat. "I know."

"We'll have to sit down soon and go over some details. I want you to know what to expect in the courtroom."

I nodded. "Okay. I can get home early on Friday, if that works for you."

"Sure." He rubbed his jaw and looked away. "Well, I'll let you eat. I have some work to do."

"Okay," I said quietly. He turned and went toward his study.

My heart ached.

I wanted to stop him, but I didn't know what to say. We'd barely had a moment alone since we had sex in his study.

Was this the same man who said he didn't want to be with anyone else a week ago?

I still needed to tell him about the pregnancy, but I hadn't. I didn't know what the hell was wrong with me. I guess I was scared. Scared of his reaction. And most of all, I was scared of losing Cooper.

He already seemed so far away. I didn't want the pregnancy to make us lose the last bit of connection we still had.

But tonight, it felt like any connection we once had was hanging by a thread.

The next morning, I got to the store early. I was hoping to get a jump on my backlog of sewing projects before I opened the store doors.

But when I saw Lauren knocking on the locked front door, I knew catching up on work wasn't going to happen. And I was glad. Talking to my best friend was more important.

I unlocked the door for her and pulled her inside, wrapping my arms around her.

"You're finally back from Seattle!" I exclaimed. "It feels like you've been gone forever."

"I've only been gone a week." She laughed as she hugged me, then stepped back to look at me. "Are you okay?"

I turned away, walking toward the stools at the sales counter. "I have news. Really big news. You should sit down."

Her eyes grew large as she followed me and pulled a seat underneath her. "Okay, I'm listening. Tell me everything."

"Well, the other day I was walking past that French restaurant, and the smell made me throw up."

She frowned. "Jean-Luc's? You love that place."

"Yeah, but lately, certain aromas have been making me feel sick. Then I realized I had skipped a period."

Her hands flew to her mouth. "Oh, my God."

"Yeah. The tests I bought at the pharmacy came back positive. Both of them."

"So, you're..."

I took a deep breath. This was the first time I'd told anyone outside of the people at the birth clinic. "I'm pregnant."

Lauren jumped up so fast her stool fell to the floor behind her. She hugged me, and I began to cry.

She handed me a tissue. "I take it you're shocked."

"I'm fine. I'm just... terrified."

"Is it Cooper's?"

"Yes," I said. "It's definitely Cooper's."

"Right. You went through a dry spell before he came along. But weren't you on birth control all this time?"

I nodded and dabbed at my wet cheeks. "Yes, I was. But I got sick with that stomach bug the morning after our first night together. I was throwing up for three days. I didn't think of it at the time, but I guess the birth control wasn't effective during that time."

"Damn." Lauren shook her head. "That's a tough break."

"Thanks," I said sarcastically.

She grabbed my hand. "I didn't mean it like that. I just... Wow. This is crazy. Pregnant?"

"I know. I found out the day you left. I've been so stressed out since then."

"You've known this for a week and you didn't tell me? You've been texting me about the interview and the store, but you didn't mention this little tidbit?"

I lifted a shoulder. "This was too big for a text. And I didn't want to interrupt your family time."

She scoffed. "I would have made time for you, silly." She gave me a sympathetic look. "I know you're stressed out about your new customers and the changes with Moonstone. But how are you handling *this*?" She gestured at my belly.

I paused for a moment. "I'm scared, to be honest. But I'm excited, too. I was never really sure I wanted to have kids before. But now that I'm pregnant, the thought of bringing a new life into the world makes me happy." I smiled. "I keep wondering if it's going to be a boy or girl, and who it's going to look like."

She grinned at me. "If it's a girl, hopefully she'll have Cooper's long eyelashes."

I laughed.

"But seriously," Lauren continued, "I'm excited, too. I know you're going to make a great mother. And I'll be with you every step of the way. What does Cooper say?"

I winced. "I haven't told him yet."

She blinked at me. "What? Why not?"

"Because I'm a big chicken. I'm afraid of how he's going to react. The trial is just four days away, and he's so stressed out. It doesn't feel like the right time to drop this bomb on him. Especially not with my dad creating more drama."

"Your dad?"

"Yes. He found out I'm pregnant."

"Shit."

I gave her a recap of what had happened with my dad threatening to expose the engagement.

"Okay," Lauren said, nodding. "I can understand waiting to tell Cooper."

"There's one more thing..." My voice trailed off, and new tears welled in my eyes.

"What is it?"

"Cooper's been acting really distant lately. I think he's starting to pull away from me now that he knows our time together is almost over."

"He hasn't asked you to stay with him after the custody trial? From what you told me, it sounded like he was feeling something for you. More than just sex."

I swallowed the lump in my throat. "Yeah, it seemed that way to me, too... for a while. Things were going so well between us. I kept expecting him to say he wanted a real relationship with me. And then there was our talk in his office..."

"What talk?" Lauren asked.

"He said he didn't want to be with anyone else. Our conversation was cut short, but it almost seemed like he was saying he wanted to be exclusive."

"Yeah, sounds like it."

"But right after that, he became a different person." My voice cracked as another sob moved through my chest. "It's like he doesn't care about me at all anymore."

Lauren squeezed my hand. "I'm so sorry, Felicity. That sounds really confusing."

"Yeah, just when everything was going so great, he got all cold on me. It was so strange." I blew my nose into a fresh tissue. "It's like he's biding his time until I move out of his house and he's rid of me."

"Is it really that bad?"

"It feels that bad to me. I feel like an unwelcome guest in his house. I know the girls still enjoy my company, but Cooper not so much." Tears rolled down my face. "And I'll have to say goodbye to the girls, too. I'm going to miss them so much."

"I know you are, sweetie. Maybe you can still visit them sometimes."

"Yeah, that would be nice. But everything will be different." I sighed. "That's the understatement of the year. With this baby, everything will be totally changed."

"You don't think he'd want to have a relationship with you now that you're pregnant?"

"No." My chest ached as I said the words, but deep down I knew it was true. "I don't think he's going to take the news of my pregnancy well. He's already said he doesn't want more children. He may resent me for giving him another one."

"Well, if he's like that, screw him. It takes two to tango. He could at least help you raise the kid."

"I'm sure he will. Cooper's not the type of guy to back out on something like this. He would never be a deadbeat dad. I'm sure he'll want to have some kind of co-parenting relationship."

Lauren nodded. "Okay, that's good. So you won't be all on your own."

"Not when it comes to raising the baby, no. But romantically, yes." I looked up at her through watery eyes. "I was really starting to feel something for him, Lauren."

She made a sympathetic noise and gave me another hug. "Here," she said with a smile. "Have another tissue. And you should add a few more boxes to your supplies list. I have a feeling you're going to need them."

"Thanks." I chuckled. "God, just look at me. I'm a mess. And I have to open the store in an hour."

"You can't take the morning off?"

"No way." I reached for the stack of bespoke clothing orders I had received. I held them up for Lauren to see.

"What are those?"

"Order forms for custom-made girls' clothes. I have to design and sew each one of these within a week."

"And you're doing that in addition to managing the store and all the rest of your merchandise?"

"Yes." The tension rose in my stomach as I thought about the work waiting for me.

"Babe, you need help around here. For starters, you should hire at least two or three employees to cover sales and the sewing. Then you need a competent manager. Your job should be fashion design. Now that you're leveling up, you have to delegate all those other tasks."

"I can't afford all that. You're talking about putting several people on payroll. I'd like to hire staff eventually, but I can't yet."

Lauren picked up my bookkeeping notebook. "Mind if I have a look at this?"

"Help yourself."

Lauren spread it out on the counter between us. We both studied it intently for a few moments.

"See?" Lauren finally said, pointing excitedly to the profit I had made the past few days. "That number is huge. You can definitely afford a few employees. Even without factoring in Cooper's financial investment."

I looked at the numbers and listened as she gave me a summary of how much I'd need to pay a few employees every week, based on her experience managing the books at the flower shop.

My eyes grew wide when I realized she was right.

Moonstone Boutique was finally thriving. Even before the interview was published, I had seen a steady increase in sales from the advertising campaigns I was running. And with the prices adjusted to reflect the amount of time and cost of materials that had gone into each garment, my business was doing better than ever.

"You're right," I breathed. "I could hire some people." I

smiled, my mind racing with possibilities. "That would be a huge help around here. And I'd be free to do what I love most of all—designing."

Lauren glanced at the front door. Three customers had lined up outside, waiting for me to open the store. She laughed. "Yeah, you're going to need some help around here."

I blew my nose and grabbed a handheld mirror to check my eye makeup, then turned to my friend. "Thanks, Lauren. For everything."

"That's what friends are for." She smiled. "I better get to work. Text me later?"

"Of course." I gave her a hug and followed her to the front door, where she walked toward the flower shop.

I smiled at the customers waiting outside. Even though it wasn't yet opening time, I let them inside. As soon as I had a free moment, however, I would post some job openings for staff members.

Hopefully, I'd have some help around the store soon. That lifted the burden from my shoulders a little already.

And tonight when I saw Cooper, I would tell him I was pregnant. It wasn't the best timing, but he deserved to know.

And I deserved to know what to expect from the father of my child.

26

COOPER

Felicity was late getting home. Again.

It was just as well. It was better if the girls didn't see her around the house much anymore. It might hurt less for them this way.

We just had to get through the next three days. Then the custody trial would happen on Monday.

At dinner, the girls asked about her. They had been spending time in the studio, drawing and playing with the fabric. I think it was mainly to feel closer to Felicity, to be in her space and to be around her things. All I could say was that she was working.

Shortly after I put the girls to bed, Felicity came home. As I heard her park, I walked out of my study and met her in the foyer. She seemed tired, but she gave me a smile.

"Sorry I'm so late again. Are the girls already asleep?"

I nodded. "I put them down half an hour ago."

She looked disappointed. "I keep missing their bedtime."

I rubbed the back of my neck. "Do you have a few minutes? I have something to talk to you about."

"Sure. I have something to tell you, too."

She followed me into the living room and settled on one side of the sofa. I sat in the armchair. My tongue felt heavy in my mouth. When I didn't say anything for a moment, she spoke up.

"Hopefully, I'll be getting home earlier from now on. I just hired my first employee today." She beamed.

"Really? That's great."

"Yeah. I didn't think I had the money to pay a staff, but it turns out I do. I just put the job postings up this morning, and by noon I had several qualified applicants. One was ready to interview this afternoon for a sales position, and I hired her on the spot."

I did my best to smile. "That sounds great, Felicity. I know you could use more hands around the store."

"I want to hire a seamstress, too. Lauren says I should hire a manager, but I'll see how it goes." She gathered her hair and pulled it over one shoulder. "How was your day? How are the girls?"

"They're fine. They just miss you."

Her face dropped. "I miss them, too, Cooper. But hopefully my workload will lighten with these new employees and I'll have more time."

My stomach tightened. She was talking like we'd be together forever.

"Felicity, the trial is only three days away."

"I know." She heaved a sigh. "I can't believe it's coming up so soon. What does your lawyer say?"

I shrugged. "He says to continue with the engagement. The private eye we hired hasn't dug up anything on Gen."

She nodded, looking down at her hands. "Is that what you wanted to talk to me about?"

My throat went dry as I looked at her beautiful face.

How could I do this? I wanted to back out, reverse direction. I wanted to pull her into my arms and cuddle her forever.

I wanted to tell her I loved her.

Instead, I had to break her heart.

"Felicity, I truly appreciate all your help with the girls and the custody trial. You've gone above and beyond everything I asked of you. And you've made a difference in their lives."

She blinked at me, uncertain of where I was going.

I drew a deep breath. Everything inside me was screaming for me to stop. But I had to continue.

"For the remaining time we have together, I think we should return to the original terms of our agreement."

She stared at me. "What do you mean?"

"We got our feelings all mixed up in this fake engagement." I drove a hand through my hair, looking at the carpet. "We both got confused about what was real and what was fake. We need to remember this has an end date."

I met her eyes. They were watery, as if holding back tears.

"You mean *I* got confused about what was real or fake, right?" she bit out. "You knew all along that you would say goodbye to me after the trial."

I looked away from her. That wasn't true, but I didn't deny it. It would just hurt more.

I swallowed down my feelings so I could get through this.

"I'd like us to stick to the contract. I need you to go to the trial on Monday wearing the ring and play the part. But we can't do anything more than that. And after the judge's decision, we have to return to the way things were before."

"You mean you want me to leave." Tears were rolling

down her face now, and she wiped them away angrily. "You're kicking me out of your house. As soon as I've fulfilled my obligations to you, you want me gone."

"I'm not kicking you out, Felicity. I'm just saying we should stick to our agreement. Things have gotten messy. My kids are confused. And that's my fault, not yours. I should have done everything differently."

"Like not get close to me?"

I swallowed. I didn't know how to answer that. The truth was I didn't regret getting close to her. Not one bit.

I didn't want this to end. But I couldn't tie her down when her business and life were starting to take off.

I'd made too many mistakes in my life. Some of them had come close to breaking me. I wasn't the same man I once was.

Felicity deserved better.

She deserved someone whole.

"I care for you, Felicity. A lot. But I need to prioritize my daughters now."

She sat in silence for a long time, her arms folded over her chest. Her eyes were downcast, looking everywhere but at me.

"I'm sorry, Felicity. I never wanted to hurt you. But I think this is the best for all of us."

I reached across the space to grab her hand, but she snatched it away. "You mean this is the best for you, Cooper."

She sprang to her feet and glared at me. Her face was hard and angry. She'd never looked at me like this before, and it made pain shoot through my chest.

"So that's all I was to you," she said quietly. "Just a business deal."

"No, Felicity, that's not true. Not at all. If that were true, I wouldn't be telling you this right now. I'm doing it now, before the trial, because it would be a dick move to wait until it was over."

But she wasn't listening to me. She charged out of the room and grabbed her things from the table in the foyer.

I followed her. "Where are you going? You can't leave now."

"Don't worry, Cooper," she said over her shoulder. "I won't violate the terms of your *agreement*."

"That's not what I meant," I said. "You shouldn't be driving when you're upset like this."

"Don't worry about me. I'll be fine. I'll be at the custody trial. And I'll sleep in your house every night until then, per our agreement. But right now, I need some air."

She opened the front door and walked into the night. Even in her angry state, she closed the door gently so she wouldn't wake the girls.

I thought about running after her and convincing her to stay.

I thought about telling her what an idiot I was, how I was lying through my teeth when I said I didn't want something more from her.

I thought about confessing that I was doing this for her, so she wouldn't be tied down to a screwed-up guy like me.

But I didn't run after her. I just let her go.

She was the best thing to ever happen to me, other than my daughters. And I had driven her off.

I went to my study and poured myself a glass of whiskey.

If I couldn't be with Felicity, at least I could be numb.

27

FELICITY

I drove on autopilot through the dark Los Angeles streets.

My destination was unknown as I navigated the highway and took an exit without reading the sign.

My mind was numb. I couldn't feel my emotions yet. But when I looked around and saw that I was in my old neighborhood, the dam broke and I started crying. I pulled into the parking lot in front of my apartment building and got out of my car.

"Please let Lauren be home," I muttered to myself as I climbed the steps to our second-story apartment.

I knocked on the door, which felt strange since I still technically lived there. But I had been living at Cooper's house for months, and I didn't want to barge in on Lauren unannounced.

She opened the door looking confused. But all it took was one look at my face for her to understand.

She wrapped me in her arms and ushered me inside where we sat on the sofa in the cramped living room.

"Felicity, I'm so sorry. Is it Cooper?"

"He broke up with me before I could even tell him about the baby." I wiped at the tears. "I was all set to tell him. But then he ended it, and... I just had to get out of there."

Lauren nodded in understanding. "What happened? What did he say?"

"He wants to stick to the terms of the agreement." My voice cracked as I answered her, and I paused to catch my breath. "He was so cold, Lauren. He was talking like I was just another business transaction."

Lauren reached for a box of tissues and handed me one, putting her arm around my shoulders. "You deserve so much better than that. After everything the two of you have been through. Does he still want you to go to the trial?"

"Yes," I sniveled. "He wants me to pretend to be his fiancée in court on Monday. But after the judge's decision, he wants me to move out."

"Wow," Lauren murmured. "That *is* cold. And strange. I thought you guys were getting so close. It sounded like the four of you were starting to become a family."

That made me sob harder. "That's what hurts so much. It *did* feel like we were becoming a family. And then Cooper just stomped it all out."

She narrowed her eyes. "So he was just using you for sex?"

"It seems that way." I shook my head in confusion. "I guess he was just having a good time with me. And then he got bored. What else could it be?"

Lauren folded her arms over her chest. "I don't know. It doesn't make sense, especially since his daughters love you."

"I was so stupid, Lauren. I was hoping he would ask me to stay, to move in with him and the girls." I laughed bitterly. "I thought he might be falling in love with me. What an idiot. Of course he wasn't. He was just using me."

She squeezed my hand. "You're not an idiot, Felicity. He was sending you a lot of mixed messages. You're not stupid for thinking there could be more."

"Guys like him don't go for girls like me," I said. "Not for the long-term. I was nothing but a good time to him."

Lauren chewed on her bottom lip. "Do you think it has something to do with your dad finding out?"

"I don't think so. Cooper and my dad are friends, but Cooper's not the type of guy to let him run his life. I don't think he would break up with me just to make my father happy."

"No, probably not," Lauren agreed.

"And now I'll have to tell him I'm pregnant even though he doesn't care about me." My hands flew to my abdomen, the reality of my situation sinking in. "I'll be tied to Cooper for the rest of my life," I whispered. "I'll never be able to get over him and move on. I'll have to see him whenever the kid goes to visit."

I sank into the couch cushion, wallowing in despair.

"You'll get over him," Lauren said. "It will take some time, but you're not going to spend the rest of your life pining away for this guy. I won't let you."

I met her eyes. "I don't know, Lauren. I... I really love him."

"You'll find someone else to love, Felicity. In the meantime, you'll have a cute little baby. And I'll be by your side, so you'll never be alone. Everything will be okay."

I nodded, but I knew she was wrong about finding someone else to love. And about everything being okay.

I had never known anyone like Cooper. I'd never felt this way about any man.

Deep down, I knew there would always be a gaping hole in my heart where he once was.

28

COOPER

*E*ach minute that Felicity was gone felt like an eternity.

I carried my glass of whiskey into my office, hoping to distract myself with work. But as soon as I powered on my computer, I knew it was a lost cause. I shut it off immediately. I couldn't focus on work now.

I went up to check on the girls. They were sleeping soundly, and I pulled the covers over Eva. She had a tendency to kick them off in her sleep.

Lily was in her own bed. I always used to find her in Eva's bed, but soon after Felicity arrived, she had stopped crawling in with Eva. I knew it was because she was doing better with Felicity's presence in the house.

My daughters' faces were innocent and peaceful as they slept. I wished I could shield them from any pain and suffering forever.

But even if I won the case and kept custody of them, things could never return to the way they were before. The girls had bonded with Felicity.

And I had told Felicity to leave.

What the hell was wrong with me?

I left the room and closed the door softly behind me. I picked up the whiskey I had set on the hall table and trudged toward my bedroom.

But first, I poked my head into the sewing studio, flipping the light switch on. The girls had been drawing in here. I picked up their latest creations and unfolded the papers.

Fuck.

My heart constricted to see my daughters' love for Felicity depicted in crayon—happy scenes of the girls together with her.

Quickly, I looked away from the drawings. It was too painful to see them right now. I folded them again, but I carried them out of the room with me. They were too precious to be lost or thrown away by accident.

In my bedroom, I shut the door and switched the bedside light on, though I wouldn't be able to sleep until Felicity was back safe and sound.

I knew exactly what was wrong with me.

I was in love with Felicity, but I was too broken to be with her.

Felicity's life was just getting started. She was young and full of possibilities. She didn't need to get saddled with a middle-aged man with a family and a slew of problems. A guy who couldn't even trust himself enough to let his guard down.

Standing at the window, I stared into the darkness below. Wherever she was, I hoped Felicity was okay. I hoped she wasn't feeling this gut-wrenching pain that I was. But I knew she wasn't exactly having a good time. I'd seen the look of hurt on her face.

If she decided not to show up at the trial on Monday, I couldn't blame her.

I had made a mess of this whole thing. I couldn't keep my dick in my pants around her. That was my first mistake. Then I let myself get too close to her emotionally. And in doing so, I gave her mixed signals. I made her think that we had a future together.

I'd gotten jealous and possessive because I thought she had been cheating on me that night she was out walking. And then the next day I told her I didn't want to be with anyone else.

We had never fully agreed to be exclusive, but that was about as close as you could get.

But then I pulled away from her like it had never happened. Like this whole thing had been nothing more than a business arrangement.

Felicity had every right to be furious with me. Hell, I was furious with myself.

I downed the amber liquid in the glass and picked up my phone. At least there would be one person happy with the way things had turned out.

When the call connected, Marsh's voice came in, gruff and blustering.

"Cooper, I don't have time to listen to your bullshit excuses," he started.

"It's over," I said flatly.

He paused. "What's over?"

"Felicity and I. I told her we couldn't see each other anymore after the trial. We agreed to keep things professional and stick to our original agreement."

For once, Marsh was speechless. He didn't say anything for so long I wondered if he had hung up.

"Are you still there?" I asked.

"I'm here," he answered. "So you're still going through with this pretend engagement?"

"Yeah. I don't have much of a choice at this point. My attorney's already submitted my background information to Judge Graves, along with Felicity's name as my fiancée. I would lose the case for sure if it fell through now."

"And she's still going through with it?" he asked quietly.

"Yeah, she says she'll show up at court." I left it at that. I didn't need to tell Marsh everything that had gone down between us.

Another long pause. "Did she say anything else?"

"No." A bitter chuckle escaped my mouth. "Just that she's pissed at me. And I don't blame her."

Marsh cleared his throat. "I never thought you would call it off just to please me."

I laughed again. "I didn't do it to please you. Believe it or not, people can make their own life decisions regardless of whether or not Marsh Hayes approves."

He grunted. "So why'd you do it?"

"Because of something you said in my office. *Not* the part about me not loving her. You were wrong about that. I do love her."

Marsh scoffed. I ignored it and continued.

"It's because you were right about one thing. I shouldn't tie her down. She has her whole life ahead of her. She doesn't need to be roped down by a guy who's screwed up his life already."

Maybe it was the whiskey making me spill my guts, but we were in relatively unfamiliar territory. Marsh and I hadn't had a conversation like this in years. Not since my divorce with Gen. Back then, he'd opened up to me about his grief after losing his wife. But since those days, we'd kept our conversations a lot more surface level.

After a long moment of silence, Marsh spoke slowly. "Well, maybe it's for the best."

"Yeah. Anyway, I wanted you to know since you were so upset about it. Keep that blood pressure down and all."

"Right. I'll see you on Monday at the trial."

"You're going?"

"Yes. You could use the moral support. And you don't need to worry about me talking to Judge Graves."

"I don't?"

"No. I'll keep my mouth shut. And, Cooper... good luck."

"Thanks."

We ended the call, and I tossed my phone on the bed.

Outside, headlights turned into the driveway. I watched from the window as Felicity parked her car, got out, and opened the front door. Her beautiful face was red and tear-stained. And it was all my fault.

But she was keeping her word and spending the night here. Just as she had agreed to.

I fought the urge to run downstairs and confess everything to her.

I'd been lying through my teeth when I said I didn't want a future with her. I loved her and I wanted nothing more than to spend my life by her side.

But that would only end up hurting her in the long run. It was better to hurt her now, when she could still bounce back. She was still young. Her life was full of possibilities.

I would just be a millstone around her neck. A heavy burden, weighing her down.

So I got into bed and waited for the alcohol to lull me to sleep, feeling emptier than I ever had.

The Fiancé Hoax

The next morning, I felt like shit. And it wasn't just the hangover.

I emerged from my bedroom, squinting at the bright light, and woke the girls. Felicity's door was shut, but her car was parked outside. Maybe she'd had a bad night, too, and was sleeping in.

I got the girls dressed and fed. I gulped down extra coffee and a few bites of toast so I could feel somewhat human.

Upstairs, footsteps came from Felicity's room. It sounded like she was waking up and moving around, but she didn't make an appearance in the kitchen. I couldn't blame her.

Eva and Lily noticed my ragged appearance and asked if I was getting sick. I shrugged it off and hustled them into the car to drive them to school.

Despite feeling like my life was falling apart, I managed to keep it together long enough to pull into the school parking lot.

Lily spotted her teacher at the door. After I freed her from her car seat, she ran off across the yard with her backpack over her shoulders.

But Eva didn't move from her car seat. She studied my face as I leaned on the open back door, waiting for her to get out.

"Okay, your turn, Eva. Have a nice day at school."

She eyed me suspiciously. "What happened with Felicity, Daddy?"

I blinked. "What do you mean?"

"How come she's never around anymore?"

"She's busy with work," I muttered.

Eva gave me a skeptical look. Clearly, she wasn't buying that line. "And even when she *is* at home, everything's different with you guys."

I took a deep breath and looked at her.

"Eva, I know this will be hard for you and your sister. But Felicity is going to move back to her own house after the judge decides where you girls are going to live. I'm sorry for all the changes at home. But I want you to know everything I've done has been for you and Lily."

I regretted telling her so much, but Eva was so smart, there was no sense in hiding things from her. She would figure it all out anyway.

She tilted her head sideways. "But you don't want Felicity to leave, do you?"

I rubbed the back of my neck. "Eva, this is grown-up stuff. I've told you too much already."

She rolled her eyes. "Come on, Daddy. You can tell *me*." She pressed her hand to her chest dramatically.

"Well, as you figured out from the beginning, Felicity moved in to help me. If the judge thinks I have a girlfriend, then..." My voice trailed off. I couldn't believe I was telling my daughter this. "Then it will be easier for me to keep you and Lily living with me at home."

"I know all that," Eva said impatiently. She squinted at me. "But you like her, don't you?"

I nodded. "Yeah. Very much."

"And she likes you."

I looked at her. "You think so?"

"Believe me. I *know*."

I chuckled. Eva was smart, but she was eight. She didn't know about adult relationships.

"You want to be with her, and she wants to be with you," Eva explained. "Grown-ups are so silly sometimes."

I chuckled and glanced over my shoulder at the school. "Aren't you going to be late for class?"

"Nope. My teacher's not even outside yet. That means we're early." Eva shrugged.

"You've got everything figured out, don't you?"

"Yes, I do. So listen to me, Daddy. I've never seen you smile as much as when you're with Felicity. And I've seen the way she looks at you. If *you* can't see it, you're blind!"

She threw her hands into the air in frustration.

"I don't know what happened," she continued, "but now you're both acting all sad and weird. You guys are perfect for each other. Like, way more perfect than Ariel and that prince guy."

I laughed.

"I'm serious, Daddy. Like two peas in a pod. But..." She pressed her finger to her lips, thinking. "I think you must have said something wrong. Something that made her sad."

"Yeah," I admitted around the lump in my throat. "I messed up."

"So, go make it better. Tell her you're sorry and stuff."

I scratched the stubble on my jaw. "You don't think it's too late?" It was ridiculous to ask an eight-year-old for relationship advice, but here I was.

"No, but you better hurry before some other guy finds her. Felicity is the full package, Dad."

I chuckled at her choice of words.

"You can't expect her to wait for you forever," Eva added.

I nodded, letting my daughter's words sink in. As pathetic as my situation was, maybe Eva really did have the best advice for me right now.

"Lily and I love Felicity. We don't want her to leave. She doesn't want to leave, either. Plus, me and Lily want Happy Dad back."

"Happy Dad?" I asked.

"Yeah." She circled her hands through the air, gesturing toward my face. "This is Sad, Grumpy Dad. When Felicity is around, everyone's happy. We're like one big, happy family!"

I nodded, suddenly speechless and choked up.

Eva hopped out of the car and gave me a hug. "I've got to go, Daddy. My teacher's waiting for me now."

I hugged her tight. "Thanks for the advice, kiddo."

Eva ran off toward the school and shouted over her shoulder, "Anytime!"

I watched as she raced toward a cluster of her friends. Within seconds, she was laughing hysterically at something. I smiled. I was so lucky to have both my daughters.

And maybe it wasn't too late to make our family complete.

Eva was right. Grown-ups could be silly sometimes. Or maybe it was just me.

As I got in my car and pulled away, I realized I'd been a fool.

I'd let the past dictate my life. I'd made some bad decisions with Gen. But that didn't mean I couldn't love again.

Sure, there was risk. I had hurt Felicity. She might not take me back. Even if she did, a million things could go wrong that might end up hurting both of us down the road.

But I couldn't give up on her just because I'd been disappointed and disillusioned in the past.

I had to show my girls what was important in life. Sometimes you have to take a risk for something important. You have to put your heart on the line for the people that matter even if you might end up hurting like hell.

Pulling onto the highway, I picked up speed.

I couldn't hide my true feelings for Felicity anymore. Not from myself, and not from her.

I had to fix things with Felicity, the only woman I'd ever truly loved.

29

FELICITY

I woke up feeling wretched.

I had cried myself to sleep in my bedroom at Cooper's house, knowing that I would soon be leaving his home. When I finally dragged myself out of bed after sunrise, I knew I couldn't go downstairs without putting on some makeup to hide the evidence of my crying spells.

Plus, I was still dealing with morning sickness. The smell of coffee turned my stomach, but luckily I didn't throw up this time. I washed my face and got dressed, trying to convince myself everything was going to be all right.

I wasn't looking forward to seeing Cooper, but I at least wanted to see the girls. My time with them was dwindling. And I didn't want them to remember me as the sad girl with bloodshot eyes.

But by the time I had slapped on a little concealer and mascara, they were already getting into Cooper's car.

Hearing the vehicle pull away almost made me start crying again, but I composed myself. Another busy day waited for me at the boutique, so I grabbed my things and left.

My new employee was in her car in the rear parking area waiting for me when I drove up. Katie, a sweet fashion enthusiast a few years younger than me, climbed out of her sedan and waved at me.

I got out of my car and went to unlock the back door of the boutique. "Hi, Katie. I'm not late, am I?"

She gave me a bright smile. "No, you're right on time. I just wanted to get here early."

"Great." I smiled at her. "I'm so glad you could start today."

"I'm super excited to work here! I just love your designs, Felicity. I can't believe I never knew this place existed."

That seems to be a common occurrence, I thought to myself. Or it was before Cooper came along.

Katie continued chattering, and I was relieved I didn't have to make much small talk. She was a nice girl, but I didn't have the energy to be outgoing today.

"I would have been in here all the time had I known about Moonstone. I have a feeling I'm going to be spending half my paycheck on your clothes." She laughed.

I smiled, happy to have found such a sweet, cheerful employee. She was perfect. "Let me give you a quick tour, then I can train you on the cash register before we open."

"Sounds good!"

I led her through the store, showing her the various clothing sections so she could familiarize herself with the inventory. I explained the custom-made children's clothing process, and she listened intently, even jotting down a few details.

"These girls' clothes are so adorable," she gushed. "I have to get my sister in here—she'll go wild over these designs. She has two daughters."

A lump formed in my throat as I thought of Eva and Lily. "Really? How old are they?"

"Five and seven. Going on about twenty-two," Katie laughed.

I chuckled, but my heart wasn't in it. All I could think about was that I might never see Cooper and his girls again after Monday.

I turned away, hiding my face from my new employee. I had to remain professional, but all I wanted to do was crawl back into bed and hide from the world.

I trained Katie on the computer system, explaining how I handled transactions and credit card payments. She asked good questions, and I knew she would do well in the boutique. She was a quick learner, and she had a few years' experience working in retail. I thanked my lucky stars I had found her. At least something was going right.

She glanced at the front door, where a handful of people were waiting for me to open the door. "Wow! You already have customers lining up to get inside?"

I smiled. "Yeah. But that's a recent development." I turned to her, noticing she looked a little nervous at the small crowd forming. "Katie, I'm confident you are going to handle this just fine."

She grinned. "Thanks, Felicity. I'm just so happy to be here! I love this place already." She threw her arms around me in a quick hug, and I smiled. I needed that hug more than I'd realized.

"Are you ready to get started?"

She nodded. "Ready!"

I went to the front door and opened the store for the customers. They all went straight to the girls' collection. I busied myself nearby as they browsed. Katie stepped forward to answer any questions and assist them with the custom order forms. I filled in any gaps in Katie's knowledge, but she had paid close attention.

Two hours later, after I supervised Katie at the sales counter for several transactions, it was clear she was getting the hang of this. I retreated to my sewing space, ready to tackle the projects I had waiting for me.

I was so grateful for my newfound success. Hiring an employee was a big step for me. So much of this would never have been possible without Cooper's help. Of course, I was the one who had put in the long hours. This entire store had been a labor of love for me. But without Cooper's investment and business coaching, I never would have gotten so far.

I only wished he was around to celebrate with me. That I could fill him in about the store's progress every evening over dinner. That we would be there for each other and the girls.

Just like we'd done for a few short weeks... until he pulled away.

Somehow, the thrill of success didn't taste nearly as sweet as I expected. Without him by my side, nothing seemed as good.

Now that I had experienced the joy of spending time with him and his daughters, feeling like a real family, how could my store's success compare?

How would anything *ever* compare?

Don't cry now.

I could fall apart later, in the privacy of my bedroom at Cooper's house when everyone was asleep. For now, I had to hide how I felt. I needed to get through the next two days at Cooper's house, plus the trial on Monday. I'd sit by his side and play the loving fiancée in court.

And after that, I would return to my old apartment. Without Cooper, Eva, or Lily.

I'd have to be content with the memories of the times we'd shared.

I planned to tell Cooper about the pregnancy after the trial. I had waited two weeks so far. What was another couple of days?

He needed to focus on the hearing, and I didn't want my news to distract or upset him when he was fighting to keep his daughters.

I expected him to be upset about the pregnancy. But I knew he would step up and support the baby. He'd probably want to be in our child's life, too.

Because that was the kind of guy Cooper was. He was there for everyone he cared about.

Too bad he didn't care enough about me.

Tears threatened to spill down my eyes, and I wasn't sure I could hold them back any longer.

I stood up from my design table. I needed to get to the restroom before I started sobbing in front of everyone.

But a sudden movement outside the glass front door caught my eye.

The door flew open, and Cooper charged in with a bouquet of flowers clutched in his hand. He was breathing hard, and his eyes were wild and intense.

Everyone in the boutique stopped what they were doing to gape at him.

He scanned the room, then zeroed in on me. He crossed the space with determination and stood before me in the middle of the store.

His blue eyes locked on mine, making my stomach do somersaults, and he took my hand.

"Felicity, I made a terrible mistake. I haven't been honest

with you. I told you that I wanted to go our separate ways after Monday. That we got too close to each other. And that we needed to split up to protect my daughters. It was all a lie."

My heart was racing. What was he doing? I was totally confused. But I was also aware of Katie and the customers watching the scene unfold before them.

"Cooper, maybe we should talk about this in private," I murmured.

He shook his head stubbornly. "No. Right here. Right now. I don't care who hears me."

I nodded in a daze. "Okay."

"The truth was that I didn't trust myself not to screw everything up again. I made so many mistakes in my past that I stopped believing in love. But that's stupid. That's like not believing in the air we're breathing. I do love you, Felicity. I've loved you for a long time."

"I love you too, Cooper." The words tumbled out without a second thought. "But... why did you say all that the other day? Why did you pull away from me?"

"Because I was an idiot." He took a breath and spoke in a lower voice. "I thought that because I misjudged Gen all those years ago, I couldn't trust myself when it came to love. So I kept telling myself everything with you was only temporary. But I couldn't deny how I felt. I knew how special you were that first night I met you sneaking into your dad's party."

He grinned, and I couldn't help but smile at the memory.

"And when you came to live with me and the girls, you made me the happiest man alive."

I nodded. "You made me happy too, Cooper. Which is why I was so confused when you grew distant."

"I'm sorry for being such a jackass for so long. I thought I was protecting myself and my kids. When really, I was hurting everyone involved. And... I thought if I was honest with you, I'd tie you down. Your life is just beginning. I figured you'd be settling to be with a messed-up guy like me. I've been through a lot of shit, and I thought you deserved someone better. Someone who's not so... broken."

I blinked at him. "Are you serious? Cooper, you're not broken. And I've been through some shit, too, you know. Just because you've been through a divorce doesn't mean you're damaged goods."

He chuckled. "I know. But a few days ago, my history felt like a big wall between us." He squeezed my hand and searched my face. "But I'm ready to knock down all those walls. I want to be the man you deserve, Felicity. I want you to stay with me and the girls, if you can forgive me."

He looked down at the flowers he held, as if he'd suddenly remembered them. "These are for you."

He handed me the bouquet. They were my favorite—daffodils and purple tulips. He had remembered what I told Lily weeks ago. Not even Lauren knew I loved this combination.

"These are for you, too." He handed me two folded papers he pulled from his pocket. "I found these last night in your studio at home."

I unfolded them and gasped at what I saw.

Eva's crayon drawing depicted me, with long brown hair, sitting at a table working at a sewing machine. Two little blonde girls worked beside me on their own smaller machines. Small red hearts floated through the air.

I looked at the second paper. Lily had drawn a peach-colored house to match the stucco of Cooper's home. In the front yard, Cooper, Eva, Lily, and I all held hands and smiled.

At the top, in big, uneven kid letters, Lily had written one word.

Family.

I was speechless. Through the tears in my eyes, I looked up at Cooper.

He went down on one knee, taking my hand in both of his.

"Felicity, you make me happier than I ever thought possible. I want to spend my life with you. Would you do me the honor of marrying me? For real?"

He took out a velvet box from his pocket and opened it to reveal a diamond ring.

This one was nothing like the gaudy ring he'd bought me for the fake engagement. This ring was perfect—romantic, vintage-inspired, and gorgeous.

I looked in his eyes, and I saw all the love there. I'd never been more certain of anything in my life.

Nodding through the tears, I laughed. "Yes, Cooper. Yes, I will marry you."

He broke out in a grin, stood up and wrapped me in his arms, lifting me off the floor. I laughed and shrieked as everyone in the store applauded. Katie cheered, and one of the customers wiped at her eyes.

But there was one more thing to talk about.

Cooper set me down, his eyes sparkling. When he looked at me, his brow furrowed.

"What's wrong?"

My stomach twisted. What if my news made him change his mind? I couldn't wait until after the trial. I had to tell him now.

"I need to tell you something. Outside."

30

COOPER

I followed Felicity through the rear exit of the store. I was confused, unsure what else there was to talk about. Her face was tight with worry.

"Felicity, whatever it is, we'll work through it."

The door shut behind us, and we stood in the sunny parking area. I brought my hand to her cheek and caressed her soft skin. "Did something happen?"

She nodded, looking up at me. "Yes, something happened." She drew a deep breath that filled her chest. "Cooper, I'm pregnant."

It took a moment for her words to register in my brain. "Pregnant?" I repeated.

"Yes. It must have happened the first time we slept together."

I stared at her in shock. "But how? I thought you were on birth control this whole time."

"I was. But the pill doesn't work if you puke it all up."

The memory of her stomach bug returned to me. I smacked my palm against my forehead. "Of course. I didn't even think of that."

She chewed her bottom lip. "I guess neither of us did."

"Did you know all this time?"

Her eyebrows knit together in worry. "No. I found out two weeks ago."

I blinked at her, speechless and stunned.

As the silence stretched out between us, her face fell.

"This is exactly what I was afraid of," she said. "This is why I didn't tell you until now."

"What do you mean?"

She shook her head. "You're obviously upset. You made it clear you didn't want any more kids. And now you have another one on the way. I... I understand if you change your mind about getting married."

A smile pulled at my mouth as I looked at her beautiful face. Then I started to laugh. A chuckle at first, then it developed into a full belly laugh.

She frowned. "Are you laughing at me?"

I wrapped her in my arms and pulled her against my chest. "Yes. But in the best possible way. You're adorable, and I love you." I paused to look down at her. "And we're having a baby!"

She squinted up at me. "So you're not mad?"

"No, I'm not mad. I'm thrilled you're pregnant, Felicity. I can't wait to have a baby with you." I bent down and kissed her.

As I pulled back to look at her, she smiled. "Really?"

"Really. I'm sorry you felt you couldn't tell me sooner." I stopped to recall the events of the past two weeks. "But I understand why—I was pulling away from you. It explains a lot, actually. But none of that matters now. What matters is that we're going to be together. You, me, the girls... and now a new baby." I grinned at her.

"But you said you didn't want any more kids."

I shrugged. "That was before I could admit what you meant to me. I was afraid to commit. And if I'm being honest, I was afraid of getting hurt and disappointed again. But a very wise soul helped me to see how stupid that was."

"Who was that?"

"My eight-year-old."

Felicity laughed. "Eva really is some kind of sage."

I nodded, my mind racing. "She and Lily are going to be so happy to have a new baby brother or sister." I took her hand in mine. "But most of all, they're going to be thrilled that you're staying with us."

"They couldn't be any happier than me." She stood on her tiptoes and wrapped her arms around my neck. I lifted her off the ground, spun her around, and kissed her once more.

As I set her back on her feet, she gave me a playful smile.

"Are you interested in getting out of here to celebrate?"

~

Felicity's new employee assured her she could handle the store alone for a couple of hours. Katie waved us off as Felicity promised to check her phone in case Katie needed help.

I laced my fingers through Felicity's as I drove her back home. To *our* home.

Inside, I carried her upstairs to my bedroom. Between kisses, we undressed each other. I lay her down on the bed. Moving my hands over her soft belly and hips, I kissed her delicate skin. I had missed the touch of her body so much.

"I'm already starting to get a bit of a belly," she said self-consciously.

I planted a line of kisses down her abdomen. "You're more beautiful than ever, Felicity."

She smiled and reached out for me. "Come up here."

I lay on top of her, careful not to crush her. She bent her knees and allowed me to settle between her soft thighs. Cradling her head in my hands, I kissed her deeply.

She moaned and lifted her hips. The soft folds between her legs were already dripping wet, and she rubbed herself against the length of my erection.

"You have no idea how horny I've been," she said. "I guess these pregnancy hormones are really kicking in now."

I grinned. "I'll be happy to be of service whenever you need."

Lacing her fingers behind my neck, she clung to me.

"I need you inside me," she murmured.

She was so wet that I only needed to position the head of my cock at her entrance and with one push, I slipped inside. She closed her eyes for just a moment as I entered her, then she held my gaze as I pushed all the way in.

I paused when I was fully inside her tight heat. "I love you so much, Felicity."

"I love you too, Cooper."

She wrapped her legs around my hips as I began to move inside her. A tiny whimper escaped her lips, and I paused.

"I'm not hurting you, am I?"

She smiled, her eyelids heavy. "No. It feels wonderful."

Her back arched upward, pressing her breasts against my torso. I moved one hand over her curves, sucking one nipple and then the other into my mouth. My hand traced the shape of her body, over her hips and thighs, then up to caress her face.

She was finally mine, and I wanted to explore every bit of her body.

Felicity writhed underneath me, and I knew she was getting close. She dug her nails into my back and clenched her muscles around my cock.

I kissed her breathlessly, and she gasped into my mouth.

"Cooper, yes," she murmured as she lost herself in orgasm.

Her muscles contracted around me, milking my cock. I couldn't hold back any longer. My body tightened and tensed before it surrendered its release deep inside her.

We were still for several moments. I rested my head on her chest, and she moved her fingers through my hair as we both caught our breath.

Finally, I rolled off her and lay on my back. I slid my arm under her shoulders and pulled her close.

"We're having a baby," I said. I was still in awe.

She grinned at me. "Yes, we are."

Slowly, though, her face fell as some new doubt entered her mind.

"Cooper, what about the trial? What if... what if the judge..."

I pressed a finger to her lips before she could finish that question.

"We're going to win, Felicity. We have to."

But deep down, I was just as terrified of what might happen as she was.

31

FELICITY

After we cuddled in bed for a while, Cooper and I returned to the boutique.

Katie had managed the place on her own just fine. I knew she was curious about why Cooper proposed when I had already been wearing an engagement ring, but she was kind enough to not shower me with questions. I had a feeling we would become friends, though, and I could fill her in later.

I took the opportunity to show Cooper the changes around the store. He was excited to see the steady stream of customers, and he spent the better part of an hour going through my financial statements and bookkeeping.

"Congratulations," he said as he pulled me against his chest. Katie had just left—I'd sent her home early and closed the store to celebrate the engagement. "You have a thriving business, Felicity. And it's all because of your hard work."

I laughed. "That, and your business coaching. Plus, the check you wrote me didn't hurt."

He buried his face in my neck, planting kisses along my

shoulder and collarbone. "That was nothing. You did the real work."

Heat flooded between my legs. "You better stop before you get me all worked up again. I told you these pregnancy hormones are out of control."

"Good," he murmured as he grabbed my rear. "I can't get enough of you."

I pushed him away gently with my hand on his chest. "Save some for tonight," I laughed. "You can show me exactly how much you've missed me."

He growled in frustration, but he backed off. "Are you ready to go home? The girls will be waiting for us."

I smiled. "I'm ready."

And I was. I was ready for anything, as long as Cooper and I were together.

Back home, we had dinner with Eva and Lily, and it was just like things had been before. Only better.

Cooper didn't say anything to them about his proposal or my pregnancy. I knew he was waiting until after the custody trial to tell them the news. But the girls picked up on the happier atmosphere, and we felt like a family once more.

We put them to bed together, and the girls requested I read them a bedtime story. Cooper and I exchanged glances as I read the book. I felt like a teenager again, sneaking peeks at him. I just couldn't stop smiling.

We kissed them goodnight and left their room. In the hallway, I turned to him.

I fidgeted with my hair, pulling it to the side over one shoulder. "I guess I should still sleep in my own bed tonight." If Cooper wasn't ready to share a bedroom for his daughters' sake, I could understand.

But he looked down at me with a lopsided smile. "Are

you crazy? We're getting married and having a baby together." He took my hands in his. "I want you with me tonight. I want you *every* night."

I grinned as he took my hand and led me to bed.

～

"Good morning, beautiful."

I opened my eyes to see his gorgeous face smiling at me.

A goofy grin spread across my face.

It was the first night we had slept together, and I felt giddy.

For a moment, I worried that it had all been a dream. Maybe I was *still* dreaming.

But as I took in his sparkling blue eyes, I knew it was real. He scooped me up in his arms and cuddled me, taking my hand in his.

I looked down at my new engagement ring. It was perfect, just like Cooper. And we were getting *married*.

"So you like that ring better than the first one?" he asked.

"Yes. Don't get me wrong—the first one was pretty, but it was a little... well..."

"Gaudy?"

I laughed. "Yes."

He grinned. "I chose that one so the judge would be able to see it from his bench."

"He'd be able to see that rock from outer space, Cooper."

We laughed, and he tickled me.

With a happy sigh, he moved his hands over my abdomen. "You're going to be such a good mother, Felicity."

"I hope so," I said. "I'm a little nervous about it."

"You'll be fine. You're already so great with Eva and Lily."

I squirmed against him in excitement. "It's going to be so much fun. I have a lot of work to do in the next few months. I'll have to hire more staff and train a manager to take care of everything while I'm on maternity leave."

"You've got time to figure that out. And, by the way, I noticed in your records how many repeat customers you have now. That's a good sign, Felicity. It means your success will be sustainable."

I sighed happily. "I can't believe how well everything is working out. Now we just need the trial to go our way tomorrow."

"It will," he said before he kissed me.

I snuggled against his body. "It will be so cute to see the girls with the baby. Do you think they'll want a little brother or a little sister?"

Cooper thought for a second. "It won't matter. Lily will fall in love with the kid no matter what. And Eva will be happy to have someone new to take under her wing."

I giggled. "You're right."

The bedroom door swung open, and Eva and Lily walked in the room. At first, I panicked, pulling the covers up, even though we were both wearing pajamas. But Cooper remained calm, and I followed suit.

Eva and Lily froze in surprise as they realized I was in bed with Cooper. Then Eva moved closer with Lily following. They stood at the foot of the bed.

"Good morning, girls," Cooper said with a smile. He sat up in bed, and I did, too. "You're up early."

"No, you're just late, Daddy," Eva said. "We always get up early on Saturdays to watch cartoons."

"Right," Cooper said sheepishly.

They were silent for a moment. Lily looked between Cooper and me.

"Do you two love each other?" she asked us.

Cooper grinned. "Yes. Very much so."

I nodded beside him. "Yes, I love your dad."

Eva tilted her head and looked at me. "Felicity, does this mean you're going to stay forever?"

I smiled at her. "I have no plans to leave."

Eva and Lily exchanged excited looks. Then Lily came closer to me. "Are you going to be our mommy?"

I hesitated, touched by her sweet, innocent question, but unsure how to answer. I spoke gently.

"Well, Gen will always be your mother. But I love you both very much. And I will be here for you in any way that you want."

Lily thought about that, then her face lit up.

"Okay."

She climbed on the bed and crawled into my lap, lacing her arms around my neck. I held her close, smoothing her blonde hair and kissing her head.

Eva surprised me by climbing up next to her sister and reaching her arms toward me. I hugged and kissed them both, my heart filling with joy.

"I'm glad you're going to stay, Felicity," Eva said. Lily nodded her agreement.

"Me, too," I said, laughing through the tears that made my vision watery. "So happy."

Eva gave her dad a knowing smile, but she didn't say anything.

"All right, you hooligans," Cooper said. "Who wants pancakes for breakfast?"

"Me!" Eva and Lily shouted in unison.

"Oh, good. You're still alive," Lauren answered my phone call sarcastically. "I've been texting and calling you like crazy."

I stood in the kitchen, leaning on the island. I'd taken the opportunity after breakfast to call Lauren on my cell.

Cooper was playing with Eva and Lily in the living room, and Inga had just arrived for her shift.

I was dying to tell Lauren my news.

"Sorry. I've kind of had my hands full."

"Please tell me they've been full with something besides work."

"They have. Cooper came to the store and apologized."

"I knew it!" Lauren said. "He called the flower shop early and requested that bouquet. When he came to pick it up, he was super excited. What did he say?"

"That he got distant and pushed me away because he was jaded after his ex-wife, basically. But he said he loves me and he wants to try this for real. And, Lauren..." I held out my left hand to admire my new ring. "He proposed!"

Lauren squealed so loudly I had to hold the phone away from my head before my eardrum burst.

"Oh, my God! Like, *proposed*, proposed? For real this time?"

I grinned. "For real this time. He did it in the middle of the store with everyone watching. Hang on, I'll send you a picture of the ring." I snapped a picture on my phone and texted it to her.

"Felicity, that's a gorgeous ring! And it's the perfect style for you. He picked that out by himself?"

"He did. And it means so much more than that giant rock I was wearing before."

"This is amazing! I knew you guys had something special. Ever since that first night at your dad's party. Congrats, girl. You deserve it." She paused. "But what about the pregnancy? Did you tell him?"

"Yes. I was scared he was going to be upset or even call off the whole thing. But he was actually happy. Like, over-the-moon happy."

"Yay! I'm so glad."

"Me too. We haven't told the girls about the baby yet, but we will soon. They're excited I'm going to stay."

"I bet. Those girls love you."

"And I love them, too." I smiled. "I never would have expected things to go this way, but... I couldn't be happier, Lauren."

"See? I told you it would all work out."

I smiled. "You were right."

"When can we get together to celebrate?"

"Soon. And hopefully we'll have something else to celebrate after Monday."

"Right," Lauren said. "The custody trial. Do you guys have a good feeling about it?"

"I think so, but Cooper is pretty nervous. We both are."

The doorbell rang, and I heard Cooper talking to someone at the front door.

"He's going to win for sure," Lauren said.

"I hope so. Hey, I better go. I'll talk to you soon, okay?"

"Okay, keep me posted. And let's all go get drinks soon."

"Deal. Love you, Lauren."

"Love you, babe."

I ended the call with a smile. I couldn't wait to see Lauren in person and tell her more about everything that had happened.

But something about the tense voices coming from the

foyer made my stomach tighten. I set the phone down on the kitchen island and walked toward the front door.

Cooper was talking to an older, well-dressed man standing with a briefcase in the doorway. Cooper looked at me as I rounded the corner.

"Felicity, this is my attorney handling the custody case. Nick Worcester, Felicity Hayes."

I smiled and shook his hand. "Nice to meet you."

"Nick, let's talk in my study," Cooper said. "Felicity, you should come, too."

Inga popped her head into the hallway. "Want me to take the girls to the park?"

"Good idea," Cooper said. "Thanks, Inga."

She went to the living room to get the girls, who cheered at the mention of an outing. They were bouncing off the walls after breakfast.

I followed Cooper into his office, and he held the door open for Nick and me. My shoulders were tense as we all sat around Cooper's desk.

Was it normal for Nick to visit his clients at home the weekend before a trial? I couldn't remember my dad ever making house calls to go over last-minute details with clients. Especially not on a Saturday.

Cooper looked at Nick. "What's the news?"

"It's not looking good, Cooper. As you know, I have a source in Gen's attorney's office. And she told me they have proof your engagement is fake."

Cooper froze. "What proof?"

"I don't have the details," Nick said. "All I know is that a witness has been summoned to testify. And there are some pictures."

"Well, we already know about the pictures," Cooper said.

The Fiancé Hoax

I cringed, remembering the private eye spying on me when I wasn't wearing my engagement ring.

"But this is the first I've heard of a witness being called to testify for Gen's side." Cooper's jaw tightened. "Do you have the name?"

"Ruth Fulton. She's an employee of Marsh Hayes."

I gasped. My father's executive assistant?

All at once, I felt sick. And furious.

My father was surely behind this. He must have told Ruth what happened with Cooper and me.

"I thought you said Marsh wasn't going to say anything," Nick said.

Cooper shook his head, his eyes dark. "That's what he told me."

"Well, apparently Ms. Fulton is planning to testify that you and Felicity faked the engagement to win the case."

Cooper leaned back in his seat. "Fuck," he muttered under his breath.

I swallowed. This was bad.

"What do you advise?" Cooper asked Nick.

Nick heaved a sigh. "There's only one option. You'll have to tell the judge the truth before Gen's lawyer drops this bombshell."

"Fine. Though I doubt Judge Graves is going to take that news well." Cooper leaned forward to scrub his face with his hands, then looked up at Nick between his fingers. "Do you think we have a shot in hell?"

Nick paused, then lifted his briefcase from the floor to the desk and popped it open. "I have some ideas for your opening statement. Let's discuss them now."

My heart sank. Nick didn't answer the question. This was really bad.

Nick began to coach Cooper on what to say. I knew

Cooper was taking the news badly, but he remained calm and collected enough to listen attentively.

Nick also gave me some advice on what to say if I was questioned. When I was no longer needed, I excused myself.

Curling my hands into fists at my sides, I charged through the house. In the kitchen, I snatched my phone from the island and angrily punched my father's phone number.

It rang twice, then he answered.

"Hello, Felicity."

"Why did you tell Ruth that Cooper and I were faking the engagement for his custody hearing?"

Dad paused, then spoke in a bewildered voice. "I—I didn't. I haven't told her anything."

"Then why is she going to testify for Gen's attorney on Monday?"

After a silence, he spoke. "I have no idea, Felicity. But I assure you I said nothing to her. It's news to me that she's planning to testify."

I was so angry that his words barely sank in. "Did you talk to Drew, Gen's private investigator? Will you be testifying against us as well, Dad?"

"No, of course not." He sounded genuine, but I wasn't sure I could trust him. Right now, I just needed some sure footing. I was confused and scared.

"I'm honestly shocked that Ruth is being called to testify. I promise I didn't tell her anything." He paused again. "Unless..."

"Unless what?"

"Unless she overheard me the other day," Dad said sheepishly.

"When? What were you saying?"

"The day I found out you're... pregnant, I might have had some angry outbursts back in my office."

I narrowed my eyes, my anger building. "So you told her I was pregnant, too?"

"No, I didn't tell her anything directly," Dad said. "But, I was probably ranting about it to myself in my office after seeing you. I was so furious about the whole thing. Maybe I was a little indiscreet."

"*Indiscreet*? Really, Dad? You were ranting in your office about our engagement being fake? It's a wonder they haven't summoned half your staff."

"I'm sorry, Felicity. I was upset. I don't really remember what I said. That day was a bit of a blur. But Ruth must have overheard something."

I gripped the edge of the island and squeezed my eyes shut. "I can't believe this."

"I'm telling the truth, Felicity. I meant it when I told Cooper I wouldn't say anything. Not to the judge, and not to Gen's attorney. I'm just as surprised as you are that Ruth would pull a stunt like this."

I chewed on my bottom lip. I was angry, but he did sound sorry about it. I unclenched my fists and took a breath.

"Okay. I believe you, Dad. But why would Ruth do this to me? I know she and I were never close, but why does she want to screw me over? And why does she want to hurt two little girls who need their dad?"

"You know Ruth has always been a stickler for the rules. But honestly, she probably didn't intend for this to happen."

I scoffed. "What else would her intentions be?"

"She probably said something without thinking it through. You know, I saw that Drew character lurking around the parking lot at my law firm last week. He must have cornered Ruth to question her. And she probably repeated something to Drew about the engagement being a farce. By saying too much, she got herself summoned to testify."

I wrapped an arm around my waist, feeling nauseous again. "She might make us lose the case, Dad."

"I really am sorry, Felicity. And I truly hope it doesn't come to that. I'll be in touch with Cooper to see if there's anything I can do." He inhaled sharply. "This is why you never should've gotten mixed up in my colleague's personal life."

I bristled, and my stomach rolled. I knew he was trying, but he still believed that Cooper and I weren't right for each other.

"Those girls belong with us, Dad. Please don't try to ruin this."

"I'm not trying to break you up, Felicity. I know you believe you have something lasting with Cooper. But remember, this whole engagement thing was fake."

"Not anymore."

"What do you mean?"

"He proposed to me today, Dad."

He was silent on the other end. Speechless, probably.

"Cooper and I love each other," I said. "You're just going to have to accept that we're together."

He started to protest, but I cut him off.

"I've got to go, Dad. I'll talk to you later."

I ended the call and hurried to the bathroom where I bent over the toilet to throw up.

I wasn't sure if it was the morning sickness or hearing this terrible news that was making me sick, but I felt awful.

Standing, I rinsed my mouth out, washed my hands, and looked at myself in the mirror.

My heart was pounding. If Cooper lost this case, it would destroy him. It would destroy everything I cared about too.

And it would all be my fault.

I should have stood up to my dad a long time ago. I should have told him that he couldn't control my life. Now his volatile emotions and indiscretion threatened to rip everything apart.

Just when things were starting to go right, *this* happened.

I walked out of the bathroom slowly. Cooper's and Nick's voices lofted through the hallway. Nick said goodbye and left, and Cooper closed the front door behind him.

I walked into the foyer, and Cooper's eyes met mine.

His brow was furrowed with worry. He reached for me, and I moved to him. We held each other in silence, each of us hoping for a miracle.

32

COOPER

"It's going to work," Felicity whispered to me. "It *has* to."

On Monday afternoon, I sat in the courtroom between Nick and Felicity.

I wiped my palms on my pants and gave Felicity a smile.

She had been nothing but supportive all weekend, brainstorming ideas and approaches with me, listening, offering suggestions. But above all, knowing she was there for me meant everything.

Marsh had called to apologize about Ruth. I knew he regretted what had happened. Though I was pissed off at him on Saturday, my anger had subsided.

Marsh was a good guy deep down, and he just wanted what was best for his daughter. I could understand that.

I knew he wasn't trying to hurt me or the case. Unfortunately, his indiscretion had done exactly that.

I met Felicity's gaze and reached for her hand to squeeze it. She wore her new engagement ring, the real one. The love in her eyes somehow made me feel like everything would work out, even if my brain was telling me there was no way I could win this case.

Being with Felicity made me feel like we still had a shot. She gave me hope.

I had avoided looking at Gen's side of the courtroom, but I snuck a peek now. She sat next to her lawyer. She had done her best to look competent, wearing a tailored suit with her blonde hair curling down her shoulders. She stared straight ahead, paying me no mind.

Behind her, her two brothers glared at me. Gen's older brothers thought their sister could do no wrong. They had never liked me, and the feeling was mutual. Based on the mean-spirited way they treated Eva and Lily—including cruelly teasing Lily about her shyness—I had hoped to never see them again after the divorce.

But the biggest go-to-hell look thrown my way came from Gen's mother, Jackie. She'd been a thorn in my side during my time with Gen. I'd always suspected Jackie was a toxic influence on Gen, encouraging her to be a social climber.

I wouldn't have been surprised if Jackie had pushed Gen to go after full custody... and the ample financial support.

Looking away from Gen's family, I scanned the rest of the courtroom. Ruth sat in the back, clearly uncomfortable and regretful. Marsh sat in the row behind us.

My eyes flicked back to Gen, and this time, she was looking at me. She wore a smug smile on her face. Obviously, she was confident she was going to win custody.

"Don't worry about her," Felicity whispered to me. "We're going to win this."

I smiled and nodded, focusing on Felicity's hazel eyes. I only hoped she was right. But I couldn't deny that the cards were stacked against me.

The door to the judge's chamber opened, and we all rose to our feet.

Judge Graves emerged in his black robe. He was heavy-set with thick gray hair, and he moved slowly to his seat.

He looked stern. Not the type of guy to be very forgiving of mistakes.

After he settled in the chair behind his stand, he opened a folder and shuffled some papers. He gestured for us to sit down.

In a booming voice, he read the case number, and my throat closed up.

This was it—the hour I'd been dreading and anticipating for months. I made myself focus.

"Geneviève Barra versus Cooper Pierce," the judge announced in a monotone. "Motion filed by Ms. Barra. I have reviewed the history of this case."

Nick stood up. "Your Honor, my client would like to make a statement."

The judge nodded with a bored expression on his face. "Go ahead."

Gen jumped to her feet. "Your Honor, I would like to speak first."

Judge Graves ignored her. "Go ahead, Mr. Pierce."

I stood up. "Your Honor, I made a mistake. Three months ago, I asked this young woman beside me, Felicity Hayes, to pose as my fiancée. I thought it would help my case if I appeared to be in a committed relationship instead of a single father. I was reluctant to do so, but I felt it was my only recourse to protect my children. I know it was wrong, and I apologize for the deception."

Before I could continue, Judge Graves raised his hand to stop me. "Mr. Pierce, I do not appreciate parents who attempt to lie in court to win custody." He leveled me with an angry glare.

Gen's attorney stood up. "Your Honor, we have further evidence of Mr. Pierce's deception." Beside him, Gen was gloating.

"Your Honor," I continued, "the arrangement with Ms. Hayes began as a way to assure custody, but it is no longer a deception. I have since fallen in love with Felicity, and our relationship is now genuine."

"Oh, for God's sake!" Gen exclaimed, rolling her eyes and crossing her arms over her chest.

The judge silenced her with a wave of his hand. "Ms. Barra, no more outbursts from you. You'll have your chance to speak." He turned to Felicity. "Ms. Hayes, please stand up to address the court."

Felicity stood up. I knew she was nervous, but she kept a calm exterior. She wore a white jacket and matching slacks, and she looked professional and beautiful.

"Ms. Hayes, can you confirm what Mr. Pierce is saying?"

Felicity nodded. "Yes, Your Honor. Cooper and I are now in a committed relationship. In fact, he proposed marriage to me. For real, this time."

There was some scattered laughter in the courtroom. But Judge Graves was not amused.

"I've been living with the Pierce family for three months," Felicity continued. "I've gotten close to his daughters, Eva and Lily, and I love them. The four of us have become a family."

The judge looked between Felicity and me, unmoved by her words.

"How convenient," he said sarcastically. "Mr. Pierce, how can you expect me to believe you or your *alleged* fiancée when you've already admitted to deceiving the court?"

My heart sank. I was going to lose the case.

"Your honor, Cooper and I are going to have a baby together," Felicity said.

Beside me, Nick looked up sharply. We hadn't practiced this.

Felicity opened the folder in front of her and held up an ultrasound image. "We're planning to get married soon, before the baby arrives. I assure you, our relationship is real. And Eva and Lily will have a home full of love if they stay with us."

Judge Graves' eyes lingered on the ultrasound image, then flicked between me and Felicity once more before he turned to Gen's attorney.

The next several minutes passed in a blur. Gen and her attorney made their statements. Ruth was summoned to speak, and she repeated what she had heard Marsh ranting about. Her testimony made us look bad, and I listened to all the arguments with my pulse hammering in my head.

After everyone had gotten a chance to speak, the judge looked over the paperwork on his desk.

Nick had gathered statements from several of my business associates, friends and employees, including Marsh. Everyone had sworn that I was a good father to Eva and Lily.

The judge looked at us. I braced myself for the worst.

"In light of the news of Mr. Pierce's and Ms. Hayes' statements, I've decided to issue a continuance. The children will stay in their current arrangement for the time being. We'll postpone the hearing to see if you indeed get married, Mr. Pierce. But I'm warning you," he said to Felicity and me, "do not enter into your vows lightly. And do not take further action to influence me. You are dismissed."

With that, he collected his paperwork and stood to move slowly toward his chambers.

Felicity and I blinked at each other, both of us in shock.

We had been expecting a decision today. As painful as it was, I assumed Judge Graves would grant custody to Gen. And now he would decide later?

Nick slapped me on the back. "This is good news, Cooper," he said under his breath.

"This is bullshit!" Gen exclaimed, causing the entire courtroom to go silent as everyone looked at her.

She charged over toward Felicity, pointing a finger at her. "You little floozy! You think because you spread your legs for him you have a right to raise my kids?"

I took a step forward, ready to intervene if Gen got any closer. "Back off, Gen."

Gen's attorney was behind her, trying desperately to shut her up. "Gen, don't say another word," he warned.

But Gen ignored him and directed her fury to me.

"And *you*! You got her pregnant to spite me! You just want to keep me from my money!"

"Gen, stop," her lawyer said, nervously looking toward the judge's chambers.

"That's enough," Judge Graves bellowed.

Everyone froze, and all eyes turned toward him. I had been so dumbfounded that I didn't notice he was standing in the door to his chambers. Gen apparently hadn't noticed him standing there, either.

He had heard everything.

He ambled back to his seat and motioned for everyone to return to theirs. Gen's face fell as she slunk back to the table beside her attorney.

"This court is back in session," Judge Graves announced, his eyes fiery. "There will be no continuance on this case. I'm ready to make my judgment now."

Felicity glanced at me nervously. I swallowed.

"My primary concern is *always* the well-being of the children." His eyes moved between Gen and me. "It's true I often favor families with two parents. But when both households are single-parent, I'm inclined to think the children belong with the mother. Mothers are usually more nurturing and attuned to their children's needs."

I blinked. What was happening? Was he going to grant custody to Gen after all?

"However, that's not always the case. After reading the statements made by associates of Mr. Pierce and Ms. Barra, it was clear that these children belonged with their father. And I had planned to make that judgment today... *until* Mr. Pierce admitted to engaging in activities intended to deceive my courtroom."

He looked at me. "There was no need to resort to such deception, Mr. Pierce. It's clear you're the more fit parent."

I held my breath.

"And now, thanks to Ms. Barra's outburst, she has revealed her true intentions. She's interested only in money, instead of providing a loving environment for her daughters. Ms. Barra, I advise you to re-examine the priorities in your life."

I could feel the fury radiating from Gen, but she remained silent as the judge continued.

"Judgment is for full custody to Cooper Pierce. Geneviève Barra will be granted limited, supervised visitation until she applies to modify the order. Ms. Barra, you'll have to prove you want to be a mother to these girls before I'll consider any changes."

It took me a moment for his words to sink in. But when they did, I felt I could breathe again.

"Thank you, Your Honor," I said.

He struck his gavel, then stood up and moved toward his chamber.

Nick shook my hand and congratulated me. I thanked him, still in a daze, and he snapped his briefcase shut before taking his leave.

I turned to Felicity, who had tears in her eyes.

"You did it," she whispered.

I took her in my arms. "We both did."

Unable to say much more at the moment, I held her. I was at a loss for words, but my heart was full.

Somehow, we'd managed to win. Despite all my fuck-ups, despite all the problems along the way, I'd gotten everything I wanted... and so much more.

The girls would stay where they belonged, with me —*and* Felicity. We'd be a family.

Behind me, Marsh clapped me on the back.

I let go of Felicity and turned to him. "Congratulations, Cooper," Marsh said, extending his hand to shake mine. "You deserve this. And those little girls do, too."

I took his hand, but then pulled him in for a hug, slapping him on the back.

Marsh turned to Felicity and smiled. "And congratulations to you, too, Felicity. You're going to be a great mother."

She looked at her father with tears in her eyes. "Thanks, Dad." They embraced for a long moment, then Felicity stepped back to return to my side.

"Well, I'll leave you two to celebrate." Marsh started to leave, but then stopped and turned toward us. He shook his head in amazement. "I can't believe I'm going to be a grandfather."

Felicity laughed. Marsh's face lit up in the biggest grin I'd ever seen him wearing. He turned to walk off, whistling a happy tune.

I took Felicity's hand in mine and pulled her in tight.

"I love you so much," I said. "I can't wait to make you my wife." I moved my hand to her soft belly. "And I can't wait to raise our children together with you."

She stood on her tiptoes to kiss me, then looked in my eyes. "I love you, too, Cooper. You've made me happier than I ever thought possible."

"School will be out soon," I said with a smile. "Let's go pick up our girls."

33

FELICITY

One Month Later

"Wow!" Lily exclaimed. "You look so pretty, Felicity!"

I smiled at her. "Thanks, Lily. And you look absolutely beautiful. Just like a fairy princess." I put a hand on her back.

We stood before the full-length mirror and looked at our reflections. Eva ran up to stand on my other side.

"And I clean up pretty nice, too, don't I?" Eva asked, pointing a thumb to her chest.

I laughed. "Yes, you do. You look beautiful, too, Eva."

Eva spun around to show off her midnight blue dress with a fitted bodice and full tulle skirt. The tulle had been embroidered with suns, moons, and stars in a shimmery gold thread to reflect Eva's newfound interest in outer space.

Lily's eyes sparkled as she moved her hands over her pale pink gown. It was a full A-line design in a similar cut to Eva's, but with tiered ruffles and rosettes on the poofy skirt. A flower garland crowned her head.

I'd designed and sewed both girls' dresses with their ideas and help, and they looked stunning.

My wedding dress was my own creation as well, and I was thrilled at how it had turned out.

It was a lace gown in ivory, featuring long, sheer sleeves and a short train. The high neckline in the front was balanced by the low back that came to a deep V at my waist. It was just my style—romantic and bohemian, elegant and relaxed.

I had spent many evenings and weekends working on this dress in the home studio Cooper had built for me. Eva and Lily had helped me with simple tasks, like cutting and measuring. Plus, they'd taken it upon themselves to stand guard at the door to make sure Cooper never caught a glimpse of the gown.

I smiled as I recalled Eva shaking a finger at him in the hallway. *Daddy, if you think we're going to let you see that dress before your wedding day, you're crazy!*

Even though our wedding would be a small, intimate affair, it had always been a dream of mine to wear a beautiful gown. So I indulged myself.

A hairstylist had done all our hair. Lily's was fixed in elaborate braids with the flower garland on top, and Eva's was loose with the sides pulled back. Mine was in a fancy chignon.

"I think we all look pretty gorgeous today," Lauren said. She moved to the mirror to stand behind Lily.

"Definitely," I agreed, looking at the lavender dress that Lauren had selected. The pale purple color brought out the deep green of her eyes and made her red hair even more vibrant. "You look amazing, Lauren."

She applied a peachy lipstick to her lips and smiled at

me. "Thanks. And, babe, your wedding dress is to die for. You've really outdone yourself."

"Thanks, Lauren." I smoothed my lace skirt over my belly and smiled. "It's a good thing Cooper and I are getting married now. This kid is growing so fast. I would need a bigger size if we waited a few more days."

Lily spun to face me and lifted her hand. "Can I see if the baby's kicking?"

"Sure, go ahead." Lily gently placed her hand on my abdomen and concentrated.

I chuckled at how serious she was. She was fascinated to know a baby was growing inside my tummy.

At four months pregnant, I had a small baby bump. We still didn't know the sex, but my obstetrician told me we'd be able to find out soon.

"But remember, it's still too early to feel the baby kicking," I said. "He or she is about the size of an avocado now."

"An avocado!" Eva giggled. "You're growing an avocado baby!" She clutched her sides and doubled over laughing. The mental image had clearly tickled her.

"You silly goose," I laughed.

Lily removed her hand. "I don't feel anything yet."

"I'll let you know as soon as I feel the baby start kicking," I promised her.

Eva perked up as if she remembered something. She tugged on Lily's hand. "Come on, Lily, let's go."

Lily blinked at her. "Where are we going?"

"We should make sure Daddy's all ready to get married. You know how he is." She shrugged. "He probably needs our help with something."

I winced as the girls ran through the room to the front door in their dresses. "Don't run, girls," I called after them. "You don't want to fall and tear that fabric."

They slowed down and gently opened the door. I watched through the window as they went outside. They walked slowly for a few steps, but the temptation to run was too great. Soon, they broke into a sprint toward the cabin where Cooper was waiting before the wedding.

"Those kids are hilarious," Lauren said, shaking her head.

"Don't I know it."

"I can see why you love them so much."

I smiled. "The Pierces are very lovable. Especially their dad."

Lauren zipped up her makeup bag and peered out the window. "Just look at that view." She gazed at the mountain ridge in the distance. "This place is perfect."

I nodded in agreement. The venue *was* perfect. Cooper had found a beautiful ranch just outside of Los Angeles that was rented out for weddings. It was gorgeous and scenic, with lots of tall cottonwood trees growing along a creek and sweeping views of the mountains to the north.

The ceremony would take place in a small, historic chapel that the ranch owners had restored to its full glory. Cozy, handsome cabins were dotted around the property for guests to spend the night if they chose.

Cooper and I had rented the honeymoon lodge, set off at a distance from the other buildings. From the pictures online, we'd be staying in high style while surrounded by nature for the next week. Plus, there would be plenty of opportunities for horseback riding—which delighted my inner child as much as it did Eva and Lily.

Inga would be staying with the girls in a nearby cabin while Cooper and I had some time alone. But I had a feeling we would be seeing the girls plenty during our honeymoon, and that was just fine with me.

Cooper had asked if I wanted to travel to an exotic, distant location for our honeymoon. But, honestly, I wanted to stay closer to home. And it turned out he did, too. We'd have plenty of time to travel after the baby was a little older.

For now, stability for Eva and Lily was more important. They needed to know that they wouldn't be uprooted, and that I was in their lives for good. With each passing week, I knew they felt more secure in their attachment to me.

Lauren's voice pulled me away from my thoughts. "I'm so proud of you, Fel." She opened her arms to embrace me.

I hugged her, then pulled back to raise an eyebrow. "I didn't expect you to get all mushy on me, Lauren."

"I can get mushy with the best of them!" She laughed, then her eyes met mine. "You, my friend, have made all your dreams come true. Let's see," she said, counting on her fingers. "You found an amazing hunk of a guy who adores you. Your business is a smashing success. And you're no longer driving the Plymouth Breeze."

I laughed, thinking of the new SUV Cooper had surprised me with for my birthday last month.

"Yeah, and I got a few things I didn't even know I wanted." I watched Eva and Lily race across the front lawn as I moved my hands down to my belly.

"I'm still mad at you for moving out of our crappy apartment," Lauren huffed. "But thank you for paying for the rest of your lease. That'll give me plenty of time to get a new roommate. With some luck, I'll find someone who won't kill me in my sleep."

I grinned. "I'm sure you will, Lauren. And you know you're always welcome at our place."

"I know. And I'm really happy for you, Felicity. If anyone deserves a happy ending, it's you." She sighed dramatically and lifted the back of her wrist to her forehead. "I'll just be waiting for my own happy ending. And waiting..."

I put a hand on her shoulder. "And you'll get it, someday soon. I know the right guy is out there for you, too."

The front door swung in and Inga appeared, her face red and flustered. She breathlessly ushered Eva and Lily inside.

"I found them by the koi pond. *This one* was coming close to falling in," Inga said, pointing at Eva.

"I wasn't going to fall in," Eva protested. "I just wanted to get a closer look."

"I thought you guys were checking on your dad," Lauren said.

Eva shrugged. "He didn't need our help."

Inga shook her head with a smile, then her eyes widened as she saw me.

"What a beautiful bride!" Inga crossed the room to plant a kiss on my cheek and squeeze my hand. "I'm so happy for you and Cooper. You know, I had a good feeling about you the first time I met you."

"You did?"

Inga nodded. "I was rooting for the two of you from the beginning. I knew you'd be good for each other, and I was right. I've never seen Cooper this happy. And you, my dear, are glowing."

I smiled. "Thank you, Inga. For everything."

"You're most welcome." With a smile, she bent down to straighten the girls' dresses and hair. Carefully, she adjusted Lily's flower garland. Finally, Inga stood up and looked at me warmly.

"It's almost time," she said. "Are you ready?"

I nodded. "I'm ready."

Inga grabbed the basket of flower petals for Lily, our flower girl, and the rings for Eva, the ring bearer. She guided the girls out of the cabin and across the breezeway that led to the chapel, urging them to stay put.

Then Inga hurried back to help Lauren carry my train.

The five of us stood outside the chapel. On the other side of those doors, Cooper and the guests were gathered and waiting. It was a small, intimate wedding, with only close friends and family. Still, I had butterflies. This was a big day.

"Okay, I'm up first," Lauren said. She winked at me. "Good luck."

"You, too."

Inga opened the door for her. Cooper's brother, Rhys, was the best man. He was waiting inside, and he offered his arm to Lauren. They walked down the aisle together, and she looked beautiful and elegant. A few of Cooper's college buddies and work friends were seated near the back, and I noticed a couple of guys checking her out.

"I'm next!" Eva announced, clutching the satin cushion with the wedding rings tied in bows.

"Okay, remember, Eva," Inga instructed, "take *slow* steps. It's not a sprint down the aisle." She made sure the rings were secure. "And try not to drop this cushion."

Eva nodded. "No sweat."

Inga opened the door for her, and Eva began to march slowly down the aisle, holding the cushion carefully.

From where I was standing, I couldn't see Cooper. But I knew he was waiting at the altar for me.

My stomach fluttered. We were really doing this. I was about to marry the man of my dreams.

"Okay, Lily, your turn." Inga adjusted the bow on her back.

Lily looked up at me nervously, her brow furrowed.

I smiled at her. "You got this, girl." Lily grinned and nodded.

Inga pulled the door open for her. Lily began to walk slowly down the aisle, tossing a handful of petals with every step.

Suddenly, I realized my dad wasn't here. He was supposed to walk me down the aisle. Panic washed over me.

He hadn't backed out at the last minute, had he?

I strained my neck, looking across the lawn for signs of him. A deep voice behind me made me spin around.

"You look beautiful, honey," Dad said.

"Oh, thank goodness," I sighed. "I was beginning to worry you had flaked out on me, Dad."

He chuckled. "No, those days are over. I'm here for you. From now on, I always will be."

He offered me his arm and I looped mine through it. I smiled up at him.

Things had changed since the trial. He finally saw me as an adult instead of a child.

"I'm so proud of you, Felicity. If your mother were here today, she'd be proud of you, too." He patted my hand, and I blinked back tears. "I love you, Felicity. I always have, and I always will."

"I love you too, Dad." I drew a deep breath. "Now let's do this before I ruin my eye makeup."

The music changed and Inga opened the door for us, arranging my train behind me on the aisle. All eyes were on me, and I felt a rush of anxiety.

My eyes met Cooper's, and all my nervous energy dissipated. He was my rock, my everything.

As long as I had him, I knew I'd be fine.

Dad walked me down the aisle and winked at me before leaving me with Cooper.

"You look stunning," Cooper said under his breath with a lopsided grin.

I smiled at him, taking in how handsome he looked in his gray suit. His intense eyes were bluer than ever, and they remained steady on me.

The minister, an older man with a kind face, began to speak.

I didn't hear much of what he said. I was focused on Cooper's eyes. When it came time to do the vows, he went first.

"Felicity, I thank God for bringing you into my life. I had given up on love before you. I had even convinced myself that I could be fulfilled without opening my heart to a woman again, but you showed me exactly how wrong I was. You've been the best mother Eva and Lily have ever had. And I promise to be the best husband I can possibly be to you. I will love you, treasure you and protect you for the rest of my life."

He smiled at me, and I blinked back tears. Taking a breath, I tried to keep my voice steady as I spoke.

"Cooper, thank you for coming into my life and teaching me what's most important. What matters most in life is not business and success. It has everything to do with the people we love. I promise to love and cherish you forever. I vow to be your partner and friend for the rest of my days. And I promise to love and support Eva and Lily, and all our children, with my full heart."

Cooper held my gaze as he listened. The small gathering murmured softly after I finished. Cooper smiled at me, then nodded at Eva, who was seated beside Lily in the front row.

Eva stepped forward with the rings, a big grin on her face. Cooper untied my ring and began to slide it on my finger.

"I give this ring as a token of my love," he said.

I untied his ring and turned to him.

"With this ring, I vow to love you from this moment forward."

He held my hand in his, and Eva returned to her seat.

The minister nodded. "I now pronounce you husband and wife. You may kiss the bride."

Cooper reached for me and pulled me against him gently. He pressed his mouth to mine and kissed me.

Everything was perfect.

The audience erupted in cheers and applause.

Eva and Lily ran up to us. Cooper picked Lily up and held her at his waist. I pulled Eva in close and put my hand on her shoulders.

"Now you're really married," Eva said.

"And we're a family for real now," Lily added.

Cooper kissed Lily's forehead. And I bent down to kiss Eva's cheek.

"Yes," he said, "we're a real family."

~

At the reception, I sat down to rest between dances. I laughed as Lauren and Katie danced with every bachelor in the room.

Cooper's younger brother had flown in from Philadelphia, and Lauren had quickly discovered he was single. Between him and a few of Cooper's single friends, there were plenty of dance partners for the single women.

Even my father was dancing. After the father-daughter dance, he danced a couple of songs with Vera, a sweet older lady from Cooper's office. I'd never seen him smile so much.

Dad had come a long way in the past few weeks. He

finally seemed to realize Cooper and I were perfect together. Also, I suspected the knowledge that he'd be a granddad soon had slowly melted his heart.

Whatever it was, he was now totally supportive of Cooper and me.

Katie smiled and waved at me as she slow-danced with Rhys, Cooper's brother. I waved back, once again grateful to have found her. Katie was Moonstone's biggest fan and supporter. I never would have been able to survive the demands of my growing customer base without her.

After two weeks, I'd promoted her to store manager. With her help, I hired two skilled seamstresses and two more employees who handled customer service and sales.

In the span of a few short months, Moonstone Boutique had gone from near bankruptcy to a thriving business with six employees. Best of all, it continued to grow.

Word of mouth had spread like wildfire. I had a backlog of orders for custom-made girls' clothes for months. Katie and I were already talking about moving to a new, bigger location so we could keep up with demand.

There were so many more changes I wanted to make. Boys' clothes. New designs and fabrics. The sky was the limit, and I loved Moonstone more than ever.

And I no longer had to work around the clock, which gave me plenty of time to spend with Cooper and the girls.

"There you are." Cooper walked up behind me and kissed my cheek.

I smiled as he sat beside me. "Hey, handsome."

He put his arm around me. "Are you feeling okay?"

"I'm fine. Just needed to rest." I nodded at Katie dancing with Rhys. "Which one of my friends do you think your brother likes more?"

Cooper laughed. "I'm not sure. I think he's on cloud

nine, though, from all the attention." He reached for my hand and intertwined our fingers. "It's been a good day."

"The *best* day. Everything was beautiful."

He kissed me again. "I'm so happy you're my wife."

I started to answer him, but the sound of quick footsteps made us look up. Eva and Lily charged toward us, and Cooper caught them both in his arms.

The girls giggled as he tickled them. "Having fun, girls?" I asked. "I saw you dancing just now."

"We're having a blast," Eva said.

Lily nodded. "Uncle Rhys gave me a piggy-back ride."

"That's awesome," I said. "Oh, you have some cake on your face, sweetie." I reached for a napkin to wipe off Lily's chin. "There, all clean."

Lily gave me a hug, then looked up at me. "Thanks, Mommy."

I blinked at her.

Mommy?

My heart, which was already full, was close to bursting wide open. I glanced at Cooper, who smiled at me. I wiped away the tears that pooled in my eyes.

"You're welcome, Lily," I croaked.

"Are you sad?" she asked.

"No," I said, pulling her in close. "I'm happy. Very, very happy. I love you all so much."

Eva came closer to give me a hug. "We love you, too."

Cooper wrapped us all in his arms. It was the perfect moment.

And best of all, we were only getting started.

EPILOGUE
COOPER

Five Months Later

"And now, Miss Lily Pierce will perform her dance to the song 'Friar Jack,'" Eva announced to Felicity and me.

I grinned. "I think it's '*Frère Jacques*,' goose."

Eva shrugged. "Same difference."

She sauntered off the makeshift stage in the living room—really, just a mat we'd put in the middle of the floor after moving the furniture.

From our place on the sofa, Felicity and I watched Lily move to the center of the mat. She wore a pink leotard and a multicolored poofy skirt Felicity had created for her.

Eva tapped a button on the tablet I'd connected to the stereo, and the piano music filtered through the room.

Lily had been focused on her ballet classes lately, and she was eager to show us what she'd learned. She'd be in a dance recital for her class soon, and this was her favorite piece.

I watched with glee as my daughter, now seven years old, moved gracefully through the living room. Her upcoming performance in the recital was a major step. Lily would never have performed in public before Felicity entered her life.

Having a loving maternal presence in the house had been a game changer for both the girls.

They were happier and more secure. Their therapist had noticed their progress and told me that they no longer needed therapy unless they wanted to continue.

Felicity and I applauded as Lily's dance came to an end and she bowed. Eva, who had just performed her hip-hop routine, joined Lily on the stage and both girls joined hands for a final dramatic bow.

Felicity grinned. "Bravo! Beautiful dancing, girls," she cheered.

"Excellent work, both of you," I agreed. "I can tell you've been practicing a lot."

The girls grinned, basking in the praise, and the doorbell rang.

"That's Inga!" Eva exclaimed. She ran off to open the front door.

"Can I have a snack?" Lily asked. "I'm hungry."

"So am I," Felicity said. "Let's go see what's in the fridge." With considerable effort and a little help from me, she rose to her feet, her hands supporting her lower back.

At one week overdue, her belly was big and round.

I put a hand on her back and squeezed her shoulder. "How are you holding up?"

She smiled. "I'm ready to have this baby."

I chuckled. "I'm sure you are. Need any help right now?"

She waved me off. "I'm fine. I'm just gonna grab a snack for the girls and me."

I was ready for our new son, too. Dr. Temple said that if the baby didn't come this week, she would have to induce labor.

Felicity and I had done everything to help the process. Exercise, herbal tea, nipple stimulation—which was my favorite of all.

Other than some false labor pains, the baby hadn't given much indication he was ready to leave.

Ready for her afternoon shift, Inga walked into the living room and glanced at Felicity. Her eyes bulged at the sight of my very pregnant wife. "Hi, everyone. Felicity, how are you doing?"

"Right now, I'm starving. This baby is one hungry kid."

Inga laughed and looked around the living room. "I see the girls had a dance recital."

I nodded as I began to push the furniture back to its original place. "We've got a couple of budding dancers in the house."

Inga helped me move the furniture as Felicity went to the kitchen. The girls followed her, debating about what kind of juice was better—apple or orange.

"Uh-oh."

I froze.

"Daddy!" Eva called. I took off before she could say another word, my heart pounding.

"What is it?" I asked as I rounded the corner.

Felicity stood in the kitchen holding a carton of juice. She looked down to see a stream of water running between her legs.

"Um, I think Mommy had an accident," Lily said gently.

"I didn't wet myself," Felicity said. "My water broke." She looked up at me with wide eyes.

This was it. Go time.

Behind me, Inga took one look and gave me a nod. "I'll be here with the girls. Keep me posted."

The girls picked up on the tension. "What's that mean? Her water broke?" Lily asked, concerned.

"It means she's going to have the baby soon," I said, trying to keep the panic out of my voice.

As the girls cheered, I ushered Felicity toward the garage door. We had a bag packed and ready to go, and I hoisted the strap over my shoulder.

"Girls, we're going to the hospital now," I announced.

"We can't go with you?" Lily asked.

"No." I shook my head. "It could take a long time. Inga will drive you to the hospital when the baby is born."

As I tried to steer Felicity out the door, she raised her hand to stop me. "We don't need to rush to the hospital right away. I'm not even having contractions yet."

I shook my head. "I'm not taking any chances."

"But I haven't even had my snack," Felicity protested. "I don't want to do this on an empty stomach."

I grabbed the carton of juice she still held. Moving swiftly, I backtracked to the refrigerator. I grabbed a half gallon of milk, a few pieces of fruit, a package of lunch meat, cheese and a loaf of bread. I packed it all in an insulated cooler bag with ice packs. Finally, I tossed in silverware, napkins, and plastic cups.

Everyone watched me silently as I rushed around. Quickly, I returned to her side and opened the garage door, anxious to get on the road.

"You can eat on the way," I said. "Plus, there are more snacks in the hospital bag. Let's go."

The girls reached up to give her a quick hug.

"Good luck, Mommy," Lily said, her arms wrapped around Felicity's neck.

"Don't worry, Mom," Eva said, using the name she'd started to call Felicity a few weeks ago. "You got this."

Felicity smiled. "Thanks, girls. We'll see you soon. And then you can meet your new brother!"

Amid cheers and well wishes, I led her out to the car.

Halfway to the hospital, Felicity's contractions began.

They seemed to come on strong, with short intervals in between them. I cursed under my breath at the traffic, wishing I could part the sea of vehicles so we could get to the hospital faster.

Finally, though, we made it.

We had already texted the obstetrician on the drive over. Ten minutes later, Felicity was checked in and settled in a bed in the delivery room.

I stood at Felicity's side as Dr. Temple checked her dilation.

I was a nervous wreck, fidgeting and shifting my weight from foot to foot. Even while panting through contractions, Felicity was handling this better than I was. I just wanted her and the baby to be safe and healthy.

Dr. Temple stood and removed her latex gloves. "I have good news and bad news."

Felicity groaned as another contraction hit her. I brushed her hair off her forehead. Then her face relaxed as the pain subsided.

"What's the good news?" Felicity asked.

"The labor is progressing very quickly. We don't usually see it go this fast for a first-time mother."

"What's the bad news?" I asked tightly.

"There's no time for an epidural."

Felicity grimaced and moaned. I wasn't sure if she was reacting to the doctor's words or another contraction.

I bent down so she could focus on my eyes.

"Hey," I said to her, and she looked up. "I'm right here. I'll be here with you the whole time."

She nodded and bit her lip. Another contraction came on quickly.

As Felicity's labor progressed, Dr. Temple and the nurses were great. They did everything possible to make her comfortable. I never left her side, helping her to breathe through the pain and holding her hand.

A nurse asked if Felicity wanted to stand and move around, and Felicity gratefully took the opportunity to walk around the room. I watched as she shut her eyes with each wave of pain, wishing I could do more to help her.

The nurse showed me how to apply pressure to Felicity's hips and lower back, and it seemed to help a little. When it came time to push, she climbed back into bed.

I gripped her hand, pushing my own anxiety aside. I had to be steady and calm for her.

"You can do this, Felicity," I said.

She looked at me, her eyes focused on mine. Then she shut her eyes to concentrate. The doctor was saying something, but I could hardly hear her as Felicity pushed.

Finally, a high-pitched cry filled the room, bringing me back to my senses.

"Congratulations," Dr. Temple announced, lifting a little, squirmy baby up for us to see. "You have a healthy baby boy."

The nurse took the baby to clean and weigh him. Breathless, Felicity looked at me with wonder in her eyes. I kissed her forehead and squeezed her hand.

"You did it," I whispered.

She beamed, all of her previous pain already forgotten. A moment later, the nurse handed the baby to Felicity, who took him in her arms. I peered over her shoulder at our son's face.

"He's beautiful and perfect," I whispered. "Just like his mother."

"Hello, little baby," Felicity murmured. She moved her hands over his face and tiny fingers.

She looked up at me with tears in her eyes. I kissed her again, so proud of my wife, and so proud of our son.

"Benjamin," Felicity whispered, using the name we'd picked previously. "Welcome. I'm so glad you're here."

After Felicity and I spent some time alone with the baby, I called Inga and told her to bring the girls. Twenty minutes later, Inga knocked on the door of our room.

I let them in. The girls were curious, but realizing they couldn't charge in like they normally did, they cautiously entered the room.

When they saw Felicity holding the baby, their eyes grew large. Inga helped the girls wash their hands at the sink in the room, then they moved close to the bed.

"There he is," Lily breathed.

Felicity smiled. "Girls, meet your new baby brother, Benjamin." She passed the baby to me and I held him securely. He'd just had his first meal of breast milk and looked peaceful and serene.

Standing at my side, they looked at their new brother.

"He's asleep," Lily said.

Eva nodded. "He must be tired after being born."

I smiled. "Do you want to hold him?"

Eva blinked. "Can we?"

"Sure." I pulled two chairs together at Felicity's bedside

and had the girls sit close together. "Remember to support his head."

Gently, I placed the bundle in Eva's arms, and moved Lily's hands to support his head. Inga kneeled beside them, a big grin on her face.

"Hello, little brother," Eva murmured, "I promise to love you forever."

"Forever and ever," Lily agreed.

I reached for Felicity's hand and squeezed it.

"I love you," I murmured to her.

She smiled up at me, more beautiful than I'd ever seen her. "I love you, too."

No more words were necessary. I knew her heart, and she knew mine.

Our love was the realest thing in the world.

~

Want more of Cooper and Felicity?

Sign up for my mailing list.

You'll get a free extended epilogue for *The Fiancé Hoax*.

Plus a free copy of *Second Chance Daddy*!

Type this link in your browser:

https://BookHip.com/QFFBJFX

BONUS CONTENT

Join my mailing list to get a free Extended Epilogue for *The Fiancé Hoax!*

You'll also receive *Second Chance Daddy* as a thank you!

Type into your browser:

https://BookHip.com/QFFBJFX

SNEAK PEEK OF THREE WEDDINGS AND A BABY!

About the Book

Three weddings as my boss's fake date.
One baby I didn't count on.

Trent "Diablo" Dillon.
He's my devilishly hot boss, and he's gonna make my money problems disappear.
The catch?
Pretend to be his girlfriend at three weddings this summer.
He needs to get his pushy family off his back.
I need a windfall.
Besides, I'm used to dealing with Trent's demands at work.

But sharing a bed with my fake boyfriend is more than I can take.
After one sizzling night, I'm addicted to his rock hard…
er, abs.

The craziest part?
I'm falling for my grumpy boss.
The one who plans to never settle down.

My feelings for him are real.
And so is this baby I'm having in nine months.

Chapter 1: Trent

I checked my Rolex as I stepped into the elevator. It was still early, so the office would be quiet.

Good.

Dillon Tech wouldn't be what it was without my employees. But I preferred not to be around them if I could help it.

They called me a loner.

They called me a lot of things.

I didn't really give a shit.

I knew who I was and what I was doing. Validation from everyone else was the last thing I needed.

On the top floor, the elevator doors opened into the executive offices.

"Oh, my God. Seriously?"

Bella's voice rang through the hall as I exited the elevator. I rounded the corner to see my executive assistant bent over a filing cabinet in the reception area.

It was hard to miss her with that hourglass figure and blonde hair falling down her shoulders. Her black pencil skirt stretched tightly over the most perfect curves I'd ever seen.

She was struggling, her ass in the air as she desperately grabbed at something behind the cabinet frame. I stood there for a moment, quiet, my mind going places it shouldn't.

I would have given anything to see her bent over my bed, casually teasing me with a move like that, a playful invitation to grab her by the waist and pump into her as hard as I could—

Fuck.

My cock twitched in my pants. Why the hell was she able to do this to me when she wasn't even trying?

I'd hired Bella Williams because she was damn good at her job, not because of her tight, curvy little body or pouty lips that made me think of *filthy* things.

That had been a bonus.

One that you're not going to follow through on.

I adjusted myself, willing my cock to cool off. I couldn't get worked up by my EA.

I was her boss.

It would be wrong on so many levels.

Besides, Annabella Williams was the best EA I'd had since I started the company.

No way was I screwing that up over a fling.

"Yes! Got it!" Bella shouted as her heels made contact with the floor, now standing upright with a sheet of paper in her hand. "That's one point for Bella and zero points for you, filing cabinet—Oh! Mr. Dillon!"

Her face turned bright red and she flipped her long hair over her shoulder. "I didn't see you."

"Morning," I grunted.

"The weather out there is incredible, isn't it?" she asked.

"Yeah," I offered.

Bella was one of those happy sunshine-and-rainbows types. Which was another reason to keep my distance. People like that made me grumpier than I already was.

I brushed past her to get to my office. I didn't need her

distracting me any more today, and I was eager to get away before she noticed the tent in my pants.

In my private office, I exhaled. The sun poured in through the full-length windows. I crossed the space and sat behind my mahogany desk.

I'd barely powered up my laptop and opened my email when Bella knocked softly on the open door with a cup of coffee in her hand.

"Mr. Dillon?" She took a few steps toward my desk before setting the mug down in front of me. "I wanted to make sure you had your coffee first thing."

"Thank you, Bella," I said. "But what about the morning reports? And the mail?"

"Coffee first, Mr. Dillon," she confidently replied. "Then the rest. You know the drill."

My brow furrowed in frustration. "So, you're ignoring my request? Is this a mutiny, Ms. Williams?"

"Not a mutiny, Mr. Dillon." She shook her head. "I just know how you are. How you work most efficiently. You need coffee before you start the day."

I chuckled. "So, you think you know me?"

"No. I *know* that I know you, Mr. Dillon." She beamed. "And now, if you'll excuse me, I'm going to give you a few minutes before I bring in your mail and the morning reports."

She turned around, her head held high like she wasn't bothered by anything I said, like she was completely unaffected by my attitude.

That was something else that drove me crazy when it came to Bella Williams. Nothing ever ruined her good mood.

She had such an upbeat spirit that it sometimes threatened to infect me. That was another reason to keep her far away from my general direction.

Optimism was poison in the boardroom. Poison in any kind of serious work, really.

I slowly sipped my coffee, my mind still too focused on Bella, even if I was mentally listing reasons to keep our relationship strictly professional. As I worked through my anti-Bella thoughts, her words floated back through my head.

I know that I know you, Mr. Dillon.

Ha. She couldn't have been more wrong about that.

If she really knew my preferences, she would be on top of me right now, that pencil skirt on my floor and my hands unbuttoning her blouse—

"Here you go. Here's your mail." Bella slid a stack of bound mail across my desk with a bright smile. "And I've got the morning reports here, too, whenever you're ready for me to go over them."

"Yep. Give me just a sec." I held up a finger as I quickly flipped through the mail.

It was mostly junk from wannabe employees and aspiring entrepreneurs, all hoping that kiss-ass handwritten letters would help them stand out from the crowd. I was ready to abandon the entire pile.

But then a familiar name on one of the envelopes caught my eye.

Grant Dillon.

My family sent everything to my office, rather than to my house. They figured I lived here.

They weren't wrong.

I tore it open to reveal a wedding invitation.

Another one.

This time from my brother.

This was the third wedding invitation I'd received from a family member in the last few weeks, the others coming from my sister and my cousin.

"What the fuck?" I said absent-mindedly.

"Is everything okay, Mr. Dillon?" There was concern in Bella's voice. "Can I help?"

"You can go over the morning reports," I snapped. "Have a seat. Let's get at it."

Unfazed, she took a seat in front of my desk, the reports held out across her lap. She read through the updates from each department manager.

I couldn't focus on a single word she said.

I was still lost in the deluge of upcoming weddings I'd be expected to attend.

Images of white dresses and tiered wedding cakes swirled in my head.

Was everyone getting married this summer except for me?

"So, marketing needs you to sign off on an elephant purchase."

"What?"

"Marketing needs you to sign off on an elephant purchase," she calmly repeated. "Or *potential* elephant purchase, I should say. No guarantee they'll be able to get one, but they still want to try."

A smile played around her lips, and she broke into laughter.

"Sorry, I couldn't resist," she said. "You were so distracted I figured I could say anything and get away with it."

"And the best you could do was ask for an elephant for marketing?" I laughed now, too. "This would've been a perfect time to ask for a raise, Bella."

"Eh. The elephant would've been more fun. We could set it up in the break room and let everyone feed it peanuts during lunch."

"Why do I get the impression you've thought about this before?"

"You show me someone who hasn't considered a break room elephant, and I'll show you a liar." She chuckled again, then her expression turned serious. "Is everything okay, though, Mr. Dillon? Ever since I brought you the mail, you've been out of it. Do you want to talk about it?"

I looked at her, surprised. It wasn't her job to listen to my drama. I always talked to her about business—that was her job. But we never discussed personal shit.

Her big hazel eyes were trained on my face, her expression sympathetic. She waited for me to make the call.

"Do you have a big family, Bella?" I asked.

She shook her head slowly. "No. I have some distant relatives in other states. But here in LA, it's just me."

I nodded, feeling a pang of guilt I didn't know that detail about her. But why should I? She was my employee, not my girlfriend.

I swallowed. *Definitely* not my girlfriend.

"Well, I have a *huge* family," I said. "They're very pushy and very loud. And apparently, they're all getting married at the same time."

"What do you mean?" Bella asked. Amusement danced in her eyes.

"This summer I've been invited to three weddings. *Three.* My cousin Patrick's getting married in Vegas, then my sister Anya in Colorado, and then my brother Grant in Napa Valley."

"Destination weddings all around?"

"Yes," I harrumphed. "Which only makes it worse."

"I love going to weddings," she said with a dreamy smile.

I shook my head. "It's not my scene."

"Oh, come on. You get to dress up, you get free food and a fun reception. If you're lucky, there's a bit of drama. And it's not your responsibility to make sure things run smoothly. What's not to love?"

"The fact that it's *my* family," I deadpanned. "There's a *lot* of drama, and I can't get out of it because I'm related to them. I'll never hear the end of it if I don't go."

Bella smiled, but she tried hard not to. "I guess that could make things complicated."

I sighed. "You have no idea." I glanced at her, trying to decide how much to tell her. "The thing is, my family is full of matchmakers."

"Yeah?" Her eyes sparkled. "That sounds interesting."

"Not when I'm the target." I bristled. "If I don't have a date, my mom will arrange one for me."

Her eyes still danced with amusement, but she had the good sense not to laugh.

The more I thought about the weddings, the more it pissed me off. My family really got my hackles up.

"Really? That sounds—"

"Don't tell me it sounds sweet," I cut her off. "It's not. The last two family weddings I attended were disasters."

"Why?" she asked, clearly trying to hide her smile.

"Because my mom set me up with dates I didn't want. She could at least run these women by me first." I drove a hand through my hair. "And when anyone in my family gets married, it's a huge production. It's much more than a ceremony and a reception."

"It is?"

Sneak Peek of Three Weddings and a Baby!

"Yes. They make it a multi-day thing with dinners and parties. It gobbles up your whole weekend. And I get stuck making small talk for three days with some girl my mom picked out."

"No offense, Mr. Dillon, but I'm not really seeing the problem here."

"What do you mean?"

"If you need to bring a date, just ask one of the women falling all over themselves to be with you," she said. "One of your... *friends*."

I bristled at that.

I might have played the field for a few months after my last serious relationship ended. But not lately.

I'd gotten sick of waking up to another nameless face in my bed. Maybe it was because I was getting older—I was forty now. These days, one-night stands didn't do it for me.

"Or ask whoever you're seeing right now," Bella continued. "Even if it's a casual relationship, it's still better than a random person you don't know."

"I don't do casual," I said, correcting her assumption. "And when was the last time I had you order flowers for anyone?"

Bella's brows pulled together as she thought about it. Fuck, she could be so cute.

"When I started working here, two years ago..." Bella's words trailed off as she replied. "Wait. You're not saying it's been two years since you were serious with anyone—"

Her mouth snapped shut, and she shook her head. "You know what? It's none of my business."

"I appreciate the restraint."

"Still. This wedding date thing is not a problem, if you ask me." Bella beamed again.

"Oh? And why is that?"

"Because you're a very rich man," she started. "And a very rich man can always *Pretty Woman* the whole thing if he needs to."

"What?"

"You know, hire an escort to pretend to be a woman you're dating. You've never seen *Pretty Woman*?"

Her mouth fell open with shock as I shook my head.

"Just don't fall in love with her, and you should be fine," she said. "Or wait. Maybe *do* fall in love with her? I don't want to spoil the ending of the movie, but you'll see what I'm talking about when you watch it—"

"I'll take that under consideration."

"Which part? Watching the movie? Or hiring an escort?"

"That'll be all, Bella. That'll be all."

Chapter 2: Trent

With a nod, she stood and walked to the door. I caught myself staring at her ass.

Again.

Fuck, Bella had me mesmerized. I'd always found her attractive, but these days something about her drove me crazy.

I didn't know what it was. She was still the same person, and so was I.

But I couldn't stop staring at her. Couldn't tear my eyes from her face. Or her body.

And the way she stood up to me when everyone else backed away... It was icing on the cake.

As the hours ticked by, I tried to focus on work. I threw myself into business meetings in the morning and worked on reports through the afternoon. I blazed through emails

Sneak Peek of Three Weddings and a Baby!

and phone calls—whatever it took to keep my mind off the weddings.

And Bella.

Her words echoed in my mind, no matter how hard I tried to block them out.

You could hire an escort.

Maybe it was a good idea. Not quite in the way she'd meant it, but that didn't matter.

I was a businessman, and if there was one thing I did well, it was business.

The more I thought about it, the more it made sense.

This was the only way I could endure the three weddings. There was no way in hell I'd risk a blind date with some random woman my mom picked out for me. Let alone three of them.

And now that my sister and my brother had invited me to their weddings, I *had* to go. As irritated as my family made me, I couldn't just not show up.

By six o'clock, I knew what I had to do.

I always worked late, and today I waited until I knew most of the employees had left. Bella would still be at her desk—she stayed as long as I needed her.

"Bella, come see me," I said, pressing the button on my phone that accessed a direct line to her desk.

A moment later, she opened my door.

"Have a seat," I said.

Bella nodded and walked to the chair she'd occupied this morning, sitting down. She crossed her legs at the ankle —finishing school perfect—and waited patiently.

"I want you to be my date for the three weddings this summer," I said. "If you agree, you'll have to pretend to be my girlfriend around my family. It's the only way to keep them off my back."

Bella's eyes widened. "What?"

"You heard me," I said. "It's a business deal, not a favor. I'll pay you for your time, just like you suggested."

"I didn't suggest you take *me*!" she cried out.

"I know. But I'm not interested in hiring a stranger to be my date. You already work for me, and we have an understanding. We can keep things professional."

She gasped, looking for the right words.

I took the opportunity of her stunned silence to finish my offer.

"I'm thinking three hundred thousand dollars for the three weddings. I'm paying for your discretion, as well as your acting skills."

I knew Bella could play a role. Anyone who could stay composed and professional when I was on a rampage was a born actor.

She blinked at me. "Three hundred..." Her voice trailed off, and she mouthed *thousand dollars,* as if she was afraid to say it.

"Yes. I'll cover all the travel expenses as well. And this is an independent arrangement. If you say no, it won't affect your job."

"And if I say yes?" she asked in a breathy voice.

Her eyes were still wide. I wasn't sure how to read her reaction.

Was it a good thing that she looked so stunned? Or a bad thing?

"Then you'll keep it a secret from the rest of the office," I said. "You understand my reasoning, I'm sure."

Bella swallowed hard and nodded. I watched her carefully. A part of me was suddenly nervous she would say no.

It's just a work contract. It means nothing either way.

"Can I take some time to think about it?" Bella asked.

It wasn't the response I'd expected. I wanted an answer now, but I couldn't blame her for needing some time. I'd just sprung this on her.

Besides, it wasn't a hard no, and that was saying something. I could work with that.

"Let me know tomorrow morning," I said.

"Okay," Bella said. She looked uncomfortable, and her hands fidgeted in her lap. "Is there anything else?"

I shook my head. "I'm about to wrap up here, and then I'm done for the day. You can head out."

She nodded and stood. "Goodnight, Mr. Dillon."

"Goodnight, Bella."

She turned and walked out of the office, closing the door quietly behind her. I let out a breath I hadn't realized I'd been holding and tilted my head back against my chair.

God, I had to wait the whole night for an answer.

Why was I so tense? Why did I care so much if she said yes?

If she said no, it would be a kick to the balls.

I'd told her she could say no, that it wouldn't affect her job. I was planning to follow through on that.

If she declined, I could still hire an escort. But I didn't like the idea of taking a random woman to my family's weddings. Bella and I knew each other. That meant something to me.

I couldn't imagine myself with a stranger on my arm, introducing an escort to my family.

She had to agree. It would spare me my dignity and save me from my matchmaking, meddling family.

But if I was being honest, there was something that excited me about spending time with Bella outside the office. I didn't expect anything physical from her, but the thought of spending three weekends with my EA made my pulse race.

I just hoped she'd say yes.

Chapter 3: Bella

Oh, my *God*.

When Trent asked me to pretend to be his girlfriend for the weddings, I had the good grace to keep a straight face.

After more than two years working for Trent Dillon, I had one hell of a poker face.

Trent was known around the office as *Diablo*—a fitting name for the devil he resembled when he was in a bad mood.

As his executive assistant, I'd learned to hide my emotions.

What kind of emotions?

Well, the frustration that I had with him for being an ass sometimes, for starters.

And, if I was being *totally* honest, the physical attraction I'd felt since I walked into his office the very first time.

He was, after all, a gift from the gods. An Adonis among us mere mortals. Physically, at least. Even on the days he was a total jackass to his employees.

Trent was the kind of man women forgave because he had the charm that made knees go weak and hearts flutter, that made logical thoughts leave the brain.

With dark brown hair and baby-blue eyes, he could do everything wrong, and with one puppy-dog look, a flex of his bicep and an arrogant grin, he was right back on top.

Just where I would want him to be, too.

Stop it, I scolded myself as I shut his office door behind me.

As soon as I was out of sight, I leaned against the wall and let out the breath I'd been holding.

What. The. Fuck.

"Hey," Angie said, walking toward me as she stepped off the elevator.

"Hey," I said with a smile.

"Ready to get out of here?" she asked.

"Yes." I nodded enthusiastically as I headed toward my desk to grab my things.

Angie was my friend and roommate—we'd shared an apartment for several years. We also both worked at Dillon Tech.

She'd been in human resources for ages, and when it was announced that Trent Dillon needed an EA, she'd told me about the opening. It was partly thanks to her I got this job.

"What's up?" Angie asked with a frown. "You look like you've seen a ghost."

I swallowed, pausing. "I'm fine. It's just… Trent's assigning me a tough project. I just heard about it."

"Let's go already." Angie ran her hand through her dark brown hair, pulling it back into a ponytail. "I could use a drink."

"Me too," I breathed.

I was still reeling. Trent Dillon wanted me to be his *girlfriend*.

Okay, no.

He wanted me to *pretend* to be his girlfriend.

But judging by the way he kept everyone at arm's length, that was pretty much the same thing.

And either way… there was good money involved in this, and I could certainly use it. In a city as expensive as LA, I was just scraping by, despite my generous salary.

"Hello? Earth to Bella," Angie teased as we rode the elevator down to the lobby. I was in a daze, and I suddenly realized I hadn't heard a word she'd said. "You're not even listening."

"Sorry, Angie," I said. "I'm a little distracted."

Angie rolled her eyes as the doors opened into the lobby. We left the building together and got in her car in the parking lot. We took turns driving to work, and this week it was her turn.

I concentrated on her story about her argument with her manager as she drove us to our apartment building and parked. Instead of going inside the building, we walked toward our favorite bar, The Grove.

It was only two blocks away, which suited me just fine. We were never tempted to take stupid risks like driving after a few drinks.

The Grove was a dive bar with a laid-back atmosphere. It featured an amateur hour for musicians to cut their teeth and—our favorite—drink specials on Wednesdays that were so cheap they had to be a loss for the owner.

I loved it here.

We walked in and nodded at Charlie, the bartender on duty tonight.

"What will it be, ladies?" Charlie asked when we sat down in our usual booth toward the back of the bar. Sitting at the bar itself felt too exposed to talk about personal things, which we usually did when we came to drink here.

"I'll have a vodka tonic," I said.

"Keto mojito. You know me, Charlie. Always watching my waist."

Angie was reed-thin and lived on low-carb food and drinks. Her model-like figure was beautiful, but she was so different from me. When I met her in college, I'd been

Sneak Peek of Three Weddings and a Baby!

intimidated by her looks and her constant focus on them, but I'd learned to love my curves since then.

Charlie grinned and nodded. "Coming right up."

He turned to leave and Angie looked at me, her eyes narrowing.

"So, tell me."

"Tell you what?"

"What's going on with you? You're *never* this distracted about work, so it must be something else."

I laughed. "You know me too well."

"We *live* together," Angie pointed out. "If I don't know you by now, I'm not paying attention very well, am I?"

I chuckled and shook my head.

"It's this thing with Trent... it's not exactly a work project, per se."

"Then what is it?"

"Can you keep a secret?" I asked.

Angie lifted an eyebrow. "You know I can."

I took a deep breath. "He has to go to three weddings this summer for family members who are getting married."

"And?" Angie prompted impatiently.

"He wants *me* to go with him. As... his fake girlfriend," I whispered, as if I was afraid to say the words.

"Are you serious?"

"Very."

I watched Angie's shocked expression as I told her the whole story.

"So you'd travel to three different cities with him?" she asked.

"Yep."

"And pretend to be his girlfriend in front of his family?" Her eyebrows rose. "*Diablo's* girlfriend?"

"That's the deal. If I agree to do it."

She shuddered. "Do you really think you could pull it off? No one is *that* good of an actress."

"I don't know. Maybe I could do it for the money he's offering. I'm supposed to give him an answer tomorrow morning."

"Sleeping on it isn't much time at all," Angie mused. "It's a big decision."

"It is," I agreed.

Angie shook her head. "I can't imagine it. You and Diablo, sitting in a tree! First comes love, then comes marriage... Bella, you could be Diablo's *bride*!"

I cut her off. "Hold it right there. The illusion won't go that far, trust me. I won't let it."

"It's still insane. You'd have to act like you *like* Diablo." She stuck out her tongue. "Three hundred grand, though? Not bad."

Charlie arrived with our drinks, and I gladly took my cocktail.

"Charlie, would you pay someone to date you?" Angie asked him.

I nudged her with my foot under the table. She ignored me.

"What?" Charlie asked, confused. "Do you think I'd need to *pay* someone? I like to think I'm a nice enough guy that someone would actually *want* to be with me."

"You're great," I said to him. "Don't listen to her. After her mojito, she'll talk more sense."

Charlie chuckled. "I'll never understand women," he said as he walked away.

I gave Angie a sharp look. "You're not supposed to tell anyone," I pointed out. "I'm telling you this in confidence. You know what that means, right?"

"Oh, come on. I didn't tell Charlie anything. I just asked an innocent question. He'll never guess."

I sighed. Half the population of Los Angeles knew who Trent Dillon was. He was a self-made billionaire with an empire he'd built from the ground up. The last thing I needed was for rumors to start circulating before I even said yes to him.

"So, you're going to do it, then?" Angie asked.

"I think so," I said.

"But... it's Trent *Diablo* Dillon we're talking about here."

"I need the money," I admitted. "You know how things are. Despite my good salary, it's a struggle to make my student loan payments each month. Our rent and utilities are so high, I can barely keep my car running. If the clunker breaks down one more time, I'm screwed. If I do this, I could buy a new car, get out of debt... This could change everything." My eyes lit up. "I could maybe even make a down payment on a house."

"I thought you liked being roommates," Angie pouted.

"I love being roommates," I said. "But I'm twenty-eight now. I didn't think at this age I'd still be trying to find my feet, you know? It's not like it's an immoral way to make money, anyway. I'm sure we'll sign a contract and everything."

God, talking about it like this made it seem so *clinical*.

Wasn't that what Trent had in mind, though? It was a business agreement, after all. There was nothing personal about it, aside from my *personal* feelings for him.

My feelings were beside the point, though.

"Do you think you'll be able to handle the close proximity?" Angie asked.

"Yeah, why wouldn't I?" I answered almost too quickly.

"Trust me, the last thing on my mind is sleeping with Diablo."

Actually, that had been one of the *first* things on my mind.

But I was wise enough to know sleeping with him would be dumb.

I took a sip of my vodka tonic. "I have more sense than that."

Angie's eyebrows rose over the rim of her glass as she sipped her mojito.

"Honey, I was talking about his grumpy mood swings," she said. "I didn't mean sex."

I flushed. *Oh.*

"Are you attracted to him?" Angie asked, her lips curling into a smile.

"No." I took another long sip of my drink.

"You are!" Angie cried out, her eyes sparkling, an incredulous smile growing. "Oh, my God, why didn't you tell me you had a crush on Diablo?"

"Because I don't," I said hotly.

Angie laughed with glee. "Don't try to deny it, Bella Williams. I know you too well—you said so yourself!"

I shook my head, my cheeks warm.

I'd been attracted to Trent since I started working for him. Not the teenager kind of crush where I tripped over my feet and doodled his name on a notepad—I was an adult. I could keep my feelings in check. But that didn't mean I didn't feel attracted to the guy. As insane as it was.

"Seriously, though, if that's the case..." Angie studied my face. "It might be hard to resist him, if you're spending all that time with the guy. What if you do something you'll regret?"

I rolled my eyes. "I've spent every workday for two years

with Trent without doing anything I regret. I see him every day and keep it professional."

"Right," Angie said skeptically. She didn't believe me.

"I'm serious," I said. "I can handle it. It's just another work project."

I was more than capable of taking care of myself and not falling for Trent Dillon. He was a pain in my ass on a *good* day.

He was also my boss, so I'd been very careful with my feelings around him. It didn't matter that he was scorching hot, drop-dead gorgeous, and the idea of being with him made me melt into a puddle of need.

This was strictly business.

"So, you've decided?" she asked.

I nodded. "I'm doing it. And *only* for what that money can do for my future."

"Well, then," Angie said, slapping the table. "We should have shots."

"That's a bad idea on a weeknight," I said.

"Come on, live a little," Angie laughed. "We're grown-ups. We can do what we want." She waved at Charlie and ordered two tequilas.

I groaned.

"We have to celebrate your windfall," Angie said, leaning over and squeezing my hand.

"I'm not sure I want to celebrate," I said.

But Angie was incorrigible, and she waved my protests away.

I sighed and sat back, preparing myself for a night that wouldn't end soon. It was okay. I liked hanging out with Angie, and maybe a bit of alcohol was a good thing to take off the edge.

Because suddenly, I was nervous.

I was, after all, going to pretend to be Trent Dillon's girlfriend.

If there was ever a tall order, this was it.

Diablo's bride, Angie had teased, but I shook off the thought. She was being dramatic, as usual.

I wouldn't let it go that far. Obviously.

Look for **Three Weddings and a Baby** on Amazon!

ALSO BY CRYSTAL MONROE

All books can be read as stand-alones.

Bosses and Babies Series

Boss's Secret Baby

Boss's Pretend Wife

Boss with Benefits

Boss Daddy

Bossy Single Dad

Boss's Little Secret

Boss Me Baby

Surprise Daddy

Doctors Down South Series

Dr. Wrong

Doctor Daddy

Doctor Grumpy

Doctor's Secret Twins

Cole Brothers

Come Back to Me

Forbidden Single Dad

Doctor's Secret Baby

Mountain Man Protector

Faking It with My Best Friend

~

The Fiancé Deal

His Christmas Gift

Printed in Great Britain
by Amazon